LAST NIGHT OF FREEDOM
DAN HOWARTH

NORTHERN REPUBLIC

Copyright © 2024 by Dan Howarth

All rights reserved.

No part of this publication may be reproduced, distributed, or transmitted in any form or by any means, including photocopying, recording, or other electronic or mechanical methods, without the prior written permission of the publisher, except as permitted by U.K and/or U.S. copyright law. For permission requests, contact [include publisher/author contact info].

The story, all names, characters, and incidents portrayed in this production are fictitious. No identification with actual persons (living or deceased), places, buildings, and products is intended or should be inferred.

Book Cover by Paul Stephenson @ Hollow Stone Press

Copy Edits by Rachel Elsa.

First Edition – 2024.

For all the "lads" out there... grow up.

ONE

Connor

On every stag or hen party since the dawn of time, there's a moment where some bellend shouts "oi oi!" From that moronic mating call onwards, it's always downhill from there.

Always.

I refuse to be that bellend.

The pub's over half full which isn't too bad for five o'clock in the middle of nowhere. Perhaps this weekend won't be a washout after all. Old boys line the bar, huddled over pints in tweed, whippets lying at their feet. As stereotypes go, they couldn't be more nailed on. Farmer types sipping a mild and hoping they don't have to go home sober. A fruit machine burbles in the corner, all flashing lights and spinning dials, so old it probably spits out shillings instead of pound coins.

I've made the fatal mistake of taking my eye off the barmaid and now she's serving someone else. The old guy is holding court from beneath his flat cap and it's hard to shake the feeling the barmaid's ignoring me on purpose.

Breaking the rule for a second time, I steal a glance at the others. All three of them squatting on little stools, dressed in their finest to frequent this place - The Dog & Duck. The lads aren't laughing - they're not smiling - they're bored - they're having a shit time. At what point of being a best man do you get to relax at a stag party? I loosen the collar of my shirt and try to get some oxygen. Smoke and heat belches into the room from a log fire – summer's barely gone and it's like they're trying to cook us.

"What can I get you, love?"

The words shake me out of it. When I face the barmaid, her hands on her hips make it clear this isn't the first time she's asked me that question. Grumbling regulars eye me like I've walked dogshit into the place.

"Same as last time, please."

"Four bitters?"

"Yeah." Then I get an idea. The twinkling bottles on the glass shelves behind her. Time to spice things up. "And a shot of every spirit you've got, cheers"

A smile slides across her painted lips. "Now you're talking."

I pay for the round, double checking the prices because they're insanely cheap compared to our local back home. The shots ripple in their glasses like something off Jurassic Park. Ethan looks up first, that blinding white smile cracking his face. Jay smirks too, looks at Luke.

"You're for it now lad. Told you that he wouldn't go easy on you forever."

"Whoa now, whoa now," Luke's got his hands up like a bank teller staring down a shotgun. "I can't drink all those."

I take my seat, nearly slipping off the ridiculous stool because it's lower than I expected. Ethan stifles his laugh. "Play your cards right and you won't have to," I say.

"Playing cards, are we?" Ethan's got his wallet out. "How much are we buying in for?"

"Chill out, Paddy Power. But there's a game incoming. When's the last time you played I Have Never?"

Ethan groans, rolls his eyes. "You can't win any money in this baby's game."

"Baby's game? Do you not remember the infamous football night out of 2011?"

"Still one of the greatest nights of my life," Luke says. "Don't tell Amy but even after the wedding, it will still be up there. Holy shit. What a night."

"Who did you pull that night?" Ethan says, eyes narrowed.

"Nobody probably," Jay says. "That was the night Mike flipped out. Remember? Turned a whole table full of drinks over cos it turned out his missus had been seeing one of the other lads. It all came out because of I Have Never."

"The sound he made when he threw that chair!" I can't keep the laughter out of my voice. "Too good. Rargh!" Not a bad impression of an oversexed leopard there. It hits the spot and the others chuckle.

"I heard the soft prick ended up going to counselling after that," Ethan says. "Wouldn't catch me dead at some shrink."

"You need to have actual thoughts to be able to talk to a therapist," Luke says. "Well, beyond – money, coke, money, women, money, coke."

"For a man about to be tied down for the rest of his life, you've sure got a lot of spunk in you," Ethan says. "Probably because you're not getting any anymore. Don't hate me because I'm living the life you all dream of."

"Not me," Jay says. He flashes his thick silver wedding ring at Ethan.

"When you get home on Sunday afternoon to those squalling brats of yours, James, you'll change your tune. Claire isn't here now. You can be honest."

"I wouldn't change a thing," Jay says. His chin jutting up, defiant. "And they aren't brats."

Ethan drags a shot off the tray and slams it onto the table. "I have never had sex with a married woman."

We look from one to the next. Jay sighs. "Prick." He snatches up the shot and tucks it away in one.

"Wait, you've had sex with a married woman, Jay?" Luke says.

"Yeah. She's married to me," Jay breaks into a smile and we all jeer in Luke's face as the realisation dawns on him.

"Get this cretin a shot," Ethan says.

"Anything but Jager, I can't stand the stuff," Luke says.

"Come on best man, do him in," Jay shouts.

You can't publicly name your Kryptonite and not expect to drink it. I select the Jager and push it towards Luke. After a couple of seconds staring at it, he pinches his nose and slides it down the hatch. We clap him. I don't need to turn around to feel the old boys' eyes burning into us from the bar. Their nice quiet evening ruined no doubt. Ah well, come Sunday, we're dust.

"I have never taken Class A drugs," Luke says.

"Pussy," Ethan says as he snatches up a shot. "A bit of chang shouldn't be illegal, it's bloody everywhere." He slides it away – the acrid scent of aniseed fills the air. Thank Christ the Sambuca is off the table, the second worst shot of all.

"I have never shit myself whilst sharing a bed with my childhood best friend," Ethan smiles at me.

"You fucker," I say. "And to be fair, we were hammered, it was my room, and Luke was only there because he lost his keys." He shrugs as I pick up some hideous green shot and chuck it back. Crème de menthe. A shudder riffles my shoulders they all piss themselves laughing.

Two can play at that game though.

"I have never paid for sex," I say.

Nobody drinks but the three of us stare at Ethan.

"Tell me when this happened," he shrieks.

"You said you did in Amsterdam one time," Jay says. "I'm sure of it."

"Behave," Ethan says, doing his best to look offended.

"Well, you look like the type of bloke to get pulled over for kerb-crawling so get it drunk," I say.

"If I was on duty and saw you driving around, I'd definitely think you were soliciting. Nailed on," Jay says.

"Well thank you for your input PC Plod." Ethan scowls and knocks back a shot of something transparent. Gin, hopefully. Get my kryptonite off the table nice and early.

"Here's another. I have never sold my mate out and made a fortune from his idea."

Silence.

They're all staring at me. Luke is shaking his head imperceptibly. Ethan and Jay look at me like I've just reversed over their cat.

"I think you'll find, Connor, that the lawyers said nothing was stolen and that Jay was amply rewarded for his hard work on the project." Ethan's voice is low, packing none of the bravado he's carried since he picked us up earlier in the day.

Jay watches Ethan, picks up his pint glass and chugs away half of his bitter. "This isn't something you can joke about," he says to me. His eyes narrow, his jaw set. There's a chance he's going to knock me out here. Then he cracks a smile. "That's only something me and Ethan can joke about. Dickhead."

"That's right old boy, just one of the many lawsuits my solicitor has batted away like flies with a newspaper." Ethan pinches his shirt, pulls it outwards, then lets go. "Bulletproof."

"Fucking Teflon more like," Luke says.

When I've stopped chuckling, I clock the look Ethan's giving me. He sniffs all of the clear shots. Finds one that makes him smile. He grins at me, that overly white, private school yearbook photo grin of his.

"Delving into our pasts, are we? I have never been on a date with someone who is about to marry my best mate."

He slams the gin down in front of me. Somehow none of it slops out of the glass. Fuck's sake.

I keep my eyes on the scratched, aged wooden tabletop and take my medicine. There's silence as I do so. The gin judders its way down and I cough. There's the taste of bile at the back of my throat. It's one of those drinks, where you have one bad night on it and can never go back. I shake my head like a dog coming in from the rain. When my vision settles, Luke is shooting daggers at me across the table.

"You went on a date with Amy? Why didn't you tell me?"

His head's cocked to the side like he's seeing me for the first time.

"You knew," I say. "I told you, back at uni. I'm sure I told you."

"You told me," Ethan says, that bloody smirk again. "Said you had a great night. Just a shame that she didn't agree in the end." He rubs his eyes, mocking crying.

"It was no big deal. We went out, had some food, went for a pint – literally one – and then that was it."

Luke frowns. "Out for food? You didn't go for fried chicken by any chance?"

Sweat beads in my hairline now. This room's too hot. Three sets of eyes are fixed on me. This weekend isn't supposed to be about my shame, it's supposed to be about embarrassing Luke.

"Yeah, a well-known chain."

Luke cracks up. "*You're* the KFC Guy? You?"

"We may have paid a visit to the Colonel."

"Holy shit, we joke about that all the time. We always laugh that there's some fella out there who took a girl to KFC on a first date and thought that was a perfectly reasonable thing to do. Turns out, I've known him all along. You sneaky sod not telling me." He sips his pint, his eyes laughing at me over the rim of the glass.

"You ever wonder that if you'd only taken her to Burger King, it might be you getting married instead of Luke?" Jay asks, trying to keep his face straight.

"Definitely explains why he's such a one-date wonder. I don't think he's been on a second date for about a decade," Luke says. "Now we know why. You need to branch out more. Go to a Nando's or a Wagamama's, man. Put your hand in your pocket. Stop taking girls to the drive-thru."

"Sounds like something Ethan would be into," Jay says.

Ethan scowls at me.

"Oh, mate. I need to text Amy about this. I can't believe it. All these years. So, so funny. Thank you, Con."

His hand goes to his jeans pocket and comes up empty. He pats both pockets, stands up and pats his back ones too.

"They're at the B&B, dickhead. You know the rules. Just the lads for your last night of freedom." I say, my one good idea this weekend is coming home to roost, at least my shame won't be online for a few days. No doubt there's a few weeks of Colonel Sanders memes to look forward to.

I need to keep the night focused on Luke and not on me, do some damage limitation. Grabbing four shots from the tray. I dish them out. One each.

"I have never been to John Eustace University and grown up to be a complete and utter arsehole." They all look at me. "Drink up boys, it's you."

They do as they're told and then, gasping from the tang of the booze, Ethan looks to me. "You didn't do yours, lad. You fit the bill."

I sup down the shot. Cheap vodka. One grade up from moonshine. It's like a kick in the jaw.

Ethan's up on his feet. His voice louder than before, perhaps the shots kicking in early. He finds his wallet, stuffed with twenties. "I'm off for a slash and then the next round is on me. Every shot and four pints of this bitter you insist on drinking, Luke?"

"It's from a small brewery. It's basically craft."

"There's a reason you can't buy this anywhere else, mate," Ethan says, marching towards the back of the pub.

We sit and sup what's left of the bitter. Ethan's not wrong, this stuff was average cold, at room temperature, it's borderline undrinkable. It coats my tongue, sucking all the moisture from my mouth.

After a few sips, I push it away, breaking the stag do code and leaving a drink unfinished. It's going to be a long weekend if this is the drink of choice.

Luke looks at me, smirks. Sips his drink. Smirks again. Then goes for it.

His arms fold into the wings, then he stands up and struts around by the table, his head bobbing. Then he opens his mouth "bwok, bwok,

bwok." He gives it some welly to be fair to him. Heads turn at the bar, staring at him and not me, thank fuck. Not that it stops another wave of heat sliding up my neck.

"Stop making a scene," I say.

Luke doesn't listen. He's gobbling and clucking and then he plods round the table and pretends to lay an egg on my lap. Ethan starts to howl from the bar, that guffawing stupid laugh of his. A few of the farmers join in too and I shove Luke away. He stumbles and clatters into the next table, sending an empty stool tumbling. He clutches his shin like a Premier League footballer who's just been fouled.

"Steady on, you prick," he says.

"I just didn't want you on my lap. You're making a show of yourself."

"Making a show of you more like."

"Oi," Jay says, suddenly Detective Sergeant Frost. His finger juts out, points from me to Luke and back again. "It's just a laugh. Pack it in and move on."

Luke takes his seat. "You have the right to remain silent." He rubs his shin underneath the table.

When I look away, every eye in the pub is on us. Behind the scowling old boys, Ethan struggles to hold himself together. Laughter bubbles in him and he shakes, on the cusp of losing it. The barmaid stands stock-still, hands-on hips, eyes aflame. "You break it, you pay for it," she barks. I wave my apologies and pick up the stool.

"Sorry, I didn't mean to hurt you, mate. Just felt like a tit," I mutter.

"You are a tit. That's why I love you chicken boy." He smiles for a second.

Ethan plonks down four pints of cider then goes back for the tray of shots. Luke scrunches his face up at the cider. "This isn't the local bitter. This is bloody Strongbow or some other piss."

"I'm not drinking that all night," Ethan says. "I need something I don't need to chew to get down. Besides, it's your stag party and you'll drink what you're told. Isn't that right, Colonel Sanders?"

I roll my eyes. "Yeah, to be fair."

"It's settled then. Pick these up and follow me. There's another room back here. Should be a bit more private than this place, not sure I can stand this amount of side-eye all night."

We do as we're told. I cop for Ethan's pint as he leads us with a tray of shots into the back room of the pub. He plonks the tray down and turns on a switch by the wall. There's a long light above a pool table and another above a dartboard.

"Ah, Jesus, Ethan. You know none of us can beat you," Jay says.

"Exactly. And we're playing for shots first and then cash." He throws his arms out wide like he's on MTV Cribs. "Let's get at it. Oi oi!"

There are not enough drinks in the world to get through this...

TWO

LUKE

The lads bring in more trays of shots, Jay passes me another Jager – and I cough back the vomit that rises every time I taste the stuff. The last thing this night needed was a bloody pool table. All I wanted from this stag was to get out into the hills and clear our heads with some walking. No nightclubs, no costumes, no go-karting, no 2-4-1 burgers in a chain pub. Just some time with my mates.

Now Ethan's on a roll – the pool shark. Already, the balls are racked up and he's looking round for someone to dominate. Being the best man, Connor takes the challenge. He breaks and grimaces as no balls drop into the pockets. Ethan smiles at him and gets to work. He's on the black by the time Connor gets another turn at the table. Connor pots two and then misses.

Thud.

Ethan whams the black ball home and straightens up. He smiles. "Still got it then?"

"Still got it?" Jay says. "Don't pretend you're not down a snooker club every night hustling old men out of their pensions."

"Some of us don't need the cash," Ethan says.

"But you do it anyway?" I say.

He smirks, shrugs.

"Come on," Connor says. "More shots for you lot." He starts dishing them out from the trays. He hands them out at random to Jay and Ethan but deliberately avoids the Jager and gives me a Crème de menthe instead. He doesn't meet my eye when he does but lingers close by as I slide the disgusting green liquid down my throat.

"You doing okay?" Connor asks me as Ethan starts setting up the pool balls and Jay throws a few darts over in the far corner. Con's voice is low, trying not to be overheard by the others.

"Fine."

"Not too pissed?"

"Steaming nicely."

"You having a good time, mate? That's what I need to know."

"I was."

His head snaps round towards me. "Was?"

"Until I found out you dated my wife and never told me about it."

There's a second of silence and I keep my face as straight as I can while his lips wobble and he tries to speak but can't.

"I – I – I"

I can't hold it in any longer and a splutter of laughter comes out. He stops stuttering over his words, gets himself together. "Wait. What? You're not... bothered?"

"Why would I be? You took her to a fucking KFC mate. Do you understand how good that makes me feel? I couldn't have written it any better!"

"What do you mean?"

"At first, I thought you hadn't told me because you were still sweet on her or something mad like that. But you didn't because you were ashamed of a shitty date, and you kept it under wraps." I clap him on the shoulder. "I mean if anything, thank you, man. You really helped me."

"Helped you?"

"Yeah. I mean if all I had to do as the next person to take her out was to do better than KFC, I was always going to look good."

"Where was it you went?"

"Pizza Express. About the classiest place you can go on a student budget. Got a 2-4-1 coupon me mum cut out of the paper."

He smiles. A grin watered down by a few shots of booze and a healthy dose of humiliation. No matter what they do to me this weekend, nothing will come close to this. Absolute gold.

"Which of you two old women wants the next game?" Ethan asks. "The Groom or The Colonel in for a second whooping?"

"I'll play you," Jay says. "I owe you for that tournament in Hawthorns Bar at uni. I needed that cash prize, and you won the bloody thing anyway."

"If you think you've got the stuff, come and have a go," Ethan says, beckoning to Jay. "You're even more of a chicken than Bernard Matthews over there. He plays like he's got chicken drumsticks instead of fingers. Fucking loser."

"Good to see Ethan keeping up his record of never losing and never treating an opponent with respect," Connor says.

Jay steps forwards and snatches up a cue. He towers over Ethan. Every inch the officer of the law. Square and broad. None of that matters when it comes to pool.

Ethan destroys him without letting Jay pot a ball.

"The undefeated Hawthorns Bar champion strikes again," Ethan shouts. He struts about the place using his cue as a guitar. Then stops suddenly.

"Hold on." He messes with a cupboard door in the far corner, it swings open to reveal a jukebox. A wooden cabinet filled with CDs and lined with yellow buttons. Fishing in his pocket, he drops in a quid and in a few seconds, Journey is blasting through the speakers.

"Come on, who's next?" He says over the music.

"We are."

We all turn at once to the voice behind us. The doorway between the bar and the pool room is packed full of lads. Ten of them in total. All dressed the same. Red and black checkered shirts. Blue corduroy trousers. Wellies. Wax Jackets. One of them, a tall tub of lard even bigger than Jay wears a dunce's hat that reads "GROOM" in appalling handwriting.

"Having a little celebration? A little dance? A right-old knees-up?"

The lad who speaks is much shorter than the groom. He's angular and lean. Blonde hair shaved up the sides. No so much Peaky Blinders as his barber just stopped halfway through his haircut.

Ethan stops dancing but the music still continues.

"It's my stag party," I say. "Having a few days away from it up here."

"No way. It's Wallace's stag do as well," the lad says. He points at the big lad who grimaces. He looks just like Wallace, that plasticine character from the films. "Farmer Wallace. We've all come dressed as him. This is what he wears every day, except without the straw and the sheep shit, like."

"We're going to do a bit of hiking and that," I say.

"Aye. A few do that round here. Always find it tougher than they're expecting in my experience. We're just here in our local for the night, get this one absolutely blasted so he's chucking up herding the sheep in the morning. Mind if we join you?"

I look to the others. They don't say or do anything. It's not like we want these random local fuckers in with us but what can you say?

I shrug.

They pile in.

"Good," says the blonde lad. "Cos we're here most nights so this place is ours by rights anyhow." He's up in my personal space then. His hand finding mine, shaking it. "Gav," he says, gives me a nod and moves on to Connor.

He introduces himself to Connor and Jay. Then up to Ethan.

"Ethan, ain't it?"

"Sorry, what?" Ethan says.

"Heard it from the door. Seen you dancing."

Gav smiles but Ethan doesn't, shaking his hand and clutching the pool cue in the other.

"Come on, Wallace, come and introduce yourself, you big dozy sod."

Wallace comes up to us. "Brian," he mutters with his head down. "My surname's Wallace. I'm not the guy off *The Wrong Trousers*. Obviously."

"Obviously," Connor says. "He's made from plasticine."

"Aye."

Wallace shuffles a few steps away and I let my giggle escape into my pint glass. Connor, wide eyed, flashes his teeth trying to keep it together because Gav's over to us like a shot.

"This is exactly why we don't let Wallace out very often. State of him." He shakes his head. "Who's your best man then?"

"This guy," I say, jerking a thumb at Connor.

Connor stands up straighter, puffing himself out. Doing that thing he does, trying to look like a real bloke rather than someone who works in insurance.

"You not got your stag on a tighter leash? Prepare him for the ongoing hell of marriage?"

"A few things. I took everyone's phone away, left them in the B&B so it's a wife-free zone. And he can only drink what we tell him to." Connor's voice drops a note as he speaks.

Gav juts out his bottom lip like Marlon Brando. "Fair play. Bit soft if you ask me but each to their own." He slaps Wallace on his shoulder. "You're getting fucking blasted tonight, aren't you? And then up to check on the sheep about four a.m. Hangover from hell mixed with sheep shit. That ain't gonna be pretty."

"Unlucky lad," I say.

Gav shoots me daggers, like as the stag I don't have the right to talk in his presence without permission. This is the kind of shite I can't stand about these weekends. All this macho stuff. Drinking to look hard in front of your mates. Trying to prove you're still a "lad" even though you're getting married. Whatever that's supposed to mean.

"We're just about to have a game of pool," Connor says into Gav's silent treatment.

Gav sucks his lips in, wearing some kind of weird smirk. "Not sure you are lads, only this is our local and we're always here. Bit awkward like, but we need that pool table."

"Our coins are on it," Ethan says. "You know the rules. Coins on the table, you've got to wait."

50p a game and Ethan's got about twenty-pound coins stacked on the table, like he's trying to stay on all night.

"Thing is lads, we need this space, we always use this space. I mean, I don't suppose you could just take your coins and…" Gav jerks a thumb back to the main lounge. Through the doorless gap, a few of the old boys at the bar are half paying attention to what's going on in here.

"Nah," Jay says. "I don't suppose we could." He straightens himself up to his full height. Wallace is taller than him by an inch or so, but he's doughy. Jay's in half-decent shape, muscles gained from pulling drunks out of dumps like this.

A couple of the other lads bristle at his tone. This Gav lad doesn't, he acts like he doesn't recognise what's happening.

"Thing is, we're gonna go for it pretty hardcore and I'm not sure some of you are equipped to keep up, if you get me?" He looks at me and Connor before turning to Jay.

"They'll be fine," Jay says without looking at us, puncturing any kind of pride we might have. "We aren't going anywhere."

"As you like it," Gav says. "But as soon as this money runs out, we're having that jukebox. Can't be listening to posh-boy shite all night. This is a nightmare."

"Journey's a classic," Ethan says, stepping closer with the pool cue.

"Fucking tragic mate," one of the new lads says.

Wallace watches on with wide eyes, perhaps Gav hasn't given him permission to speak or he's too dumb to get involved. Gav smiles. "This lad knows it. Absolute tripe. We'll put the classics on, don't you worry. Everyone loves the Stone Roses."

"Something like that..." I say.

Gav smiles. "You'll learn to if not. Come on, let's show there's no hard feelings here. We aren't going to fall out over some shitty Eighties rock, are we? Let us get some shots in. See if you boys can keep up. Had a few stag parties in here before. Not many of 'em can cope."

"Bring everything you've got," Jay says. "Bring it all on."

THREE

Ethan

They want to play me for the table. Of course, they do. It's written all over their faces that they don't think I'm any good. Any money it's because they've heard my accent and assume that because I pronounce all my syllables, I can't pot the balls when I need to.

"You can break," I tell the doughy sack of shit they're calling a stag. I mean, Luke's no specimen but at least he looks human, Wallace looks like he belongs with the cattle.

Wallace sets them up slowly and chalks his cue. He's one of those people that do everything slowly. Finally, he breaks, there's no real vigour to it and his technique is OK but nothing special. None of the balls find the pockets.

I scan the table but there's no need. I've already plotted out some shots that would put me one ball away from the black before I have to pot anything remotely difficult. I sigh, pretending to take my time.

What's better here?

Completely crush him and grind him into dust or…

"Gav lad," one of the morons who's watching shouts. "Get us a round in out the kitty."

Gav pulls out a bundle of notes big enough to beat a man to death with, peels a couple off and hands them to the moron. "Get them in yourself, I'm talking."

The moron scuttles off to the bar. I should thank him really. He's put this night onto another level now. There's some fun to be had with these boys.

I pot a couple then fluff the first pot that's vaguely difficult. Wallace comes to the table and pots a couple too. Then another couple. I pull one back but leave the balls so that I can clean up if I need to. Wallace bags another couple, one a fluke, one an average pot. He's only got one yellow ball left and then he's on the black.

Playing down your skills is harder than you'd think. You spend so long honing them and getting good at something, to then pretend that you aren't takes some effort. I adjust my aim. The balls still go in but off the jaws of the pocket rather than dropping straight down the middle. Try and make it look lucky rather than good.

It works. I get onto the black and then fluff it on purpose. Wallace gives his last yellow a decent whack and it rattles round the jaws of the pocket, slams into the black and pots it. Game over.

"Unlucky lad," I say. "I thought you might have me then until that happened."

"Me too," Wallace grumbles.

"He should've won, dozy bastard," Gav says. His hands thrust into his pockets, keeping all those crisp banknotes in. "I'm sure he'd beat you the next time."

"Are you?" I say. This is my territory now. Don't smile. "How sure?"

"First time I've seen Wallace lose a match in ages. He won't lose twice in a row."

Wallace grunts something that sounds like he agrees.

"We could always have a little wager, spice things up. I mean, we're in a little local in the middle of nowhere. It's not like we're off out for a night of Class As and prostitutes, is it?"

Gav looks at me with his small, cold eyes. He frowns. It's my accent, I'm sure of it. It's going to cost him a lot of money.

"Look, let's start small. A hundred quid. See how we get on? Between us all, we can afford to lose that, surely?"

Wallace looks to Gav like a puppy waiting to be told to stay by its master. Gav nods. "How much you got with you? No cashpoints for a fair way and I tell you now, we don't take cheques."

"You make it sound like I'm going to lose," I say.

Over Gav's shoulder I can see Jay, the ghost at the feast. He shakes his head over the top of his pint. Warning me off. Holding me back. Just like at university with that bloody project he never stops going on about.

He's a goddamn loser, that's the problem. He's never taken a risk in his life and that's why he's working for a police force that's on its arse and is stuck with two kids.

That's not me.

"Just don't bet any more than you can afford to lose, pal. That's all I'm saying." Gav takes the bundle of notes out, stacks a hundred quid on the table. I pull out the same and wedge them under the pound coins already stacked there.

Gav's just quoted the first rule of gambling at me – don't bet more than you can afford to lose. But beyond that, people who gamble a lot have their own personal code that applies. And my first rule is always – take any sucker dumb enough to bet against you for every penny they have.

***

Forcing myself to lose makes me want to throw up. It goes against everything I stand for. Most people have that element of pride. The innate need to do your best in everything you do. People like me, high achievers, we strive to *be* the best not just do our best. It's always worked out well for me and turning that off doesn't just happen.

I bite my lip, literally, through the raucous celebrations of this other group as Wallace drains the black ball in games worth two hundred and then four hundred quid. My fingers are tight on the cue, white knuckles clenched to bursting. We're getting to the crux of it now. I've got him where I want him. He's all powered up, strutting to the table like he's a snooker god, like even the Patron Saint of Snooker Ronnie O'Sullivan couldn't beat him. But he's playing to the best of his ability and I'm only getting started. There are other gears here and I'm going to make him pay.

By the time the cheering dies down, I've already set up the balls. I've been careful not to make eye contact with the lads, but I do sneak a glance over. Luke and Connor stand together talking rapidly into each other's ears. They've always had that, that bond, but right now, they look like they're planning to get the hell out of here.

Don't panic lads, I've got this covered.

Jay is a different story, he's just stood there, gawping. His mouth is actually hanging open. His head's totally gone. As a group, we're four hundred in the hole, but I'm about to dig us out. This last game's key. Putting it all on the line. The biggest stakes always bring the biggest rewards and now's the time to bring it all home and blow the doors off this weekend.

Jay looks up and meets my eye. I let slip a tiny wink, a little cute one just for him. He cocks his head to the side. He straightens up from his depressed slouch. Didn't take much for him to cotton on for once.

He nudges the others, has a little word behind his cupped hand. Their body language relaxes as well. It helped that they came up to me after I lost two hundred notes and made a show of trying to talk me out of playing any more. Without planning it, they helped me to raise the stakes. Their panic earned us another few hundred quid. They focus on me as I make a show of fishing out some more notes from my pockets and approaching Wallace.

Tell the driver to get the car running, chaps. All hell's going to break loose.

"Wallace, Wallace." The hillbillies stop cheering and jumping and whatever the fuck they're doing. They turn as one. The men in their ridiculous costumes.

"One last game. Let's put it all on the line. Come on. I nearly had that one."

Wallace steps towards me. Towering. "No," he says. The local accent is flat on his tongue. "We've got enough here."

"Come on," I say. "That's how gambling works. No matter how much you take someone for, you're supposed to give them a chance to earn some of it back. That's just manners." I want to say etiquette, but I don't feel like he'd understand.

"No. I don't think we should. It's getting too much."

There's a murmur of approval from his friends.

There's only one way to get him to commit to another game. Something that I won't be proud of in the cold light of day tomorrow.

"That's a shame, Wallace. I didn't think you were such a goddamned pussy."

The group falls silent like I've just slapped one of their mothers. The lads in the other group bristle and without looking back at my lot, I know they're poised to jump if I need them. But I won't. It's not going to go down like that. This lot are going to come around to my way of thinking any second now.

"I'm not. We're just talking about a lot of money."

I pull the rest of what I have out of my pocket and slap it on the table. It does the job. It calms the rage. It's the entire kitty for the weekend. Nearly £500. Equal to what Wallace has won tonight in total. "Come on. Last chance. Think about what a crazy weekend you'll have if you win all this?"

His best man whispers something in his ear, like a trainer pumping up their fighter in the corner of a boxing ring. Wallace eyes me up. Stands up to his full height and puts his money where his mouth is.

"Rack 'em up then."

"You get on that, I'll be back in a minute."

Like any dog, Wallace does as he's told. I pass my cue to Jay, make my excuses and head out for a piss.

***

There's a lot of money on the line and some fresh air will clear my head. I walk out of the back room and into the main part of the pub. It's rammed with people now. Most of them men, all of them huddled over their pints, nursing them nice and slow.

No-one bothers me as I pass. No-one even looks up from their conversations about mining or sheep or whatever they talk about in this godforsaken part of the world. The front door swings open into a darker world and I step through, gulping down cold air. A chill dances across the nape of my neck and I wipe away the cold sweat that's bunched there.

Cold air crystallises my thoughts and when I look down at my hands, I realise they're shaking. Adrenaline leaches out of me, any nerves about the forthcoming game running like a current out of my body and into the ground.

It's not the money that gets to you in games like this. I've played for more. It's the pride issue. Reputation. That's what's on the line really. The lads have a certain expectation for me. I want to impress.

I *need* to impress.

Leaning back against the brick wall of the pub, I stare at the stars. They are legion up here. Down in London, there's never the time or the inclination to look up, at least not beyond the penthouse suites and rooftop bars. I take a few steps forward, away from the pub and into the darkness of the car park and the winding country road that led us here.

My vision clears and I lean on the wooden gate, looking up into the growing black, eyes adjusting to find the detail of every single star. I'm not one for nature but fuck me, this is something. For the first time in my life, I welcome the feeling of being small. Being insignificant. The cold falls away and I let myself gaze up at the heavens like I've never done it before.

Voices shake me away from my vigil. Low muttered words. Off to my left. Somewhere behind the pub. I need to go back in anyway. I don't want anyone thinking I'm chicken shit and crying off from the high stakes.

Hands in my pockets, I walk back to the front door, but I pause, holding the handle. Instead of entering, I follow the sound round to the side of the pub. I walk slowly, quietly. I don't poke my head round the corner to see who's speaking. Their words tell me everything I need to know.

"You got enough money to cover me here, just in case?"

"Yeah, yeah. We all have. Enough money, enough of everything. This is *your* night. You know what to do. You know how to beat him."

"I don't need no pep talk. I can beat that posh prick."

This makes me smile. It's been a lifetime of class insults. Especially from yokels like these two. Southern this, posh that. I don't need to apologise for my background or my income. Fuck them both. But the part that really makes me smile is that he thinks he can win. Because he's got no fucking chance.

"What do we do if this all goes south?"

"Why would it? It's never happened before."

"You know. I get worried."

"It's your stag, just enjoy it. You won't be getting another one, so make the most of it, get pissed up and everything else will work out."

"But what about –"

"What about nothing, it'll be fine."

I don't wait for the rest of the motivational speech, it's time to get inside and take advantage of the weakness.

***

He's good but I'm better. The gloves are off now. There are no missed pots. No sloppy safety shots. Wallace's eyes are heavy with whisky now but I'm seeing clearly. Every angle, every roll of the ball. Like I'm plugged into the Matrix.

Right from his break, I punish him and pot four of my seven yellow balls. He answers with two of his own but then it's on me and I can see it all so clearly. I blast my three remaining balls away and leave myself set up with a nice, straight pot on the black.

It all came down to this. Unlucky Wallace, my son.

I switch hands, going southpaw for the final humiliation. Wallace's jaw clenches as he watches on, powerless, but he doesn't say anything. Just stands there like a lummox, his cue wedged into his meaty hands.

I take a breath and gently roll the black ball into the pocket.

Bedlam. The lads are on their feet. Jay and Luke and Connor piling on me, knocking the table, and sending the rest of the balls flying. Money scatters onto the felt and they're cheering, screaming. Jumping up and down, mobbing me.

I don't join in. I smile and that's it. Even at the centre of it. I stay calm. Zen. When they've finished mobbing me, I pick up the money and pocket it. Then I make a point of seeking out Wallace and shaking his hand. He looks dazed, like he's just picked himself up off the canvas. Punch drunk, or just actually drunk. I shake the best man's hand and he grips it tight, trying to crush my fingers. I don't back down, I squeeze back and meet his gaze.

He releases my hand and I don't hold it in, I throw my head back and shout at the ceiling. "Get in there!"

He stares at me, his features narrow and set. Then he smiles, it barely qualifies as one but it's the best he can do. "Get on and enjoy it all while you can, pal. Make the most of it."

I turn away from this freak and back to the lads. They're dancing and shouting and laughing. Music thuds in the background. Glasses clink. A thousand pounds burns a hole in my pocket and the night's just getting started.

"Oi, oi," I shout to them, getting them whipped into a frenzy.

This night is ours.

FOUR

Jay

As much as it pains me to admit, Ethan is fun to be around. He's really delivered here. No matter what's gone on between us, I doubt I'll forget that feeling. When that black ball dropped home, it felt like we were back at uni again. All the weight slid off, freeing us. Any hangover from work or thinking about the kids just fell away and for those few seconds, my voice raw and loud, I was back, I was me.

I sip some cider and eye the locals. The initial buzz is over, we're in the most dangerous time. As amazing as Ethan's been at pool, this is how fights start. Someone spouting off, someone riling up the locals. It's like with football when the away team scores a late winner. The whole crowd turns, nasty, feral. Just like that.

We're finishing off our drinks and my lads are chatting away loudly. They're not giving out any abuse, but the locals are huddled together, and it doesn't look good. Something isn't right. We need to get gone.

"Come on lads, let's get out of here," I say.

Ethan looks at me like I've just suggested we get together and go to church. "Leave now? Are you kidding? I own this town. We've won a fucking grand!"

"You won five hundred quid really because you put five hundred in."

"Don't get smart, Jay. It never has suited you."

"And it's never exactly been a problem for you has it? You can't stand here in this pub – their local – getting pissed up with their money and expect no repercussions. Whether you're trying to or not, you're rubbing their faces in it. We need to go."

"Go where?" Luke asks. "It's my stag, I don't want to go to bed before last orders. We've just won a ton of money, let's piss some of it away."

I shake my head. "Come on, you know what I do for a living. I know how fights start."

"Well maybe you should stop being Detective fucking Rebus for a few days and just enjoy what's happening," Ethan says. "Maybe even say thank you."

"I won't be doing that."

"You never do. It's like the Marsden project all over again."

"Don't fucking start."

Luke and Connor flinch at my raised voice and gritted teeth but Ethan doesn't. He smiles. "There it is. I knew you hated me."

"I don't hate you, Ethan. But I think you've pissed off the locals and we should go. Now."

I take the lead, walking past them, towards the doorway that splits the pool room from the rest of the pub. The barmaid appears in the gap, blocking my way. She's wearing a grin and holding a tray full of shots.

"Oh, sorry, love," she says, not moving out of my way. "I heard all this cheering and thought seeing as we've got two stag parties in tonight, I'd bring a few more shots through. On the house, like."

"Very kind of you," I say, manners taking me on autopilot out of her way.

She totters into the room and places the tray on a table in the corner. "Lads," she calls, breaking both groups from their conversations. "Would you care for a few free shots? Celebrate what's coming for you all?"

"Oh, aye," Gav says. "Thanks, Maria. Spot on that."

"And you lads," Maria says, gesturing at my lot.

"We're just about to –" I say.

"Nice one," Connor says, snatching up a drink.

There's no choice now, I take the last remaining shot. A fucking Jager, of course, and raise it as Gav proposes a toast.

"To friends old and new," he smiles at us all. There's something sharp to his smile, his eyes too pale to show any joy.

Maria scuttles out and we neck our shots. The glasses don't even hit the table before Wallace speaks.

"I want another match."

Of course, he does.

I turn to the others, to show them my "I told you so face" but they're all looking at Wallace, not at me. There's something about their faces, their features set hard, it stops them looking like the lads I know. For a second they could be any lout on a Friday night in a kebab house. Too much ale and violence on their minds.

"How much are we talking about here?' Ethan says, "because short of owning your mother, I've taken everything you have."

A hiss from the locals behind Wallace, but the big man doesn't flinch. It's as though the air in the room thickens, all the oxygen removed from it. There's no getting back to laughing and joking.

"Something more than money," Wallace mumbles. "I want to play you for pride."

He stops talking like he's waiting for Ethan to respond. Nothing comes. Like any good businessman, Ethan stands silently, waiting for his opponent to finish.

"How's this – we'll clear off and leave you alone in here if you win. But if we win, you lot have to piss off. And how's this, yeah, the loser and his mates have to do a forfeit or dare that the winner chooses. Could be anything."

"Anything?"

"Anything."

"Anything like head up the farm and skull fuck one of your sheep?" Ethan says.

My shoulders sag before I can stop them. Air rushing out of me like a child's balloon. What the fuck is doing? We've not had that much. A few pints and a few shots. Enough to get a buzz but you can't say that. Ten of them and four of us. Play the percentages, lad.

"Laugh all you want," Gav says, "but those sheep are worth more dead or alive than any man in this room."

"Okay..."

"I think you're just making your ignorant, London, Tory boy jokes cos you don't have the balls to take Wally on again. You got lucky last time out, and you know you can't do it again."

Ethan raises an eyebrow at us, amused Gav hasn't clocked he's been hustled.

"I think I've got the stones for it, mate," Ethan says, chucking on his worst Dick Van Dyke cockney accent. "And I'm looking forward to sorting something special for you when I win." He steps forward and claps Gav on the back then gives him a thumbs up.

Ethan drops a coin into the pool table and unleashes the balls with a clank of metal. He starts setting them up, his cue propped against the wall. Gav comes closer to him, right in Ethan's personal space, their noses an inch apart.

"We ain't going to back out if we don't win this. We expect the same of you. Got it?"

Ethan smiles – his most infuriating shit-eating grin. Part of me wants to see him get knocked out. In the fifteen years we've known each other, that smile has made my piss boil more than anything else, like he practises being a dickhead in the mirror.

"We aren't backing out and we definitely aren't losing."

"I'm going to enjoy seeing this, Ethan," Gav says. He's still standing too close. Should I step in? Putting a hand on him is likely to make it all kick off.

"Look, Ethan," I say, trying for a diplomatic solution. "Why don't you give them their money back, we'll take a few bottles back with us to the rooms and we'll carry on drinking there."

Gav rounds on me. That look I see so often in pub car parks and in the gutters outside nightclubs. That smaller man, thinking he's David and I'm Goliath, reckoning that the bigger they are the harder they fall.

Men like me don't fall, pal.

"Just give the money back and sort it out? Is that how it is? That's fine, is it? When you've come in here and let posh boy take our money. When you're staying at the town B&B. When you've come up here in that black Land Rover that costs more than our houses and that's never been dirty before. That's all alright, is it?"

Wallace walks over and stands next to Gav, the pair of them mismatched but equally amped up. Equally dangerous. The other locals wait for their cue.

My lads fall silent. Every trace of booze has dropped from my system now. All details resumed. The floor is steady beneath my feet. The message creeps from my brain out down through my skin. *Get out.* Every instinct as a copper tells you to run towards trouble, to help, to do something, but all I want to do now is to run away.

"Look lads, we don't want any trouble. We'll just get off. We'll find somewhere else to drink, somewhere else to stay. It's no bother. Seriously," I say.

"You're staying."

I turn round at the sound of the voice, looking past the stools and the tables lined with empties. There's a serving hatch to the bar, the light of the fruit machine twinkling behind the barmaid as she leans through. Her courtesy and customer service face are long gone. Her features are set almost as hard as her voice.

"We settle things properly in this place. If there's a quarrel, it gets resolved. If it festers, it just leads to more problems, and I will not have fighting in my pub. Understand?" She looks across at our group with that cold gaze and then smiles at the regulars. "As you were lads."

Gav smiles at Maria, gives her a curt nod. Opens his hands out wide like he's wondering what else we expected.

Without saying anything, Ethan pulls the money from his pockets, he dumps it all on the table. Tens and twenties and the occasional fifty falling onto the felt and onto the floor. "We're done. No quarrels in here, right?" He says.

Gav swipes the money off the table, notes flying everywhere like Scrooge McDuck's wet dream. Notes slide under tables, nestle against the skirting boards in the corners of the room. Nobody moves to pick them up. A thousand pounds lying like trash on the floor.

"You're in it now, Ethan. You get me? You're playing. You want to walk out? Fine. You earn it. You win and you go, nobody will touch you, you take your money back to the B&B and off you pop. If we win, you still do the forfeit. No pussying out. You do it and we're square. Yeah?"

It's a rhetorical question.

We're doing it.

"Come on then," Ethan says. All confidence gone from his voice.

"Just in case you change your mind," Gav says. He points to the doorway. It's packed with the locals. Men and women, grizzled, shaped by the landscape of this remote community. Dead eyes and cut hands. Mud-stained boots and frayed jeans. Some of the men are preceded by beer bellies but their necks and shoulders are still powerful, capable.

Locals sup their pints and my hands twitch for a drink. I snatch up a half dead pint of bitter and down the lukewarm contents. I'm not even sure if it was mine. Anything to ease this tightness in my chest.

Wallace gets a pound coin out. "Call it," he says to Ethan.

Ethan chooses heads and wins. Decides to break. He chalks his cue, takes his time. His shoulders rise and fall out of rhythm. He takes aim and smashes the balls apart. A red ball flies into the pocket and we cheer. My fist bunches so tight my fingers ache.

With his next shot, he sinks another red and then rattles the pocket on a tough shot. He doesn't leave Wallace much to go on but as Ethan steps away from the table, his face is pale.

"Go on, Wallace, lad." One of the locals shouts before the room falls silent again.

Wallace is moving differently to the previous game. Holding the cue with an ease he didn't have before. There's something athletic to him now. He checks angles and double checks them, bent low to the table. Ethan chalks his cue over and over, his eyes never leaving Wallace.

Wallace bends his huge frame forwards, pulls back his cue and takes his shot. The yellow ball rattles the pocket and bounces away to a groan from his entourage. It trickles down the table and bumps another yellow that drops into the pocket.

The cheers from Wallace and his friends rip through me like a physical blast of heat. Connor's shoulders slump. Luke hisses under his breath, going through every swear word he knows. Ethan doesn't react at all, his eyes remain on the game.

With a smirk, Wallace mumbles "sorry" to Ethan, who doesn't look at him. Shrugging, Wallace turns back to the table. He doesn't bother concealing his smile as he goes to work. The first pot he makes is a simple tap in but after that he's a machine. He nails three long pots with a precision even Ethan can't manage. After those, it's a formality. The last two yellows drop easily, and he leaves himself a simple shot for the black.

He's facing Ethan as he leans in to make the final pot. Ethan's not moved – his hands brilliant white on his cue. "This one's for you, Tory boy," says Wallace. He closes his eyes as he takes his shot, rolling the ball into the pocket. As it thunks home, the rest of his stag party go berserk, shouting and cheering. Howling like dogs.

We're fucked.

Ethan slams his cue down. "Let's get the fuck out of here. Now," he says.

He strides past me but stops short of the door. There's nowhere for him to go. Despite the commotion from Wallace and Gav, the locals are unmoved. Some of them still hold their pints. The fire exit is barred shut. We're not going anywhere.

"Didn't think you'd be leaving without your forfeit, did you?" Gav says. There's a light in his eyes now. Like an actor on stage. "I expected more from you, Ethan. You don't try and wheedle your way out. You fess up when you've let your mates down, 'cos that's what you've done."

"You haven't, Eth." Luke says. "You did your best."

"He fucking tried to mug me off. Me! Well, you got what you paid for then lad. Now the night properly begins." Wallace is spitting as he talks. Piggy eyes stretched too wide. A smile going beyond a few pints worth. There's something else there, something wrong.

"Let's get this over with," Connor says, his voice brittle. He looks like he's shrunk into himself. "We'll do the forfeit but one rule, it can't end up online. We've got jobs. We've got lives."

"Nothing we do tonight will end up on the internet," Wallace says.

"That's a promise," Gav chips in.

Everyone's all smiles then. Our lot because they've promised us something, their lot because they're about to get what they want. Whatever the fuck that is.

"Come on then," Ethan says. "Let's get on with it. Whatever this forfeit is. Whatever you want. Let's get it over with and let's get on with our weekend."

The locals snigger. Not just the stag party. All of them, the ones crammed in the doorway, the barmaid. As the current of laughter runs through them all, the base of my back tingles. There's nothing good coming out of this. Humiliation, maybe pain lies ahead.

I try to slow my breathing. Try to remember times I've battled my way out of trouble. Exchanged punches with suspects, been cornered. Memories disappear like smoke.

"Just tell us what you want us to do," Ethan says. His voice is flat. His head hangs, his good posture destroyed by the weight of defeat.

Our defeat.

"First, you're going to get a history lesson," Gav says. "None of you know why you're here, do you?"

"For my stag do," Luke says. "They all know."

Gav shrugs. "One last night of freedom, eh? It wasn't just about girls and booze. You know how this tradition came about? Centuries ago, before we modernised it and took the meaning away? Of course, you don't."

"Get on with it," Ethan says. "Come on."

Without saying anything, Gav steps forward and cracks Ethan across the face with the back of his hand. Ethan's chin snaps round to the side. He stays on his feet. Fair play to him.

My hands ball into fists at my sides and Connor surges forward from next to me. I put a hand across his chest, stopping him. "Don't," I say. "It'll only make things worse."

"Smart man," Gav says. "Listen to the big boy. Don't make things worse."

Connor simmers down, stands straight. Attentive. The good boy he usually is.

"What men used to do, real men, they used to take their friends into the woods, and they'd hunt together the day before a wedding. When they'd killed something, they'd cook it and share the spoils together. That's where all this came from. A simple act of hunting and sharing meat."

"What's that got to do with anything? I couldn't give a shit." I say.

Gav smiles again, turns to Wallace. "I think this one is the strongest. He's going to be fun."

Wallace guffaws. Almost like a child as he puts his hand up to his mouth. "Tell 'em, Gav. I don't wanna wait."

Gav claps his friend on the back. "So, this is how it's going to work. You've got an hour to get your shit together, get out of our pub and find yourself somewhere to hide. After that, we're coming for you. Old school style. We're going to hunt you. One by one or in a group.

Makes no odds. But come Sunday morning, there's only one man left standing."

"And what? You're going to hurt us? Kill us?" I say. The sarcasm winning out this time.

"Yeah. Exactly that," Gav says. He turns to the barmaid leaning through the serving hatch. "Maria, can you help me out a little here please? Is Bessie back there?"

Who the fuck is Bessie? Some old bird they wheel out to tell tourists they're only pissing about.

My stomach clenches as Maria returns to the hatch. She's holding a shotgun. She passes it to Gav, her eyes hard, her mouth turned into a grin. Gav takes it from her, checks for cartridges and cocks the weapon.

Any hope I had that this was a joke dies at that sound.

I've seen weapons before on the job. I'm pretty sure it's real.

"Shotgun ain't the most practical for a hunt," Gav says, looking at each of us in turn down the barrel. He lingers on each of us. There's no warm piss running down anyone's legs, but the cold steel sensation of fear tickles my spine.

"This is just for show in these situations. Make it clear we ain't fuckin' about, like."

"Jay, do something," Luke hisses.

He looks at me, and I give an almost imperceptible shake of my head. He's got a gun, what can anyone do?

"That's it," Wallace says, snapping his fingers and pointing over. "He's gonna say it."

There's a second of silence as I swallow, trying to relocate my bollocks. "Look lads, I don't like to bring it up but I'm a police officer. OK? There's simply no way you can do this and get away with it. What will people say if three of us don't come home?"

"Wahey!!!" They all shout together. All these fucking savages that are holding us at gunpoint. They laugh and cheer and slap high fives.

What the fuck are they doing?

"We were wondering how long it'd take you. You lot, you coppers, fuckin' pigs, can't hold it in for long can you? Of course, you're a copper. You think we didn't know? James Frost. Sorry, Detective Sergeant James Frost."

He points the shotgun at Connor. "Connor Grant. Accountant at Bingley Shreeves."

Then to Ethan. "Ethan Stanley. Investment banker, kind of. Money launderer, kind of. Entrepreneur of a sort. Professional gambler, almost."

Ethan opens his mouth to speak but closes it again.

The shotgun finds its way to Luke.

"Luke Connolly. Personal financial advisor."

Gav sighs and looks at Wallace. "Lots of fuckin' boring jobs this time, eh? Where are all the outdoor workers? Labourers? People who are in good nick?"

Wallace shakes his head. "Sad. It'll be too easy."

"I'm a police officer. People will come looking for us. I know how this works," I say.

One of the old boys crowding in the doorway steps forward. Straggly beard. Pot belly. Sad eyes and a shake of the head. "You'd think so, wouldn't you? But that ain't how it goes. Martin Compton, the Chief of Cumbria Police, where'd you think he grew up? Been married twenty odd years now, maybe more. You read much about missing people in these parts?"

I shake my head, can't meet the old lad's eye. The answer's plain.

"Course you haven't, when I was a copper round here it was part of the fittings, almost in the job description. You look after the place and the people, that includes their traditions. *Our* traditions. Most men in this room are married, they ain't sitting in a prison cell are they?"

"Doesn't look like it."

"Too right," says the old boy, blending back into the crowd. "You'll do well to remember that for the next forty-eight hours, Sergeant."

There's nothing else to say, nothing else to do. I try to keep my head up, literally, but it's a dead weight. My whole body wants to crumple in on itself, fold down into the smallest package possible and give up.

I have no ideas. I have no plan.

This is happening.

The silence is broken by Gav cocking the shotgun again. He raises one eyebrow, his eyes whiter than before, wider.

"It's your time you're wasting lads. You've got an hour. Get gone. Get hiding. Get running. But you can be assured of one fucking thing. Next time we see you..."

He points the gun at me and pretends to shoot. His lips sneer a word.

"Bang."

FIVE

Jay

"Do something, Jay."

The blessing and the curse of being a copper. When something, anything, happens, all eyes turn to you. A pub fight. A bereavement. People just wanting advice on a broken car headlight and the law about their MOT. Any trivial fucking thing and they expect you to know the answer.

Sometimes it makes you proud being that person, that rock for other people, knowing that those around you respect you and that you'll step up to help. It gives you strength, but at the same time it can suck the life out of you when there's nothing anyone can do.

Like now.

Every eye in the room is on me as this idiotic Gaz cocks about with his shotgun, being the big man and waving the fucking thing around the place like he's in *Scarface*. He's chatting total shit but he's serious. Firearms aren't my speciality, but I've been on the scenes of enough assaults and brawls to know the difference between a chancer and someone who follows things through.

Gav and Wallace and their cronies aren't joking.

Ethan starts mouthing off, giving forth about lawyers and influence. He's one sentence away from saying "don't you know who I am?"

Connor looks over at me, eyes wide with questions. Reality is sinking in for him too in his own quiet way.

"We need to get out of here," I say. My voice a rumbling bass beneath Ethan's nasal whining.

Without instructions, Connor pulls on Luke's elbow and leads him towards the door. The locals are laughing as Ethan gets shriller and red in the face.

I see this a lot at work. People in the big houses and the fancy jobs, they can't accept that crime touches them too sometimes. And not just the white-collar, tax-dodging stuff you read about in the papers. Violence comes for everyone sooner or later. An assault, a road rage incident, a breaking and entering while they sleep upstairs. There's this same righteous indignation every time. Because they're minted, nothing bad can ever happen to them.

If we weren't neck deep in the shit, I'd be laughing in Ethan's face about now.

I put a hand on his shoulder. "Come on, Ethan. We've got to go."

"Do we though? Are they really going to do anything or is this just some stupid stag do prank pulled by a load of hillbillies with nothing else to do?"

"They're serious mate, come on."

"I bet that's not even a real gun," Ethan says, waggling a finger towards Gav. "It's probably a fucking water pistol or something. An air rifle at best."

The black metalwork and wooden butt of the gun shimmer under the pub lights. It's as real as me and Ethan.

"Seriously. We need to move before someone gets hurt."

"Listen to your friend," Gav says. "Fifty-eight minutes before we come to bury you, posh boy. No-one's joking here."

"You're taking the piss out of us. Taking the absolute bloody piss." Ethan's voice is approaching a pitch only dogs can hear. His eyes round and white as he speaks.

I drag him away and the four of us are standing by the door that separates the main bar area and the back room. The place is packed with locals. Hard eyes. Set jaws. They don't part for us.

"Come on," Luke says. "We've got to go. Let us out."

"What's the magic word?" One of them says, local accent dripping from the words.

"Please!" Luke wails.

The man smiles and the crowd parts barely enough for us to get through. Our path to the door is full of shoulder barges and snide kicks. Laughter echoes around us until we stumble out through the front door and into the night.

A few cars dot the car park at irregular intervals. Apart from the lights on the front of the pub, the landscape ahead of us is coated in darkness. Various shades of grey and purple and black. In the far distance, Christ knows how many miles away, lights twinkle. Safety across valleys and rivers and gorges and lakes. Would that be Carlisle or Barrow? Somewhere similar.

There's no chance of us making it that far.

Cold assaults us and as I tug my shirt around me, it offers no warmth. All that stag do bravado extends to not wearing a jacket. It's not winter yet but after being roasted in the pub, any change in temperature feels horrendous. The lads' pale faces all turn to me and I'm about to speak when Connor points past me and mutters something I don't catch.

Following his gaze, I turn. Gav and Wallace are in the car park. The locals pile out as well, crammed into the doorway. Gav holds the shotgun at his hip, a rookie stance but his hands know their way around the weapon. So much of this is just for show.

"Just in case there was any doubt in your minds, lads."

He lifts the shotgun to his shoulder, points it over our heads and up at the stars. He pulls the trigger and the night rips apart with a bang that resonates through my head as Gav cocks the weapon and unleashes another round. Ethan's hands find his ears and we're all bent double, crouching, hiding, even though this lunatic isn't shooting to kill.

There's a ripple of applause from the locals. A chorus of laughter. The remnants of the noise still rumble around us, lingering on the hills and in the valleys. Somewhere in the distance, a dog barks into the night.

"Nobody is here to fuck about," Gav says. "Now, go."

Wallace steps forwards. "Fifty-five minutes and counting lads." That cartoon grin again. "Make it fun for us, yeah?"

The lads look to me again. Waiting for some wisdom or divine fucking intervention. I have no ideas.

"Let's get going."

And we break into a run.

***

Everywhere around here is dark and unfamiliar. Streetlights are infrequent, one outside each house or shop but nothing in between. We jog down the road from the pub, its divots and potholes hidden by the dark. Each of us stumbling and lurching as we struggle with our balance. Eyes searching for the next hazard and heads turning to look for pursuers.

No-one's coming.

Not yet.

This should be funny, a few pints and shots in, lads stumbling all over the place - but it isn't. Sweat coats my back and cools even as I run. The temperature is dropping and we need some proper gear before we go any further tonight. It took us ten minutes to walk to the pub from the B&B. The key scrapes my leg as I run, jagged teeth through the material of my jeans.

"Where are we going, Jay?" Luke asks. He's panting and I wonder when he last did some proper cardio.

"B&B. Let's get the hell out of here."

"Yeah. Alright. Makes sense."

We run the rest of the way in silence, Luke and Ethan at the back. Connor's a few paces behind me. I'm leading the way, as per. It's impossible to sprint in the darkness on this surface so we lope and jog as best we can. Mud splatters up my jeans and soaks into my trainers. Pain thuds in my joints as my weight shifts and lurches.

After a few minutes of silent running, we reach the B&B. Stopping at the low stone wall, I put my hand on the wooden gate and steady myself. Blood thumps through my temples. Cold air in my lungs. It's not the exercise that's got my heart rate up but when I look at the others, they're slumped forward, hands on knees. Red faces and blurry eyes.

If anything, the exercise has helped me. Some fresh air, some distance from the pub and those people. A couple of deep breaths calm me down and calm seeps through me.

Then it comes, out into the night. Laughter. It starts as a trickle but then it gushes out and Ethan is howling laughing, like he's front row at The Comedy Store. Side splitting laughter. It takes him a minute to get himself together and when he does, we're gawping at him like he's gone mad.

"Come on, lads. You've got to admit, that was pretty funny back there," he says.

"Funny?" Luke says. "What was funny about having a gun pulled on us?"

"Mate, it can't have been real. Blank firing at best. In the pub, I thought it was real, but it can't be. It doesn't make any sense. None of it is real, surely?"

"Your fear was pretty real," I say. "You were as scared as we were."

"Yeah, of course. But think about it, what's funnier for them? To hunt people down and kill them, like they could even get away with it, or to pretend that's what they're doing and scare some strangers out of their local boozer?"

"It was real, Eth. I'm sure of it. We need to get our things and get the fuck out of here. We'll find somewhere else to stay, miles away. Con, there's got to be some nice places nearby, right?"

Connor fumbles for his phone and then gives up. He's taken them and locked them in his room to keep us away from our other halves. "I don't know. This place is out on a limb. That was the point."

"Fine. We'll get the keys, get packed up and get gone. We can find somewhere else to get pissed in the morning. Sleep in the car if need be," Ethan says.

"Aren't we all over the limit?" Connor mumbles, almost to himself.

"No coppers are going to be out looking for drink drivers round here, OK? It'll all be fine. Let's just get inside," I say.

The wooden gate squeals open at my touch, killing any retorts dead. There's no chance of being caught over the limit somewhere this remote. If the worst comes to the worst, I'll have a chat, copper to copper.

We half-jog down the path to the B&B. In the daylight, there was a touch of neglect to the place. Nothing serious. Splintered wooden window frames in need of a paint job, an overgrown front garden. Everything in need of modernisation. But in the darkness, lit up by the soft lights inside, it's beautiful. The sanctuary we need.

I open the front door and hold it as the lads troop in. The reception area is empty. A radio whispers the news from behind the counter. A brass bell sits on the wooden sideboard. My hand tingles with the need to press it but we walk past. The less fuss we make the better.

Up the stairs, aware of the muddy prints we're leaving on the carpet. There are only four rooms in the place and Connor's booked them all. A bumper weekend for the woman that runs it. My room is furthest from the stairs.

"Grab your stuff and get down to the car asap. No more than five minutes, yeah?"

They mutter their agreements and let themselves into their rooms. Fire doors swinging shut behind them. Fumbling with the key, I get the door open and snap on the light.

Shit.

The room is immaculate. Bed neatly made. Cups and kettle cleaned and returned. Everything in its place. All my things are gone.

Turning back into the corridor, the other lads are already there. Their faces tell me all I need to know. Connor's hands are kneading away, gripping and grasping each other. Luke's jaw is set firm. Ethan's chin is upturned, that familiar defiance. "We need to find the owner," he says. "Because this, is definitely not fucking funny."

We troop back downstairs and the owner, Valerie, is sitting behind the desk. A fresh cup of tea steams on the countertop, the radio turned up to a more audible level. "Sorry I missed you, boys. I was just getting a little top up."

Valerie is a slight woman with a mane of blonde hair that's too big for her body. She looks like her bones are hollow, avian. Her thin fingers fold over each other and she leans back in the office chair as she speaks.

"Where's our stuff?" Luke asks. There's a quiver to his voice.

"I don't know what you're talking about," Valerie says. She scoops up her cup and sips the tea, not once taking her eyes from Luke's face.

"Yes, you do. We arrived here with things. Clothes. Bags. Mobile phones. Cash. Car keys. They're all gone."

"Ah yes, *those* things. They're gone. We packed them up into that car of yours and had it towed away."

"What?!" Ethan can't hold back any longer. His hands splay on the counter, and he leans over towards Valerie. She doesn't flinch. She just raises the cup to her lips again and drinks.

Words spin and tumble in my mind but none of them stick. They're like snowflakes melting as they touch the ground.

"After you left, Wallace and Gavin came round. Told me that you four had been chosen. It's an honour you know, it really is. We see quite a few of them here. Most of them in fact. Some of them are lovely lads, just like you. Polite and clean. Some of them though," she shudders. "Ground's the best place for them."

"You knew?" Connor says.

Valerie nods.

"We spoke over the phone when I booked, and you knew the whole time? You told me about local walks and pubs and everything. You were so nice and calm..." Connor steps forward and mashes his fists onto the countertop. The brass bell jumps and lets out the ghost of a ding. Valerie smiles at the bell but there's no humour in her when she looks back at Connor. I step forward, take his arm, pull him back.

"Please," I say. "I'm sorry about him. But we need our things. We need our car. We need to leave."

"You're the copper," she says. "Thought it'd be you taking charge. You're the one I'm banking on to survive it. You're built like an elk. Not like the rest of these wimps." She eyes the others and shudders.

She cuts off my attempt to speak. Eyes sharp. Her face bent around her words.

"Oh, don't look so surprised, man. Bloody hell, you coppers aren't the only ones with brains. We've been doing this for *generations* up here. You think we haven't had a cop involved before? Jesus, they used to help us run the thing for a while, when that new Chief Constable was still a bobby on the beat."

"This is fucking wrong," Ethan shouts. "Help us. Please. This isn't right, just let us go. Nobody will know."

Valerie splutters. "My whole village would know. Me and Robbie Hampton have been taking the cars and the possessions for years. He disposes of the cars sometimes, sometimes we fake a car crash. Got a scrap metal place – you've made him a few bob tonight."

She sips her tea.

"You've made it easier than most though, leaving all your phones in the rooms." She winks at Connor. "Thanks for that one, *best man*. Usually, they steal them in the pub. Makes the whole thing a bit more sordid adding robbery into the mix. Now, it's just tradition."

"Please," Ethan says. "I can pay you whatever you want. Buy you a new life somewhere else. A lovely city pad. Fancy car. Anything you like?"

"This is what I like," Valerie spits. "This place is my home, and the stag parties are part of it. It's tradition. My daddy took a life just like his daddy before him. My husband Jeff, God rest his soul, he took one too. If I'd been blessed with sons, then I'd have expected them to do their duty. If we lose our traditions, we lose our way as a people. I'd rather die myself than turn you loose."

Connor turns to me. "Do something, Jay." The whites of his eyes burn against the soft light of the room. Feral and bright.

I shake my head. "We've got to get going. This shit is serious and we're losing time."

"He's right," Valerie says. She necks the last of her tea, tilting her head back as the liquid slides down her sinuous throat. "But don't forget your leaving gift." She points to four deep green canvas rucksacks.

"What the fuck is this?" I say.

She tuts. "They always lose their manners in the end. Just a few little pick-me-ups to make the game interesting. Torches. Energy bars. That kind of thing. Just do me a favour?" We all look at her. "Make a proper fist of it. It makes for a much better wedding when the groom's had to work for his prize."

Without saying anything, I step forward, seize a pack, and step out through the front door into the cold. It takes a moment, but the others follow me out into the night, packs on and no fucking idea where we go next.

SIX

Connor

This is hopeless.

For a few minutes on the jog between the pub and the B&B, when the fresh air hit, there was something that felt like belief. Away from those animals in the pub, it felt likely that they were joking. A blank firing weapon. Some sort of sick local dare to scare tourists away from the best seats in the pubs. It all fell into place.

But the sight of that empty room. All my stuff gone. The room looking like I'd never been there. Ethan's car gone.

This isn't the first time they've done this.

This is not a joke.

Outside the B&B, everyone starts talking at once. Jay trying to take the lead and get us organised, Ethan bitching and moaning like usual, Luke panicking, and me... What am I doing? I'm shouting and saying *something* but I'm not thinking anything through. Just talking on instinct. I take a breath. Clear my head.

"Lads! Just shut the fuck up!"

They fall silent. For the first time since we've all met up, they look at me. Actually, see me. This whole evening so far, I've been side-lined. As the best man, it's time to step up and take charge.

"Standing here bickering right outside this fucking B&B isn't helping anyone. Everything we say is being listened to. I point to one of the upstairs windows where the angled glass of the open window reflects the streetlight. A curtain twitches behind the pane.

I pull the lads in close and whisper. "Walk off in any direction you like but make your way back in two minutes time."

They all nod. Without another word, we break apart and take different paths off through the village.

***

We meet behind the barn. Mud splatters up our jeans. My shoes take on liquid like a punctured dinghy. The animal reek of straw and shit is almost physical in the back of my throat. The solitary streetlight is doing its best, but shadows lie thick in the corners. Darkness gathers around us, waiting to pounce. Luke is the last to arrive, out of breath. The lads wait for me to speak.

"If we're going to survive this, we've gotta work together. Jay and Ethan, put whatever there is between you aside, nobody needs to be the alpha here, alright? We just need to be a team."

"Says the man taking sole charge." I can't make out Ethan's features in the shadows, but I assume he's joking and move on.

"They've given us a chance here by giving us equipment. We've got to use it the best we can."

"Do you think they want us to escape?" Luke says.

"No. I think they want it to be more of a challenge," Jay says. His words hang over us for a few seconds before I speak again.

"Open your rucksacks and see what they've given us," I tell them.

They do what they're told. I reach into my bag and feel more than see everything inside. A torch, heavy duty with a thick plastic handle.

My hand slides over plastic, crinkling as it moves. Ethan's torch flashes on, blinding me.

"What are you doing?" I hiss.

"Seeing what they've given us." He shines the torch into his rucksack. Apart from the torch he's got a luminous waterproof jacket, a folded laminated map, five protein bars and a dented metal canteen for holding water. I wonder how many poor bastards have used this thing in the past and how many of them now lie rotting under these hills.

A quick glance with Ethan's torch into the other rucksacks reveals the same contents. Each waterproof shimmers in the torchlight, reflective and striking. There are variations in some of the products, in brands and models, but we've all got the same things.

"Not much to go on, is it?" Jay says. "They've not even given us any water."

"Plenty of that in streams and whatnot, old boy. I'm surprised it isn't raining now, we are in the North after all," Ethan replies.

I could tell him that drinking out of streams without proper checks is a sure-fire way to finish the day shitting your guts out in a bush somewhere, but one thing at a time.

"Let's hope it doesn't rain," Luke says as he unfurls his waterproof from his rucksack. Not only is it at least three sizes too big, but it's luminous orange. Reflective stripes line the arms and the back. A rain jacket made for runners and cyclists, so they don't get wiped out on country roads. Or in this case, designed to make whoever wears it a moving target.

"Before we do anything else, does anyone want to swap protein bars?" Ethan says. His words come through his nose, the emphasis he puts on them makes my chest tighten. "I can't *stand* peanut butter. Anyone want to switch for a choccie one?"

"Are you allergic?" I ask.

"No. I just don't like it."

"Well shut the fuck up then. We might end up eating each other at this rate. A bit of peanut butter won't hurt you."

He scowls, the lines of his face harsher in the torchlight than they were in the pub. Heavy fingers tap me on the shoulder and I jump. Jay stands behind me.

"I've found where we are on the map." He points to it, holding it up as Ethan tries to shine the torch at an angle that doesn't reflect directly on the laminate surface.

We all peer in. The map is sparse. It's vaguely familiar from Google Maps, back when I was researching places to come for a hike in the Lakes. The topography of the area, one of its selling points at the time, is now set against us. Red loops show steep rises. Thick copses of trees. A network of streams and marshland. This terrain wants to kill us almost as much as those psychos in the pub.

I study the map and when I look up, the others are staring at me. Luke's eyes are wide, eyebrows raised in a question. Panic scampers inside me. Taking command isn't what I'd imagined it to be. I'd envisioned forcing people, mainly Luke, to drink shit mixes and do forfeits, it didn't extend to life-or-death situations.

My voice is level and calm when I speak. "There's a plateau on top of a hill a couple of miles away. A wood runs up there and down the back of the hills which will provide cover and the rise itself will give us some visibility. I say we head there. What do you think?"

I did well until the last sentence. Sounded like I knew what I was on about. Ending with a question is always a mistake, something I learned in office politics years back. Don't end a presentation or a meeting with an open question. If you're pushing an idea, don't let someone else's ideas be the last word. We're a long way from a boardroom here but the theory still works out.

"We've got to try and think of all the angles here," Jay says. "They've done this for years, lived here all their lives. Has anyone else done this? Has anyone hidden out there? Those are things we need to ask ourselves."

And how the fuck would we know the answers?

I don't need to say anything in response because Ethan is straight on it. "Won't we be colder up high? What if there's no shelter? We'll freeze to death."

"You can't freeze to death if the temperature doesn't dip below freezing, mate." Luke says.

"Well, it'll still be fucking miserable. We're going to be soaked. We're in our bloody going out clothes. All my hiking gear was in my rucksack." Ethan eyes us all up and down. "Designer gear most of mine, you're probably all better off, I bet Next and Burton use coarser fabric."

We're dissolving into a bunch of squabbling teenagers. We're about half a mile from the pub and we're falling apart.

"Does anyone else have a different suggestion?"

They look at me. Heads shake. "I think this is the best we've got," Jay says. "If we can make it up there and hide out, we can make another plan once we've got something to work with. Put some distance between us and them."

"I'm freezing," Luke says. His hand delves into his rucksack, and he pulls out his luminous waterproof.

"No way," I tell him. "It'll make us sitting ducks. Too obvious."

"It's Baltic out here. I can't stay like this."

"You'll warm up when you're moving."

He makes to put the jacket on. "I'm not arsed. I'll take it off later or something."

"Just do as you're fucking well asked, Luke." My words squeeze through the gaps between my teeth. He gets like this after a few scoops. Sullen. Annoying. "You can put it on later when you're really desperate."

"Because you will be," Jay says in his police officer voice, the one that tells people they've the right to remain silent.

"I'm desperate now," Luke says, sliding on the cagoule. He stares at me and Jay, daring us to rip it off him. Neither of us move.

"Is anyone else starving?" Ethan asks, changing the subject. Away from the torchlight, there's the rustle of a packet. "I'm so hungry I could even eat this peanut butter."

"Five bars each. Don't waste them," I say.

"Do you think Uber Eats will send someone to the hill we're going to get slaughtered on?" Ethan asks, his words lost between chewing.

Some people don't ever listen. Five bars for the whole weekend and he's eaten one within twenty minutes.

I don't have a watch. In a world where there's a digital screen within three feet of you at all times, there's no need. I ask Jay what time it is. We've got over half an hour before they set off after us.

"We need to stop chatting shit and get moving." My heart batters away like there's five of them inside my rib cage.

"We're ready, we're ready." Ethan says, swallowing down another bite and clearing his throat. "But I want to go on record saying that this is a bad idea. We should just run down the nearest road and find another town, somewhere that'll help us. It can't be far."

"It is far, that's the point." Jay says. I feel rather than see him shaking his head in the darkness behind his torch. "You're welcome to take your chances but I'm heading for this hill. It seems the best way."

"It all just seems so *futile*," Ethan says. "Heading through the fields and hiding out. We can make a break for it now. Get running on a half decent surface. The nearest town can only be what, a night's walk?" He snatches the map off Jay and starts pouring over it, squinting into the torchlight. After a few seconds, he turns the map over and then hands it back.

"You in now?" Jay says.

Ethan nods.

"Look, the quickest way to the hill is over the fields here." I point off into the darkness.

"Across that? It's boggy as fuck, I'll bet," Luke says. A whine rising in his voice.

"Ah just get fucking moving lad. I'll get you up there if I have to drag you."

"Start whenever you like."

I roll my eyes. "Right, torches off. They'll be watching for us so we're moving by moonlight as best we can, yeah?"

Grunts of agreement.

Jay snaps off the torch and stashes it in his bag. There's the rustling of rucksacks being adjusted and swung onto backs. After a moment, my eyes start to adapt to the almost darkness. It's not that bad, I can see in broad strokes. Jay stands tall, like he's about to go yomping across the Falklands. Ethan shifts from foot to foot. Luke is just slumped, already defeated.

"Come on then, stay as close together as we can, alright? No wandering off."

I take the first steps out into the field. Mud and water immediately lapping at my shoes, soaking through my socks and the ankles of my jeans. The chill rushes up the backs of my legs.

Perhaps this is a mistake.

Behind me, the other lads mutter under their breath, probably thinking the same thing.

"Think I've stood in cow shit," Ethan mumbles.

If that's the worst thing that happens to him this weekend, we've done well.

SEVEN

Ethan

This is what happens when you leave the city. I've always said it. People flock *to* the city for stag parties, not away from it. In London or even Manchester or wherever, we'd have had it all on tap. Girls. Booze. A bit of chang if the mood had taken us. We could've holed up in some bar with a bucket of champagne or a bottle of vodka and got nicely off our faces.

Now, here we are, ankle deep in cow shit. This is nearly as bad as drinking in a Wetherspoons.

We plod, heads down, across the rutted fields. Connor leads the way. His slim form bobbing ahead of me. Jay is next to him, a head taller and half again as wide. He's got his thumbs looped into the straps of his rucksack, wandering around like he's on a family stroll. All he's missing is a faithful dog and those awful little shits of his.

Luke's breath is already thundering along. Panting. He's stumbling more than the rest of us. As though he can't see as well as we can. I mean, I don't do cardio – the gym is solely for toning and sculpting – but even I'm doing better than him. I try to watch him as we walk next to each other. He's pissed, as he should be, but there's something else to him. He's been off all evening. Not quite the "lad" I remember him being at university. The world's knocked some of the sparkle off him over the last few years. Maybe he'd say the same about me.

Between the moonlight and the terrain itself, it's hazardous out here. My balance lurches with every step, feet sinking into holes or down ruts in the mud. It's an actual potato field by the look of it and even though we're clinging to the edges of it, every step is a gamble.

We've been walking at least twenty minutes and that crummy B&B doesn't look like it's getting any further away. That'll be the first place they look. Surely. They'll predict that's where we'd retreat to. Know that we'd have gone back there to try to get our things or to get the hell out of here in our car.

No doubt that bitch of an owner will have a good laugh with them. Take the piss about how we complained or what we did. Not that it matters now. The next time we see those lads, it'll be terminal.

I fall into step as best I can with Luke. Connor and Jay plough ahead like the true alpha males they think they are. Every few minutes one of them will look back and they'll continue the muttered discussion that I can hear but can't quite decipher.

"Is this what you had in mind when you said you wanted a weekend of outdoor activities?" I ask.

Luke chuckles. "I thought it'd be a few walks, a nip of whisky on a hill somewhere and a whole load of time sat in country pubs chatting shit. Nice and quiet."

"I told you that we should've gone to London, a few drinks in the Shard. Christ, even the Northern Quarter in Manchester doesn't have this much bullshit in it."

Another chuckle. "So much for my last night of freedom. Could be the last night ever."

"Nah. We can outlast them. For sure."

"I don't know. I'm already fucked. My head's booming."

"We've been walking about twenty minutes. You'll find your rhythm. Why ask for this type of weekend if you're not up to it?"

He plods along in silence for so long I wonder if he's even heard the question.

"Because of Amy," he says eventually.

"What do you mean?"

He sighs. His steps heavy in the mud. "She's been having doubts about it all. About me."

"So, you can't have a beer with your mates?"

"Just not near strip clubs or brothels or other women."

I could slap myself on the forehead. The screamingly obvious screams into my face. "You filthy little dog."

"Fuck off."

"You've been at it."

"Of course, I fucking haven't. How can you say that? We're getting married."

"Amy isn't the type to get paranoid over nothing. Just tell me."

We plod on in silence. A headache starts somewhere at the base of my skull. Dull throbbing where my neck meets my head. A hangover on its unstoppable rise even before we've fully sobered up.

"It was an office party. Some girl made a move on me. Nothing *happened*, not that bad. But she kissed me."

"You're too bloody sexy for your own good. I want you, Luke. I *need* you." I make a few kissy faces, but he doesn't laugh, and I can't make out his features well enough to see if he's smiling.

"When that girl kissed me at work, it was like "wow, maybe I don't have to get married. Maybe I don't have to do anything." You know?"

I honestly have no idea what he's talking about. "You know me. Never been one for the grand gesture or the big commitment."

"Apart from Yvonne."

"We're talking about Amy."

"This girl started texting me, nothing naughty but it was nice, like, to talk to someone else and discuss something else. Not worry about home improvements or flowers for the wedding. Just to chat to someone."

"Everything is easy at the start of something. When it's all new and fresh. Before someone bogs you down, becomes too familiar."

"Amy found the texts and then it came out about the kiss. Since then, I dunno, mate. Everything's been off. Wrong. She's getting cold feet. I know it. She's not said anything to me but she's not happy."

"Do you still want to get married?"

He pauses just a split second too long before he answers.

"Yeah. Of course."

"Yeah, right."

"I do. And shut up, all right? I've not said anything about this to anyone. I love Amy and we will get married."

"Sure, about that? I mean, sure you'll last that long?"

"I'm fucking sure. She's my reason to go on. And I'm not the one who chowed down on twenty percent of his rations. Think about yourself first, mate."

I always do. It's my superpower.

The peanut butter bar rages in my stomach and I stifle another acidic belch. The thought of only lasting on them until the end of the weekend brings up another load of gas and I cough to disguise it as it threatens to become a retch. Needs must.

Your last meal is something you despise. Surely that's a crime in itself before we even get onto what these savages have planned. Even in prison they get a Dominos or whatever before they die. I spit into the mud, and we trample on.

"I'll tell her that I'm sorry when we get home," Luke says. "Stop fighting her on it. Accept that I was wrong and go back and make everything work. Make sure she knows we've got a future together."

If we get home. I don't correct him.

"That sounds like a good plan. Make sure you get some sympathy as well. Somewhere down the line this is her fault as well as yours."

He doesn't laugh like I'd expected so I double down. Go again.

"Of course. We're only at the mercy of these murdering scumbags because of you pal, if you could've settled for a life with no commitment then we'd have been fine but oh no, Lukey boy needs the whole package. The marriage. The mortgage. The life insurance."

He stops walking and a few paces on, I stop myself. When I face him, he's tensed up. Shoulders bunched. Head down. Hands in fists.

"How can you say this is my fault?"

"It's a joke, mate. I thought you knew all about them? You definitely used to."

"Well, it's not fucking funny. All right?"

"All right. Should we keep walking? I don't think we should get too far from the others." I take a few steps and he doesn't catch me up. I turn back. "Are you coming or are you just pretending to be the world's ugliest scarecrow?"

"Everything is a goddamn joke to you, Ethan. Every single thing. And that's great when you're nineteen and living like pigs in shit at university but that's all gone pal. We've all moved on and all you do is piss about."

"I work twice as hard and twice as long as anyone here. I don't piss about."

"You speculate with money you never earned, Eth. It's all a gamble and one that doesn't matter to you because you've got plenty more where it came from. Everything you do has no risk. It never has. That's why Jay's still pissed off about the project and you think it doesn't matter."

"Jay got paid what he was owed and you've had too much to drink. We all have. We need to get up this stupid fucking hill and get some rest. Sober up. Start again."

"You were always the same. Money just made everything so easy for you. Eton Ethan. That was your nickname on our economics module, you know? They'd all take the piss out of your accent. But then it didn't matter because when you didn't like that, you had daddy pull some strings and transfer you to archaeology or whatever it was and then again when you didn't like that."

"It's not a crime to be born into money."

"It isn't. But there's no daddy now, no easy way out. Your money can't help you. So, for once in your life, stop cocking about and get your head in the game. We need you."

"Fair enough," I say.

He walks towards me. "You owe me an apology for saying this is my fault. It fucking isn't."

"You're right." Heat rises at the base of my neck, despite the chill of the night.

A deflation of his shoulders. I sigh. "It's not. Sorry."

He's barely a stride away. Close enough that I can see his face in the moonlight. His eyes widen at my apology. His hand on my shoulder. He blows out a sigh. "I didn't mean what I said either. I'm just pissed."

"Frightened?"

He nods.

I look away to where the other two have stretched the gap between us without looking back. Heads down. Tromping across this field. We've come further than I'd realised. The ground is starting to slant upwards. Now I've stopped, my muscles tighten. All I ever do at the gym is for show, maybe Luke's got a point.

I shake my head. Fuck that.

"Come on." I squint into the darkness. The outline of the hill curves up in the distance. Jet black against the starry sky. Like the curve of a whale surfacing. Mimicking the others, we stomp across the mud in silence other than our laboured breathing. The breeze nudges me in the back as we go. Cold tickles the nape of my neck. Our lack of conversation hangs pregnant in the air like the sky before it rains.

All we can do is walk. One foot in front of the other. One minute at a time until we survive this fucking weekend. There's nothing to be done or said now that isn't essential. Keep trying to stay alive and hope for the best.

My ankles grumble up the slope, my calves tense beneath my jeans. I'm bent forwards, against the incline that has snuck up on me in the darkness. Its gentle outline giving way to a tougher climb than expected. We've caught up with Connor and Jay, either they've slowed, or we've put a spurt on. The ache in my side suggests the latter. They don't turn or acknowledge our presence. Each of us trudges on, lost in our own worlds. Focussed on not tripping, not stumbling, not stopping. All that matters is the higher ground and the supposed advantage it gives us.

After what feels like days, the incline levels off. The pressure in my legs releases and I let myself slump forwards. Luke and Connor do the same. Jay stands there, hands on knees, bent forward. He's trying to hide that he's fucked. Like staying on his feet gives him some power that we don't have. To hell with that. If you're tired, you rest. Same rules apply in the gym.

"Is this it?" Luke says.

"Reckon so," Connor replies after a short pause. "We didn't want to turn the torches on to check. We're a bit exposed up here. But yeah, this is probably it."

A copse of trees lurks a hundred yards away. Black shapes swaying. An incessant, shushing from their leaves. They'll provide some shelter but not a lot. It's got to be better than nothing.

I surprise myself by saying what the rest of them must be thinking. "How long do you think it'll take them to find us?"

Nobody replies. We just sit there. Listening as the wind tugs at our sodden clothes and the grass. Nobody wants to be the one to state the inevitable. That these cretins chasing us know this turf better than they know their own mothers, which would be *intimately* if I had to guess.

After a few minutes, I stand up, shaking the dull ache from my legs, I stretch out, slap myself round the face a little to try to sharpen up. My shoulders are hunched against the cold. I jog on the spot, pumping my arms and legs as hard as I can to keep myself awake. Every impulse in me wants to curl up and sleep this out. Sleep through the night and never wake up again. But you don't survive by dozing, instead you wake up hogtied and at the mercy of these sadistic pricks. That's never going to happen.

I choose how this ends.

The view from the hill is of almost complete darkness. Moonlight does its best but beyond the general rise and fall of the land, there's little to see that isn't lit up. The B&B glints, its shape just about visible at this distance. Each streetlight is a pinprick, like a row of lit matches dotted across a black tapestry.

I follow the line of lights to the left, about half a mile back is the square shape of the old pub. Are they still there? Are they off somewhere else gathering weapons and supplies? Perhaps getting some advice from the old-timers about how to make their kills? It's impossible to know. Somehow the waiting almost seems worse than what's to come.

Almost.

"What time is it?" I ask to no-one in particular.

"It's been an hour," Jay says. "A couple of minutes ago, I make it."

"Maybe it was just some sort of joke? Them fucking with us?" Connor says. His voice small against the vastness of the night.

There's a *whoosh* into the sky from the direction of the pub. A burst of red light and then something travelling high into the darkness. After a second, it ignites. A marine flare. The darkness turns red as it effervesces in the air. A cloud of red smoke and light hanging above the terrain. Movement highlighted near the pub. Indistinct at this distance but definitely there.

Two more flares go up. That same deep red colour. Vivid against the plain black canvas. We stand and watch, four of us in a line. The red light illuminates our faces, baring our worries for the others to see.

On the breeze is a sound. Faint. Shouting. Cheering. It's visceral and barely there but the wind has brought it to our ears and nobody else's. It is for us and us alone.

The light, blood red in the sky. The howling and baying. This is where it all starts for them and where it starts to end for most of us.

EIGHT

Connor

This is no game. This is no stag party prank.

After the red flares fade, leaving nothing but the scent of phosphorus and gun powder to drift silently over us, there's only the roaring that barely reaches our ears. Travelling on the air like demented whispers. An engine whines, just about audible and a car races off. It's more guesswork than things I can see.

Tightness clenches my chest, and I force myself to gulp in a few deep breaths. The fog of the booze has completely worn off. My senses are sharper, all thoughts are individual and distinct.

Until that flare went off, it felt like there was a chance this was all a joke. A small chance. That maybe we'd be filmed and put on YouTube or Lad Bible or some other internet shit bin, but that flare going up changed it all, those shouts. I wrap my arms around myself and when I look at the others, their thoughts are written in their knotted brows or bitten lips.

They say it's the hope that kills you, but in this case, I think it'll just pin us down while these local psychos beat us to death. There is no doubt they're coming and they're going to find us. Everything in me tells me that's the case.

We've got to move. Got to get out of here. Surely there's someone nearby who would help us, in the next village or hamlet or whatever they're called? Not everyone around here can be complicit? There's got to be one or two that would help. Put their necks on the line to end this ridiculous tradition. Do something kind for a stranger and make a stand. The endless blackness of the valley swallows up my optimism, leaving me empty.

I take another look at these men standing next to me. All of them focused on something other than each other. Staring in the distance like they can teleport themselves away from this place and off to somewhere safer. Jay is closest to me, and he doesn't meet my eye when I watch him. His eyes are glazed, not through drink, there's a distant quality to them.

We haven't always been this way. We met as boys. Scared teenagers. Here we are nearly twenty years later, much older, and slower but still the same as we were then, scared. Back then our worries were trivial, the kinds of things that weigh on teenagers but they're never able to discuss. Worries about living away from home for the first time. Coping with university work. Social concerns – do people like me? Am I getting laid enough?

We helped each other through all of those things. That I'd known Luke most of our lives gave us a head start but we were both out of our depths at university, struggling to get to grips with moving away from our small town and our network of friends. Cooking for each other and making bungled attempts at fry-ups and spaghetti Bolognese, nursing ourselves through hangovers and navigating nights out, working as each other's wingmen when the need arose, sometimes more successfully than others.

Ethan came in from Luke's course. To this day I don't know why Luke chose economics, a boy who could barely add up the items on his shopping list. We met Jay through the football team. He was one of the few lads to see through the jocular bullshit of the team and actually have a half decent head on his shoulders. Shame he was no good at the sport.

Despite three years of living in each other's pockets, I look at them all now, even Luke who I see all the time, and wonder how well I know them. After decades apart, pursuing other things, are they still the same lads? Am I the same person? There are times I go for a pint with Luke and I'm not sure who he is, let alone the others.

Questions rattle through my mind. Memories of stupid conversations and even dafter arguments. Pub fights and winning goals.

I scan the faces of the others in the minimal light, my eyes lingering over their mouths and their eyes. New lines and old ones. Familiar faces drawn in a new way.

Two questions bubble to the surface, more important than any others.

Would these lads die for me?

Do I want to die for them?

NINE

Jay

Someone has to take charge and it's going to be me. My jaw clenches at the thought but it's what needs doing, for everyone's sake.

We all stand and watch the flares burn themselves out. After the first few there's a pause before two more go up. Gunpowder lingers on the air. As the red-light fades, I survey what I'm working with. It's not much. They look beaten already by a two-mile trek. Thank Christ for regular physical tests at work, keeping the gut away.

Connor was all piss and vinegar when we made our plan, but he looks like a corpse now. Pale and shrunken. He needs to step aside.

"Lads, we need a plan. We need an aim. OK?"

Slowly, they turn to look at me. Tearing their eyes away from the darkness. "We've got two nights to survive here. They'll be the hardest part. It's already cold and we've got no shelter. All I can think is that we try to keep moving as much as we can. Staying up here of course, but if we move into the woods, it should be warmer. We've got to stay active. The cold settles on you the second you stay still."

"What about a fire?" Luke says. "I've got a lighter with me."

"We could use some heat," Connor says. "It's a solid plan."

I shake my head. "We'll be seen from miles around if we light a fire, lads. Look at how the pub is lit up – it'd just broadcast where we are. We've got to stay as incognito as possible."

"Incognito. Here he is, Tom Clancy," Ethan says.

There's a curl to his lip that I've never liked. It's not just the tone of his voice that puts you down, there's a look to Ethan sometimes that makes you think he'd happily spit on you if he knew he could get away with it.

"You got any better ideas?" I say, trying to keep my voice light.

"Not really."

"You could just keep it buttoned for once then, yeah?"

"Or else what? You'll arrest me?"

"Don't, Ethan. Come on."

He crouches down, puts his hands over his face. "You're right. Sorry. It's just all this... It's fucking ridiculous, we shouldn't be here. It shouldn't be like this."

"But it is. There's nothing we can do to change it, what matters now is how we survive it. We've got options and we've got a chance to get out of this."

"You think they're going to let us walk away?" Luke says, his words a mumble.

"I do, yes. I think it's their tradition. There's going to be a code in there somewhere. But if we survive this weekend, even if it's more than one of us, I think they'll let us go. One way or another."

"That's fucking naïve," Luke says. "You know what I think, I think that even if we do survive, we're not getting that car back, our phones back, nothing. I think they'll have people on the roads and they'll take us out regardless. We aren't getting out of this alive."

"Not with that attitude."

"Not with any attitude," Luke says.

"He's right," Connor says. "There was a chance this was a prank until the B&B. Even after that, I thought there was a chance until the flares, but they're coming. I know they are. Chances are, we'll die unless we're smart so what can we actually fucking do about it?"

I'm losing them already. Two minutes in charge and they're turning on me and each other.

"Look. Don't lose your heads. They won't come at us without any light at all. We'll see them coming. That's why we came to the higher ground. It gives us an advantage."

"I'd say their advantage is local knowledge, more men and probably a shitload of rifles," Ethan says.

I don't need to be able to see him clearly to make out that sneer he's wearing. Part of me wants to leave him here. Let him sort it all out for himself.

"Remember that fight we had at uni?" I say. Three heads snap to look at me. "Second year. Out on the streets of Stoke-on-Trent."

"Outside that club, Dreams," Luke says. "They spelled it with a double e and a z on the end."

"That place was a living, breathing STD," Connor says. "I think I once got chlamydia just looking at it."

"God, I hated that place. If you called it a shit heap, it would be unkind to an actual heap of shit," Ethan says. "Do you remember that kebab house opposite? Christ, why did we eat there? I'm sure they cooked rats or seagulls or whatever."

"We ate there because after twelve pints and twelve shots, you'd eat a scabby dog if it stayed still long enough," I say. "I'd probably eat one now."

A couple of them snort at that and the pinch at the back of my neck loosens.

"Hard to forget that fight," Connor says. "It's the only time I've ever punched anyone in my life."

"Apart from James Malkie back in primary school," Luke says. "Didn't you fight him over some football stickers?"

"He stole the one I needed to complete the album. He had that coming."

"You got us into that fight, Ethan. I remember that much. You came onto that lad's girlfriend." I say.

"She came onto me, is how I choose to remember it," Ethan says.

"Choose being the operative word," I say. "You hear a lot of that in statements for the defence."

"And how innocent were you PC Plod, the long arm of the law using its muscles to smash people's faces in? That's not exactly appropriate, is it?" Ethan sniggers at his own joke.

"Self-defence. Nobody would've convicted us. There were more of them than us."

"That ginger lad who kicked off at us, spilled my chips everywhere. Sauce all down me. Looked like I'd been stabbed. Had to chuck that shirt away. It was my lucky bloody shirt that one," Luke says.

"You didn't wear it when you met Amy, can't be that lucky," Connor says.

There's a moment of silence before Luke replies. "It was my lucky shirt up to that point. Alright?"

"Just wondering what to put in the best man's speech is all. I want an accurate record."

"Don't be a tit, Con."

"Lads, come on." I say. "I don't want this to get into bickering. There was enough of that when we all lived together. What I'm getting at is this - we're not fighters or bad lads, any of us. Yeah, we were a bit daft and looking back, probably aren't that proud of some of the things that happened, but you know what, we won that fight. Six of them. Four of us. They absolutely shit their pants and ran off in the end. All it took was for us to stand up to them. It's a pretty good outcome when the only real casualty was a tray of chips."

"You say that, but they weren't your chips," Luke says. Even Ethan laughs at that.

"What I'm getting at is lads, these lot are mates, yeah? They know the area and all that. But we're mates too. Sure, we don't live together anymore but we've been through a lot of shit over the years. I'm telling you – this is a fight we can win."

"A fight we can win?" Connor says, "they've probably got fucking guns mate. A few kicks to the shins and a slap round the back of the head might not cut it this time."

"We don't have to take them on directly, Con. Let's just ride this out. Play it smart. Help each other out. Come on, man. You've got to stay positive. There's no reason to die here."

My voice is weedy in the vastness of the night around us. The words are right but maybe I'm saying them in a way I don't believe. I'm not sure I do, but someone has to do something to pull us together. If we fall apart, we'll be picked off before the night's even over.

"If you ask me," Ethan says, knowing that nobody asked him, "We'd be better off splitting up. I don't know too much about hunting – don't say it, I've never been fox hunting in my life – but is it not easier to catch a group of us rather than individuals or pairs? Is all this honourable intentions stuff not just going to get us killed faster?"

Connor and Luke both mutter at this but I don't pick up anything distinct.

"No. I think we're stronger together. We have the high ground, we can help each other. Look at this, we're up here because we worked together to find the best place to wait this out. We decided that between us."

"What if it wasn't the right choice," Ethan says. "It's a democracy but what if we need every man to be an island right now?"

"And how would you feel if you're hiding out somewhere and you hear a shot, knowing that out there on these fucking fields one of your mates just got a bullet in his head? Hey? How would you feel hearing that?"

"I'd feel a damn sight better being there than being knelt down next to him knowing that I was next." He looks at the others, chin raised like he's challenging us. "Come on. Tell me you're not thinking about yourselves too? Of course, you are. We all want to survive, don't we? Better to make it home and attend some funerals than we all die together. There's honour if we all die together, but we will still be fucking dead. I'd say we're better off taking our chances and just going for it however we see fit."

"Have you always been such an arsehole, Eth? Seriously. It's like I'm seeing you for the first time, mate. Away from all the uni stuff, all the hitting on girls and splashing the cash. Take all that away. Do you even see what a cunt you've become? Has anyone ever told you?"

"I get told on a daily basis, but the thing is, your opinion doesn't matter to me. It never did when we were dossing about in the Midlands and now our actual lives are on the line, I give even less of a shit. We need to survive. That's all there is to it."

"Don't do this, lads," Connor says. His voice is reedy and strained. "This isn't helping. We need to stick together. We need to stay calm. Please, Ethan. Think this through. We've all had a beer, but we need to think straight."

"The voice of reason, is it?" Ethan says. His voice a low hiss.

"You need to calm down," I say, my voice getting louder than I intended. I've stepped in closer to Ethan. I can see the top of his head. His hundred odd quid haircut. Even now his hair looks better than mine ever did. In his physical space, my senses are taken over by a scent of aftershave so thick it almost stings my nostrils.

Ethan doesn't step back. He turns his chin up at me. Jutting his features towards my face wearing a look I've seen hundreds of times. Always the second before it all kicks off. People queuing up to take a pop at the big lad. It's always been that way.

"This is what you want, isn't it?" Ethan says. "This is you, Jay. Whether you want to admit it or not. Stepping into people's spaces. Wanting them, *begging* them to kick off, to let you get stuck in. Because you're not real mate, you're not all there. You want that violence. That's you. I know it. You reek of it."

"And you reek of being a selfish prick. You say I smell of something, Jesus, have you heard yourself? You can't see beyond the end of your own nose, mate. That's why you're alone. That's why we all have something going on in our lives and you're just traipsing round bars bothering women."

"A life you'd love. I've seen that forced smile on your pictures with the wife and kids. It's because you know you've settled. Your job defines you, *pal*, and that's because your other choices have been absolute shit."

My hand is round his throat before he's finished his final word. I grab him so hard, so fast, that his head snaps back and there's a gurgle in his throat that gets blood pounding in my temples. My fingers close around his flesh, and everything fades into the distance. It's just that sensation of squeezing, squeezing...

There's a slap at the back of my head and the world rushes in. Ethan's hands claw lamely at my chest, his words are stilted, choked. The shouts of the others. Pulling at my arm. I follow the feeling of the slap and look down at Luke, he stares up at me. Fists balled. Shouting something but it's just noise. My brain can't process words.

I let go of Ethan's throat and he sinks to his knees in the mud, clawing at his neck and gulping in air. Water runs from his eyes and down his cheeks, it glimmers in the moonlight. There's the split-second urge to kick him while he's down there, to give in to the red mist and finish this once and for all. Luke's hand squeezes my shoulder, pulls me away from the heap that is Ethan.

Luke's eyes are wide, his feet spaced in a defensive stance as he talks, ready to run. "Jay, you really lost it there mate. You can't do that. You can't hurt people like that."

"I know." Over his shoulder, Connor is kneeling next to Ethan, the pair of them huddled together, collaborating against "the bad man".

"Is this how it went at work? Was this the problem?"

"Nah, don't want to talk about that, mate. Seriously. I'll apologise."

I step past Luke and over to Ethan. He looks up, one hand on his throat. He looks at my offered hand like I've just shit in it and clapped, then spits onto the ground between my feet. I leave it there a second longer before pulling away and turning back to Luke.

"You want to get yourself looked at," Ethan says, his voice scratchy like he's just woken up. I don't turn back around. "If you get out of this and go back to work, get your Plod psychiatrist to check you over. See if it's all working up there. No way a fucking lunatic like you should be wearing a badge."

My hands ball into fists but I don't turn back. Don't say anything. If I see his face, look into those eyes, the other two lads won't be able to stop me this time. There's no way.

"But then, maybe they're already thinking about that, eh? What with that suspension hanging over you? Something to keep from dear little wifey. Funny how you lord it over us all, the perfect family. Two point four children. A decorated officer. But you aren't perfect. You call me out for being a cunt when you're just a fucking hypocrite yourself. *Mate.*"

My eyes find Luke and his gaze drops to the floor. Instead of the boiling sensation of rage, cold runs over my skin, the breeze finally getting through. Gooseflesh rises on my arms and there's a clarity that only shame can bring. When the adrenaline slides from your system, the righteous fury gone, all that's left is the realisation that you fucked up. Again.

I should be raging at Luke for telling the others about my private business but when I look at him, willing him to make eye contact, there's nothing left in me but a shake of the head. He keeps his eyes on the ground and I don't need an apology. He knows.

"I'm sorry, boys." They all look at me. "Ethan, I shouldn't have laid hands on you. I won't do that again."

"Good," he says, getting to his feet. "We're supposed to be better than those animals, not the same as them."

Connor goes to say something, but I cut him off. "I know, Eth. I apologise. It won't happen again."

"Better hadn't."

I choke back my response, chewing it down like eating rancid chicken. My hands ball into fists and then unclench. I nod, short of the words to say anything but "fuck you".

The silence that forms is shattered by muted shouting and the roar of engines. We bunch up, standing closer together involuntarily. Each of us on our feet and instinctively following the sound. I look at the lads' faces in the moonlight, they're already pale and tired as though the last hours have aged them beyond their years. There's no doubt that I look the same. My bones are cold, aching already. Not from the physical exertion but the evening itself, tiredness and alcohol, stress and rage. Those things leave you empty, running on fumes once they're done with you.

"Haven't been manhandled like that since a six-star brothel in Bangkok. Left me black and blue for weeks," Ethan says into the cold.

Connor starts laughing. "I don't doubt that's true."

"Just a joke, old boy. I never pay for it," Ethan throws him a wink.

Beneath his words, there's a rumble. Something deep. Like when a lion growls in the zoo and it reverberates in your chest. Connor and Ethan continue their weak banter and after a few seconds it gets too much.

"Shush, one minute." My finger finds my lips like it does when I tell my kids off. Ethan goes to say something but thinks better of it for once.

The rumble continues, picking up momentum, gaining volume. The others hear it too now, but we turn round, scanning the view for any movement or source of the noise.

Then it gets louder, closer, worse, all at once. Headlights rip along the road by the B&B. Whilst I've been up here asphyxiating Ethan, the stag hunters have regrouped. They've snuck off wherever they needed to go, back to their hovels to get their equipment. We've made a rookie mistake, we didn't watch them. Nobody kept an eye out. They're outflanking us.

"What the hell are they doing?" Luke says. A tremble ripples across his words.

"Oh, Jesus," is the best I can do.

We should've thought of this, we should've had it in our minds from the start. Out here, when you're herding sheep or bothering cows or whatever the fuck they do, you need to be able to get around. They don't traverse over these valleys in cars or tractors, they need something a bit more versatile.

The quad bikes rev and sputter as they bunch up on the narrow lane outside the B&B. Their headlights, presumably LEDs, light up the trees and the frontage of the house so brightly that even from here I can almost make out every leaf and every brick.

The rumble of their engines splits the night open. There's a rustling nearby, some animal woken from their sleep. Based on our luck this evening, it's probably a fucking mountain lion. I turn back to the road, the quads are still sitting there, the riders presumably planning their next steps. There's no sign of a baying mob, just those three machines.

"We're never going to outrun a quad bike," Luke says, spouting the bleeding obvious. "What the hell are we going to do?"

"We've got to play it smarter," I say. "Hide better. Move quietly and quickly. Start by taking that fucking luminous kagoule off, yeah?"

As if to taunt me, a blast of thin, chilled rain blasts across us all. It stops as quickly as it starts but there's more to come.

"Not on your life," Luke says, missing the point – it'll be his life on the line if he doesn't take it off.

We all watch the headlights, waiting for the moment they swivel and point straight at us. My muscles bunch up against the chill and my stomach gurgles so loud the others must hear it.

After what feels like hours, the headlights scatter. One quad disappearing with a roar from the direction that it came - off to the right. The other ploughs on to the left, back towards the pub. The third, just sits there, the engine ticking over. It's hard to see what's going on. There's the creak of a gate and a few seconds later, the quad bike swings round and enters the field that leads to the hill. The headlights point towards us as the rider closes the gate again.

On instinct we all drop to the ground. Mud splattering onto our jeans and shirts, grass between my fingers and tickling my chin. Another sharp burst of rain shudders across my back and I bite my lip against the cold.

"Has he seen us?" Ethan asks.

"Don't think so," Connor says, propping himself up on his elbows to get a better view.

"He'd need the vision of a hawk to see us in the dark," Luke says.

"He's doing some guesswork. They've done this before, don't forget. They'll be playing the percentages, thinking about where people have gone in the past."

"Makes sense," Ethan says.

The quad roars, the gate now shut. It pulls off to the left, combing the edge of the field. The low stone wall and overgrown hedges lit up. He's taking the long way round. If he'd gone right, he'd have found us quicker. There's nothing else to do but watch this maniac combing the ground for signs of us.

The quad skirts the edges of the field before getting to the dividing gate. The quad stops, the gate swings open and then the quad scoots through. He's now in the same field as us. Next to me, I can feel Connor shaking. Whether it's from cold or from fear, makes no odds. I put a hand on the crook of his elbow. Try to keep him calm.

The quad blasts away to the far side of the field again. Its lights showing us every curve and rut of the land.

"What are we going to do? He's going to come up here soon," Connor mutters. All authority he tried to take as best man is gone.

That's fine. Someone needed to step up and I'll do it. This isn't getting up in front of a few pissed up relatives and cracking some lame jokes, this is about staying alive.

"Fucking leg it now, I reckon," Luke says. "Take our chances in the woods. Climb a tree."

"Actually, not the worst idea," Connor says.

"It's a shit idea, there are no leaves on the trees. They'd shoot us down like game birds," Ethan says.

"He's right. We need to stay mobile. When he comes up here, we can see him coming and make our move. Stay together and go the opposite way he does." They look at me and nod as I finish talking.

"Cheeky bastards only sending one of them," Luke says. "Bit insulting."

"The others could be anywhere," I say, "and they'll be moving as quietly as us so don't let your guard down."

Beneath us, the quad circles down to the bottom of the slope. Churned up tire tracks visible in the moonlight. Someone's potato crop taking a battering. A small price to pay for the prize they're chasing.

The engine turning over as the rider plans his next move gives me solace for a second instead of dread. It's a big piece of kit. Rugged. Well suited to his environment. Luke's right, this rider is on his own. If we can get him off the thing and nick it, maybe help isn't so far away after all. Maybe it'll give us a fighting chance of all getting out of here.

I'm just about to whisper something to the lads along those lines when the engines revs and without warning, the quad bike charges up the hill straight towards us.

TEN

LUKE

"He's fucking seen us!"

The words are out of my mouth before I realise that I've shouted. The quad bike is blasting up the slope and everything is noise and headlights and movement. The rider is shielded by the burst of the headlights, barely a silhouette. He can't have heard me over the revving engine and the rumble of tires. I can barely hear myself.

The quad cuts a jagged path up the slope, zig-zagging as he sprays the light in as many directions as he can. Crouching, I watch him slalom uphill. Ready to sprint or hide, whatever it's going to take. Next to me, Connor grabs my wrist as he sees me about to pelt.

"Wait," he half shouts. Then he looks down at me. "Your fucking jacket. You're like Blackpool illuminations." He's not wrong. A luminous dickhead and an easy target. There's no time to take it off and stash it. If I ditch it, I'll miss it later when it starts pissing down in earnest. Maybe the cold will kill me more humanely than this lot hunting us.

Closing the distance, the quad cuts down our options. Lying low on the brow of the hill, the other lads watch too, their faces thrown into relief by the headlights. Wide eyes. Even Ethan. Unflappable Ethan looks to be shitting bricks. At any other time, I'd have my phone out recording him for posterity and endless social media abuse. But not now. Up here, there's nothing Zuckerberg can do for us.

"The woods," Jay shouts. Pointing to the dark husks of the trees. "Get over to the woods."

Him and Ethan lie closest, and they lead the way. We scuttle like escaped prisoners, bent double, trying to avoid the searchlights of Alcatraz. Jay cuts out a big lead, Ethan close behind. Beneath my ludicrous waterproof, sweat slithers down me as we run. My knees sing a song of sweet pain. After years bunched up in an office chair, they're not built for this.

Jay and Ethan disappear into the darkness of the trees with me and Connor, who is panting like an obese Sunday League player, about fifty yards back. My arms and legs are doing all the right things, I just can't go any faster. Con's got a couple of strides on me but he's not catching them.

Squinting into the blackness between the trees, I can't see Ethan and Jay. They've been swallowed by the darkness. Have they run on, unaware that we're lagging behind? Are they waiting just out of sight to show us the way?

The quad squeals up the hill. Roaring like a caged beast. It skids to a halt. The driver's back is to us, and the headlights shine deep into the trees. There's movement there, but it's indistinct. I stumble to a halt. Con does too. Without a word, we drop to the floor, barely twenty yards from the quad itself. The rider kills the engine and it's like going deaf. Its lights still burn, illuminating the woods. Silhouetted, the rider pulls out a walkie-talkie and puts it to his ear. It's one of the lads from the pub, one that hung back and supped his pint. Not Wallace or Gav or any of the old boys. He's not even wearing a helmet.

"Yeah, it's Benny," he shouts into the thing. "They're up by Nag's Head Woods. Just seen them running into it. Send everyone you've got, and we'll flush 'em out."

"You didn't say over," comes the reply. Unmistakably Gav's local drawl.

"Fucking over, you prick, over."

No laughter from the other end.

"You seen all four of 'em or what? Over."

"Hard to say but yeah, reckon so. Over."

"Only reckon so? You either did or you din't. Over."

"They're here, alright? Bring the lads and the fucking guns. We'll be home in time for a fry-up. Over."

"Aye. Over."

"Let's fucking rush him," Connor says. His voice almost inaudible. "Two of us. One of him."

"Rush him? And do what? Push him over?"

"We can take his quad bike. Get the fuck out of here."

"What about the others? They're in the woods."

"We can come back for them. Go and get help from elsewhere. We've got a bloody map."

"What if we can't take it? He might be armed."

"What else are we gonna do? We can't lie here and wait for him to turn around. We'll be dead meat."

"We need to get back with the others. End of. We're stronger together. Come on."

I get up, bent barely above waist height. Silently, Connor does the same. He's always been good at doing what he's told. We scurry across the ground, moving in a wide circle around the quad, dodging anywhere the light from the headlights falls.

Momentum picks up as we barrel down the far side of the slope. The woods run on for as far as I can see. Hulking dark shapes against the moonlit sky. We sprint another hundred yards or so beyond the headlights. I check back over my shoulder a few times, looking for Connor but also the rider. He doesn't turn to see us. He remains focused on the glare of the headlights, his radio still in his hands.

"Come on," I say to Connor, changing direction and darting into the trees.

Roots and fallen branches immediately snag at my feet and I'm off balance. My calves protest as my ankles roll, struggling for somewhere to properly stand. I lean forwards, and grasp the trunk of a tree for support, like a sailor caught in the high seas. Connor slams into the back of me. Pain flares in my thigh as his knee finds the sweet spot, deadening the flesh around it. I bite my lip and grunt. Sound travels here.

"Sorry," Connor mutters. "You all right?"

I bend my knee up as high as I can. I can still walk. It'll be OK. Back in our uni days, I played football with worse. "Yeah, yeah."

"Where now?" Connor's breathless. Panting down my ear like a lover.

"We just circle round, try to find the others. Things'll be easier once we're all together."

He puts a hand on my shoulder as I go to walk. I shrug it off. We need to get going. "It's not too late to rush him," he whispers, his face so close to mine that I can feel his breath on my cheek. "We can do it. We can take him."

"Con, we can barely run down a hill. We need to keep moving. He could have a weapon up there. Hack us to bits or blow our fucking heads off."

"He said to bring the guns... You heard it too."

"Stop moaning, let's find the others."

"You always do this, dismiss me. I'm the best man, why aren't you listening to me?"

"Because you're the best man to deliver a speech, not the best man to keep us safe. That man is Jay, and we need to find him."

Connor goes silent. That sullen look I've seen from him over the years. Miss out on the school football team – sulk. Can't get a ticket to see his favourite band – sulk. Girl doesn't want to go on a second date – sulk.

"I didn't mean it like that," I row back because I can't stand his silence. "I just mean that Jay's got some skills that we don't and overpowering a mad cunt on a quad bike is likely one of them."

He doesn't smile. Doesn't respond. Typical. Even Morrissey doesn't sulk like this.

"Come on, lad. Let's get going before the rest of them show up."

ELEVEN

Connor

We run through the roots and trunks. Branches rip at me. Sharp, musty fingers searching for flesh. My rucksack jiggles from shoulder to shoulder, the straps too long, the contents too light.

We take turns to lead the way, running almost blind despite the piercing headlights from the parked quad bike. The angle of the light means it doesn't reach the ground, humps and fallen trees create blackspots that in contrast are blacker than ever. Anything sharp or lying at an angle becomes a trip hazard. Right now, a twisted ankle is a death sentence, not just for the person who falls but for the others who have to pick him up.

Luke pants and blunders along in front of me, leading the way despite his total lack of fitness and knowledge. Our lives in microcosm. His luminous orange kagoule rubs against the backpack, the grating sound of the plastic goes through me. Probably broadcasting our position to every lunatic in a ten-mile radius.

But that's Luke. He's as he proudly puts it "his own man". He's not wrong there. He knows his own mind to the detriment of all other opinions and options. A great person to have when you're sorting a night out or planning a five-aside tournament. Not exactly useful in a life-or-death situation. Stubbornness like his puts good people in danger.

As we half-run, half-stumble through the forest detritus, my jaw clamps shut over the things I could say right now. I bite down hard on the comments that can get me ostracised or worse. This is typical Luke, but it's also typical me. When there's any element of recognition or responsibility, I try to take it only for the bigger boys to take it away.

It doesn't matter to them that I organised this weekend. Not unless they're assigning blame, *then* it'll matter. It's not like the TripAdvisor reviews for the B&B mentioned a bunch of old-fashioned, inbred psychos. These mad fuckers have been at this for years and they've kept it well hidden.

Getting muscled out of the decision making, that's what fucking hurts the most. To have Jay be so magnanimous at the bottom of the hill to my decision making, but to have seized control by the time we reached the top – well, that's just me. Too slight, too quiet, too easy to push around. Happy to stand back and let the real men make the decisions.

Luke stops so suddenly in front of me, that I have to step round him as there's no time to stop. My shoulder crashes into his and we both tumble to the ground. Back into the mud.

"The fuck are you doing?" He hisses.

"What are you doing? You just stopped."

"We need to try and find the others, I don't know where they are. We should shout to them. Try and get back together as a group."

"It's fucking silent, Luke. Don't start shouting. He'll hear us."

"He knows we're in here, the rest are on their way. What's one lad going to do about it?"

"Luke, don't. You're fucking bright orange, if you stand up and start shouting, you may as well start shouting "kill me, kill me"."

"It'll be fine. They fucking know we're here."

"Don't."

In the residual light of the headlights, he gives me a look. That look. The one I always get. The classic *"poor Con thinks his opinion matters"* look. Somewhere between pity and condescension. If it's not teachers or employers, it's girls and friends.

Every single time.

He cups his hand to his mouth and shouts, still making eye contact with me. "Jay! Ethan!"

No answer.

"Don't," I hiss. "Just lie low, for fuck's sake."

He doesn't look away, crouches on his haunches and shouts again. "Jay! Ethan!"

There's a rustling from the entrance to the wood, the driver getting interested. Surely. He makes to shout again, and I pounce. I launch myself forwards, pushing him, my momentum taking him over onto his back. He stares up at me from the forest floor, sodden, his eyes wide.

"What the fuck, Connor?"

"Shut up," I hiss at him. "Keep your fucking voice down and just listen for once. You're making a scene. Listen and do as you're told, for once in your fucking life."

He struggles to get up, like a turtle on its back. Limbs circling. Then he gains some purchase and hoists himself back to his knees. His face is twisted into a look I've rarely seen, just a couple of times when it all kicked off on the football pitch.

"Don't fucking do that again." He goes to shout, an intake of breath.

I push him down. Springing forwards to pin him on his back. My knees finding the crooks of his arms. Keeping them in place. He struggles under me, but my weight is set and he can't get up.

Leaning down, I shove a muddy hand over his mouth, my fingers wet on his lips and cheeks. I expect him to bite me, but he doesn't, just wriggles from side to side.

"Stop, Luke. Just stop." He meets my eye and does. His face scrunched in fury. Hatred there that I've never seen before.

"You can't go shouting, you need to listen to me. They'll find us and they'll kill us. You're the stag, they'll really enjoy killing you. Believe me. These lads are not messing about. Do you get me?"

He nods.

"Are you going to shout?"

He shakes his head.

"While we're at it, we need to take this stupid coat off as well. You're drawing attention."

He struggles, shakes his head again. My hand slips off his face. His eyes are wide, too white, like a rabid dog's, rolling back in his head.

"Fuck you, Con. You don't own me. Jay! Ethan!"

I try to put my hand back over his mouth and he sinks his teeth in the side of my palm. I act without thinking. My fist smashing into the side of his face. There's no accuracy, just fury. He grunts. Shouts out again for Jay and Ethan. This time, it's calculated. Bang. Right on his chin. His teeth *clack* together, and he goes quiet.

Have I gone too far?

He looks at me, head cocked to one side. Eyes watering, shimmering in the strange light.

This is the first time it's come to this. In all the years we've known each other. The first time we've come to blows. There's a pause, a second of silence and stillness between us. Eye contact and nothing more. Then his face changes into a snarl and his hands whip out, catching me off guard. His fingers grab my throat and mine do the same to him. We're grasping and choking each other. Nails into skin.

I lean into it, his face reddening beneath my grip. His fingernails scrape at my skin, it's red raw. Then he pulls them away and starts pummelling my stomach with his fists. It catches me out and I loosen my grip. He takes a huge gulp of air and stops punching me, trying to grab my wrists.

I don't let him. Still pinning him down, I lean forward and yank down the zip of kagoule. The sound is almost comical in the silence of the wood, like something from a kid's TV show. While he struggles beneath me, I wrench the coat down. Tugging at the thin material.

"What the fuck are you doing?"

"You're going to get yourself killed, Luke. Just take it off."

"It's fine. I need to stay dry."

"You'll get yourself killed!" I snarl, my hand finding his neck again.

"Okay, okay," he splutters out, wriggling from my grip. With me still half-kneeling on him, he props himself up on his elbows and manoeuvres the jacket off. Orange plastic slides through the mud. He chucks it at me and then shifts his weight, so I have to get off him.

"Happy now? I'm piss wet through and miserable as hell. Yeah? That what you want?"

"Yes." I snatch the waterproof from him and stash it in my rucksack. Mud splatters onto the contents, coating the packaging of my protein bars. It doesn't matter. They'll likely taste like shit regardless. "Because all I want is for us to stay alive."

When my bag's zipped up, I catch him looking at me. His rucksack is caked in mud where he's been lying on it. His face is grey, even in this light, the colour that flooded it moments before has drained away.

"You aren't right, Con," he says, his gaze wandering from my face and towards the quad bike. "What the hell was all that? Eh?"

Even if I had the answers, I doubt I could put them into words. It all happened to me, rather than me making it happen. It's been years since I've had any aggro. Like most normal people, I spend my life avoiding conflict. Walking away from arguments, leaving the pub early if it looks like it's going to kick off.

But tonight, with Luke?

What the fuck?

"I'm sorry. It's the situation, I guess. Does strange things to you. I dunno."

"Like you're the only one suffering."

"We need to get out of here, find the others."

He puts a hand on my arm, the same grip he had round my neck a few moments before. "We aren't leaving until you promise me that this shit isn't happening again."

"It's not."

"You chewed Jay out when he went for Ethan, then you go for me? Hypocrite much?"

"You don't get it."

"Tell me."

"Do you not think this is on me? Seriously? All of this shit? I arranged all this. You're all here because of me. I fucked it. I brought us here. The best I can do now is get us all out of here in one piece."

"It's on me mate. You know it is. If it wasn't for all the nonsense a while back, we could've gone to Vegas or Magaluf and we'd be sitting by the pool sipping cocktails and staring at birds in bikinis. That's on me."

It is on him, to be fair. If he could've kept his eyes and his hands to himself, maybe things would be different. But that doesn't let me off the hook either.

"It was a stupid idea to come here. My stupid idea."

"Well yeah, I guess it was a bit dumb. When have I ever wanted to be caked in cow shit and chased by a bunch of fucking mentalists? It's like you don't know me at all." He laughs but it's hollow. I follow suit. Going through the motions. "It's not your fault, Con. No-one thinks that. You've got to get over that and get over yourself. We'll get through this. All of us."

I wish I could believe him. Wish I could shake this feeling that I've doomed us all, or all but one of us. He gives me this strange smile. A grimace almost, like he's forcing himself to act normally but his face isn't listening to what he's saying. I smile back. Can he see the same look on my face? That hesitance in his eyes, reflected in mine.

In all the years we've been friends, we've never come to blows. Nothing has come between us. School, football, girls, booze, music, money, careers. Nothing. Until tonight. I look away. Unable to meet his eye any longer. This is a watershed moment. There's an almost imperceptible shift there, like when a glacial plate moves. It's millimetres out of place but that movement has set it on the path to slide into the sea and collapse. We've both crossed that line tonight. Laid hands on each other.

Can things be the same again? Should they be?

I've never been the violent type and neither has Luke. The few people that punched me as kids, I cut out of my life. Friends who crossed that line for any reason never came back. Is that what I should do now? Is that what Luke should do? Cut each other out, is that what we want?

He watches the lights of the quad, they haven't moved or changed in the time we've been here. The others are surely on their way. It won't be long until they pile in with their weapons and their blood lust. Despite the violence between us, we're the rabbits, not the dogs. We need to get moving. We need to get away from here.

"Luke, pal," he looks up. "I'm sorry, I shouldn't have done all that. I'll do anything that gives us the chance of a happy ending. I just got a bit too carried away. The drink and all that." I sigh. "I'm scared."

"Me too. Apology accepted, alright? Let's get out of here. Find the others. More of them will be here soon."

He waves a hand at me as he scuttles away into the darkness between two trees and blending into the black. I follow, clutching my rucksack stuffed full of his dirty kagoule. My jaw clenches as we walk, tension still riding up my cheek and down into my neck. Our apologies should make me feel better, but then it hits me.

He didn't say sorry at all.

TWELVE

Ethan

They're coming. All of them. Every inbred fucker in this village is coming out for the hunt. The bastard on the quad bike chatters into his walkie-talkie and some inane banter between him and Gav tells us it won't be long until they all arrive.

These lads are depressingly well set up. Quad bikes that they'd already own for farming duties. Makes total sense. Walkie-talkies is the smart one though. No mobile phone traffic. No geo-tracing or triangulation of phone masts and all that shit the police use to track people down these days according to every cop show ever made. Their rifles will all be registered and logged on the national database. Necessary for hunting and farming purposes no doubt. All above board.

They're going to get away with it.

Whatever happens out here is going to remain between them and whoever survives. Like the shittest version ever of "whatever happens in Vegas, stays in Vegas". It'll stay here all right. Three of us. Buried up in the trees or hidden in a hollow. Maybe fed to the pigs or ground into meat for the dogs. Our city bones worked into the rural landscape to feed the trees and the vegetables and the crops. Like something out of the Holy Bible or worse, The Wicker Man.

Jay hides behind a tree nearby, crouched like he's Bruce Willis in Die Hard. He's ten yards away but he's made no attempt to talk since the quad arrived. We just hauled arse and got the fuck out of there. For the man who is so keen to take charge of the situation, he's had little to say since the bigger boys rolled up. Sure, the police have to be brave, but without his uniformed chums here, maybe he just doesn't have the stones for it after all?

My jaw sings as I move my head and watch the silhouette of the quad bike rider pacing up and down on the rise before the entrance to the woods. Of all the things that have happened to us on our trip so far, the only physical pain I've suffered has come at the hands of one of my own friends.

I watch Jay. What happened to this guy? He used to be okay. He was a decent enough lad at uni. Never quite the life and soul and never quite the wingman he made himself out to be but always someone it was half-decent to spend time with. You wouldn't mind an afternoon pint with Jay, a couple of games of pool or whatever. He was solid, not like the cretins from my course.

But now, ugh. I taste blood and spit onto the ground. Tonguing my teeth, I check none of them are loose. The last thing I need right now is a dental emergency. Wrenching out an incisor in the woods like an extra on a low rent horror film. What a fucking peasant.

Part of the problem of keeping up with old friends is how seismic every month that passes is. Fifteen years out of university and we've seen each other what, once a year? Twice a year? In years of weddings and thirtieths, we saw each other more. But were there a couple of years when we didn't see each other at all? It's hard to remember, life gets in the way. And now every time we meet up, it's shoved into the weekends and crammed between business meetings and children's birthdays. It makes the changes even more drastic when you notice them. Makes you feel more isolated and out of touch than ever before.

People change when they join the police, that's a fact. Their belief system skews. In comes a heightened sense of justice or what they perceive to be justice. A part of them dies. You see it in their faces. That sense of humour, the ability to be carefree and just shut off, it's gone. Disabled like an obsolete computer system. That's how it is and that's how Jay is. He thinks he's in charge, doing the best for everyone but he's only applying his own view on things - squinting at us through a copper's eyes. He doesn't see the full picture. Not like the rest of us. We don't have the blinkers on.

"We need to go," I hiss at him. Jay doesn't take his eyes from the quad bike. "Get the hell out of here before they all turn up."

"In a minute," he grunts back.

"What are you waiting for?"

"Intel," he says, every inch the G.I. Joe action figure he believes himself to be.

"We're not in an episode of Spooks, pal. Let's just get going."

"No," his teeth clench together, brilliant white in the quad's headlights. "We need to know what we're dealing with."

That's that then, decision made by Chief Constable Ball Bag over there.

There's a scurrying over to the far side of my vision. Without thinking, I follow it, but the shadows are pervasive everywhere the quad's light doesn't reach and it's hard to make it out. Could be animals clearing out, could've been Connor and Luke. They're too far away to call out to, not without drawing attention to ourselves. If it's them, they just have to make their move and hopefully we'll find them later on.

There's a roar of engines. Far away at first but coming nearer. The darkened shape of the quad driver turns towards the sound. The crowbar or whatever he's holding in his hand casting a mean, sharp shadow as it dangles by his side.

He yacks into his walkie-talkie, guiding the rest of them towards him. Waving his arms, like they can't see where he is, the one lit up part of the whole goddamn valley. They rumble closer, the sound getting louder. Four sets of headlights come into view. The brightness from them makes me squint, eyes virtually shut against the light. Jay does the same. We both shrink down in our positions as every part of the trees is momentarily highlighted in ultra-high definition. Then the lights swing away as the quads park.

Shadows jump down from the driver's seats. More quads than before. Each quad carrying a couple of men, one even carrying three. The shadows greet each other, the sound of human chatter filling the forest is incongruous to the silent, black night we've been living in until this point. Somewhere overhead a bird screeches, woken from its slumber in a fury. It swoops off, a sensation of displaced air, rather than something I can see.

Ten men. Ten of them to catch and kill four. Is that enough or am I crazy for liking those odds? We take a couple each. As much as Jay behaves like a typical copper, surely, he can handle himself? Most of them can, that's why they get into it.

Chatter and banter floats down the slope to us. Local voices. Raised and proud. This is their land, their place. Out here, they can act with impunity, and they know it. There's a swagger to them as they wander around, chatting shit and passing round a bottle of probably supermarket own-brand whisky.

"Let's fucking go," I hiss to Jay. This time he looks at me, still in his stuntman crouch. He waves a hand, flicking me away like I'd deal with an annoying waiter. My fingers squeeze my legs through my jeans, going numb with the pressure.

"We need to see what's what."

"There's ten of them, that's what."

Before Jay can say anything else, there's another rumble. Like the quad engine but louder, deeper. The locals turn to watch the vehicle approach, lights getting bigger and brighter as they near the woods. Annoyingly, the camber of the slope hides some of the Land Rover from view. It parks up and two men get out. Older blokes, moving slower than this lot. Lumbering Wallace, flanked by the smaller, sharper movements of Gav, waddles over to the driver.

The older man's words are indistinct, muttered and low, the occasional one makes its way to me but not enough to really fathom what he's talking about. After a few seconds of this, the group all cheer as one, "to your son-in-law!" Flesh on the back of my neck sings, rippling and alive.

All the younger lads pat the second new arrival on the back. He swings a rifle case from his shoulder and hands it to the other old boy. By the light of the headlights, the one I'm guessing is the father-in-law, crouches down with the case across his knee. He unzips it and pulls out the gun, its shape sleek and long as he straightens up, holding it aloft.

Again, he mutters something incomprehensible, which brings a collective titter from them. With all the pomp of someone receiving a knighthood, he passes the rifle to Wallace and the cheering starts again. There's something primal to it. Primitive in its own way. As though we're only a bonfire and a burning witch away from being back in the sixteenth century.

Wallace cheers the loudest and the longest, still yelling as the others drop off. After a few seconds, he stuffs a cartridge into the rifle, cocks it and blasts a shot up into the night sky, away from the woods. My senses split in two, as though my brain rattles inside my head. The cheering that follows it is muted in comparison to the shot. My ears ring with the violence of it all.

"Get in there, big man!" One of them shouts.

The family rifle. This family heirloom finding its way into the hands of the next generation. This is my daddy's rifle that he used to slaughter someone before his wedding day, now he passes on the gift to you, my love. The conversations these people must have. Can't they just pass on an old watch or some artwork like in our family? What the fuck is wrong with them?

There's more cheering and I look up from the ground, watching as the two old boys throw open the back door of the decrepit Land Rover and there's cheering as more guns come out. Rifles, none with scopes, but long, smooth shapes being swung around and pointed. The clatter of shells. All so familiar from grouse shoots and clay pigeon shooting at the estate in the summer. Except this time, we're the fodder.

I'm about to turn away when there's a hand on my shoulder. I freeze, my muscles tense. One of them has found me. I'll be dragged out and shot.

"Don't shout, you tit," Jay whispers in my ear. "Don't give the game away just yet, eh?"

"What the fuck?"

"Let's get out of here, we've seen enough."

We turn our backs on the yammering, excited chat, those bastards baying for our blood, and creep away into the darkness of the woods.

THIRTEEN

Luke

A dull ache creeps up the bottom of my face, seeping up both sides like mould creeping up a wall. My hands bunch into fists at my sides, everything in me tensed against the cold. Without the kagoule, moisture coats my skin, seeping through my shirt and jeans easily, and it's not even fucking raining.

I march at the front, Connor hangs back. When I look round over my shoulder, he's clutching his right hand in his left, like he's the one who suffered just now. He could've broken my jaw, really fucked me up, and stopped me being able to eat. Those rancid protein bars are the only thing between us and starvation, and even they would've been a nightmare to chew. I rub my chin, trying to knead some feeling back into my face.

We need to get out of here. The headlights are dimming with the distance and the sounds from the locals have faded to nothing. On the TV, there's always the sound of woodland creatures in a forest, but there's nothing here. Just my own breathing and traipsed footsteps as we bundle along through the undergrowth.

Everything we do feels too loud, takes too long, is too difficult.

I want to fucking scream, I want to cry. Most of all, I want to get home, to see Amy again. To have some of the conversations that have been on the cusp of being started. There's so much to say, so much to make right before the wedding. All along it's like she's doubted me, doubted that we could ever get this far. That we'd never move in, that we'd never get engaged, that we'd never get down the aisle and commit.

It's not like there haven't been mistakes. Indiscretions. Things even Connor doesn't know about and things that Amy never can. Things I'll have to take to my grave. Wherever that ends up being. Hopefully not here. Left alone and unacknowledged in a shallow grave, doomed to never be found - or propped up like meat in a fake car crash. I swallow. Not a great look carrying around so much pity for myself. So much fear. This is a stag do after all. A place where no self-respecting man can back down. That's how it's supposed to go.

I shake my head, giving it a wobble like we used to say in school when someone needed to calm down. Thoughts clack together like marbles. Spinning away into different corners of my mind. Two stand out. The dull, repetitive bass note of "keep going, keep surviving". The mantra that keeps us all going, humming on a frequency so low that we mostly don't bother to listen for it.

The second is just Amy.

This is the one that sucks the air from my lungs. Makes my breath catch in my throat as I exhale. All those times I took her for granted. Slipped into the daily grind of work and going out. Time spent in her company but not really in her presence. Watching the match and ignoring her. Chatting with mates on my phone and only half-listening. It's easy to come to accept someone as part of your life. Like a piece of furniture that you sit on every day. Safe, reliable, and never moving. That's my relationship.

Now there's a strong chance I'll never see her again, those things bring the sting of tears to the corners of my eyes. Wasted time. Time I'll never get back with her. It's enough to make me give up, to curl up in a ball in the rain and wait for them to find me. To let them do what they want to do to me. Don't even make it quick. Maybe I should wander up the slope, dressed in neon, hands raised high. Ready to be gunned down like one of the psychos in a suicide by cop. Let someone put me out of my misery.

"Come on, lad. Pick up the pace," Connor says from behind me.

He's almost standing on my heels as we pile through the scrub of grasses and weeds. Knee high ferns deposit water onto my jeans and it slides down my calves to saturate my already sodden feet. I stumble over a rock I can't see and feel my weight shift forwards, beyond something I can correct.

My head snaps to the side as Connor yanks me back by the rucksack. Stopping me from hitting the deck. I stop, try to gather myself a bit, but he barges past me. Turning to talk back at me as I pick up the pace and try to keep up.

"You still drunk, Luke?"

"Dunno. Probably not."

"Hmm. Wore off for me too. Your ankle okay? No damage?"

"It's fine. Let's get going. Find the others."

Behind us there's commotion from the top of the rise. The headlights multiply but we're too far down the slope to pick out any detail of either the sound or the shadows. Connor stops without warning, hand cupped above his eyes. He squints up the slope, head bent so that his ear is pointing towards the shadows that move. Like a cartoon character trying to listen through a wall.

"We need to move," I say, not looking up the slope but scanning the black spaces between the trees for the movement that will lead us to our mates. It's all still. They're not close by.

"Just a second, something's going on."

I follow his gaze, shifting my weight from foot to foot, not just to test my ankle but to stop myself from getting too antsy at the delay.

"There's more of them now, Con. They've properly found us. We haven't got long."

I take his arm and guide him after me. When the rumble of another vehicle arrives a few minutes later, he doesn't stop. Neither of us do. The only way forward is heads down, one foot in front of the other. That same mantra of step, step, step. To get anywhere, you can only take one step at a time, as quickly as possible.

Trees and plants try to trip us, hold us back. Branches snag our clothing and any exposed skin. Tangled weeds and roots grasp for our shoes. The occasional sinkhole of mud and rotten leaves that pulls, determined not to let go without sapping energy in return.

There's silence in the woods until the shot.

Bang.

Energy crackles through the air. On instinct, I drop to my knees in the mud, hands over the back of my head. Full brace position. The shot rings off every surface, rattles around inside my mind. When I open my eyes, Connor is in the same shape as me. His head darting around like an animal, searching for a predator.

"What the fuck was that?" He asks.

I don't have the energy to hide my expression. There's no mistaking a gunshot.

"Hunting rifle, I reckon."

"Is that better or worse that they have guns?"

Do we want to die quickly or slowly?

When you haven't planned on dying for another fifty years, it's one hell of a loaded question.

"Doesn't make any difference pal. They're coming. That's all that counts."

We pick ourselves up, careful not to make eye contact. A lingering shame like leaving a one night stand the morning after. Something intimate hanging between us without the capacity to discuss it.

Connor goes to speak. I see his lips move but instead of his voice, there are others. Shouts from up the hill. Too far away to be distinct but loud enough that the anger and aggression of the tone rings loud and clear.

These locals, these butchers, howl into the night. A pack of feral dogs on the hunt for fresh meat. They're armed now, that much is obvious. The warning shots have been fired.

Now they need some prey.

They need us.

Engines rev and churn at the top of the hill. There's another shot that clatters through the night. We don't duck this time, it's not aimed at us. They can't see us yet. They're just getting warmed up, loosening those muscles and getting their eye in.

We don't need to discuss anything, we put our heads down and sprint into the blackness, trainers rattling off roots and vines as we run. Momentum giving us a nudge in the back. Egging us on to breakneck speed.

There's a cheer and a roar from the top of the slope. The thud of footsteps and rustle of foliage.

They're coming.

FOURTEEN

Jay

We run.

Trainers skidding and sliding on the mud.

We run.

Slamming into trees and dodging branches.

We run.

Trying to watch ahead of us but keep looking back over our shoulders.

We run.

Breathless, aimless.

We run.

Until our sides rip under the claws of a stitch.

We run.

And somewhere behind us, they follow.

***

"It could be worse," Ethan says. "They could have dogs. Dogs would be worse."

Dogs would be the worst-case scenario. He's not wrong. But bringing out your best asset takes the fun out of the chase. The whole point of this hunt is the opposite to hunting animals. With animals, you need to keep them calm. Stress out your deer and the venison is tough to eat. With people, if that's what you truly want to hunt, then keeping them as frightened as possible is surely part of the thrill?

"They'll bring them tomorrow if they haven't caught us by then."

"Surprised it will take them that long."

"They want us scared, Eth. That's a big part of it."

"They've got what they want then."

It's an old police cliché to put yourself "in the mind of the offender". There's a lot of cerebral bullshit written about it. Some of the older cops used to take the piss out of me for reading policing journals. Calling me Sherlock for weeks on end. In fairness, they were right, most of it was shite, including the article about the mind of the offender, but applying logic, it's easy to see how it works.

It's just a case of asking questions.

What resources do they have? Plenty.

Have they committed the act before? Definitely.

What is their motivation? A tougher question but one I don't need to search too hard for an answer to. It's the same motivation we had for coming here. Bravado. Balls. Stones. Male pride. Whatever it's called these days. Stag dos are about letting loose but they're about proving yourself to your friends.

Can you drink as much as them?

Can you fight if it kicks off?

Are you funny?

Are you handsome?

Are you good with girls?

Are you enough of a man?

Can you kill a man?

We stop, crouched behind an enormous tree. An oak perhaps? The trunk wide enough to shield us both. The lights at the peak of the hill are distant, their reach fading long before our hiding place. Like something from a Scooby-Doo cartoon, we both peer round a side of the tree. Me down low, Ethan stood higher.

The locals are not coming quietly. There is no stalking or trapping. No staying downwind. We know they're coming, and they want us to keep that thought front and centre in our heads. Their shouts fill the air as they fan out in twos and threes. Some of them have headed in another direction, wandering off to the left or the right, pursuing what they might think are leads down gullies and clefts.

Two pairs are ploughing straight on down the slope. They're far enough away that they can't hear us or see us yet but they're coming for us. They take their time. Sensible footwear and clothing. Choosing their steps carefully.

One of the pairs is a couple of blokes I don't recognise from the pub. The other pair is Wallace and Gav. The stag and his best man. This odd pair walk together. One oversized, the other small and lean. Rifles cutting across their shadows. Held casually, like an everyday item.

A sliver of cold juts between my vertebrae at the sight of them. The relentless way they move. Patient, with the knowledge that they'll get there in the end. They'll find their prey. Like a zombie hoard. That inevitable march to our destruction.

"They're going to find us here if we don't get going," Ethan says.

"Just give me a minute, I want to see."

"There's nothing more to see. There are loads of them, and they have guns. What more do you need to know?"

I look up at Ethan and pick myself up off the floor, forcing him to step back. His feet drag through the mud and leaves. Up close he still smells of the night out. Expensive aftershave and an undercurrent of booze. Although I'm standing here sober, I'm not sure he is.

"Don't be a dick, Eth. We're all on the same side here. We've all got things we need to get home for, okay? I'm just doing what I think is best."

"So am I and I happen to think running like fuck is the best plan of action."

I lean backwards, looking round the tree, then back to Ethan. "I'm trying to work out where they're going. Figure out their next move."

"This isn't *Criminal Minds*. You're not some shrink. Just put your head down and fucking run."

"In a minute."

Hugging the tree, I peer round, using one eye. Shit. Where are the second pair? Gav and Wallace are easily visible, tramping their way through the low bushes and the weeds. The second pair though, they've moved. Leaning further forwards, craning my neck, I scan the hillock. The second pair aren't there. They must've snuck off, disappeared from view when Ethan distracted me.

For fuck's sake.

"The second pair stalking us have gone. They've fucking disappeared. This is because you distracted me. We need to move. Now."

"I could've told you that. Let's go. Down there, that slope, get some momentum."

Shit. It's impossible to know which way is safest now. "Fucking dickhead," I mutter.

"Fuck you, Jay. Like you're the best of us when you go round chinning your mates."

"Should I settle for ripping them off instead?"

"I didn't rip you off."

My fingers twitch, tempting me to close them over his windpipe. I swallow. Dry and bitter. Parched. My mind on the empty canteen in my rucksack. Apparently violence never solved anything, but people who say that criminally underestimated its ability to make you feel better for a few minutes.

"Try not to always be a cunt, eh, Eth? Maybe just dial it down for a day or two?" His face snaps towards me, eyes blazing and at the bottom of my peripheral vision, his hands twitch. I don't flinch.

"Come on, that way," I point to the downwards slope Ethan mentioned. "It's as good as anywhere."

Before he can give me some more shit, I take off. He waits a second and follows me. My rucksack rustles on my shoulders. A sheen of water and sweat covers my skin, cooling as I run through the increasingly chilled air of the night. Ethan pants somewhere behind me. Office boy feeling the exertion.

My trainers slip and slide across dead leaves and mud and whatever shit nature collects in this place. My trusty walking boots, stolen by some hag at the B&B. Probably being burned as we speak. Nothing but evidence now.

We pile towards the lip of the slope. The darkness that drapes the forest is darker here, more dangerous. I skid to a stop. Digging in my trainers as deep as they can go. Ethan slams into me and we teeter on the brink but settle back, not falling. Not yet.

"You sure?" I ask.

"Hey!" A shout from behind us. Gav. An arm outstretched in our direction. His silhouette pointing at us like a dagger.

"Just fucking go," Ethan says.

Footsteps rush towards us. Plants and dead leaves rustling. The rattle of rifles. There's nothing else to do. We can't let them get in range. I don't look at Ethan, just trust he'll follow. I fling myself down the slope into another level of black.

The slope's gentler than I expect and my feet slam into the mud, momentum threatening to topple me, headfirst, but I pull it back. Straightening up. I run like hell. Legs and arms pounding like an Olympian.

My right foot smashes into a log and I stumble. There's no time to say anything before Ethan does the same. He calls out, there's a thud. He picks himself up. Dragging his leg. Carrying on. I dodge between saplings, like an agility course. A deadlier version of Tough Mudder we did all those years ago. No t-shirts at the end of this one, lads.

I can't see Gav and Wallace. Can't hear them either. My breathing is all there is. Pounding in my ears. Blood flooding through my head, a tribal pulse as I run and run. Ethan doesn't talk for once. We just sprint. Down into the black. Running away from certain death.

The slope drops away with no warning and I lose my balance. My feet stretch out, searching for purchase but there isn't anything. One trainer lands in thin air and my weight shifts. I put my arms out and slam into the ground, trying to roll, mud filling my senses. My head smashes into something hard, bending my neck all wrong. Pain shooting up my right side. I roll like a car in an action film. Flipping. Coming apart.

Ethan's shouts somewhere around me. I come to a stop. Face down. Cold water flowing around my body. Mud sucking at me. Gasping, I pull my head up. Coated in the foul smell. Something flies up from this swamp I'm lying in. It buzzes in my ear and I slap at it, sending a flare shooting across my shoulder blade. Pain so deep that I cry out.

I pull myself to my knees. Sodden and sobbing. Pain owning me. Taking me over every inch of me.

Ethan's sitting up a couple of yards away. I can see from his face that it's bad news. I drag myself over to him, my right arm clutching the rest of me like someone's tried to twist it off but didn't finish the job.

"My ankle. My fucking ankle." He's clutching it. Rocking back and forth. With shaking hands, he pulls his fingers away from the ankle. There's blood there, not much. It shines black in the moonlight. Viscous and slick.

"Can you stand?"

"Haven't tried yet." His words hissed through gritted teeth. Each one an effort.

"We've got to get up, got to get going."

There's more shouting from the top of the slope. It's a fucking big slope and we must've rolled more than half of it. Maybe it would've been easier to break our necks and die, spite the bastards chasing us. Perhaps it would've been kinder.

Offering Ethan my good arm, I pull him to his feet. He grunts and growls like a trapped dog but once he's on his feet, he takes a few test steps and grimaces at me. "Got lucky old boy, got fucking lucky. Just a cut I think."

"Come on."

We limp and lumber forwards, dragging ourselves through the pain barrier. We get about fifty yards and I lean against a tree. "I'd fucking kill everyone for some painkillers," I say, my words more gasps than coherent syllables. Another two days of this. Even if I survive it'll need surgery and physio.

Tears form in the corners of my eyes and I wipe them away, smearing mud and moss into my nose and mouth with my sleeve. Grit between my teeth. The dense taste of earth. I want to scream. Give us away. Have it all over and done with.

"Shit. My bag. Wait here." Ethan hobbles away. Moving as quickly as he can. Swearing with every step. Leaning my back against the tree, I watch him bumbling back towards his sodden rucksack.

There's a rustling from the slope. Movement making its way down. Two shapes creeping down, carefully. Again, that patient way of moving.

A noise from over my shoulder. Heavy. Almost deliberate. Definitely not an animal. The second pair. It has to be. Circling round. A classic pincer movement that we've walked right into. It can't be that simple. They can't have flanked us that quickly.

Ethan stands ten yards away. He's rummaging in his bag. Making all kinds of noise. Giving us away.

"What the fuck are you doing?" I hiss.

He doesn't answer. He's digging in his bag like a dog burying a bone. Rummaging around, searching for Christ knows what.

"Ethan. Shut the hell up, man."

No answer. Just the scraping of hands on material. Then it's footsteps over broken branches. A snatch of muttered orders.

"My father told me something once," Ethan says. His voice not loud but not quite a whisper. The rummaging sounds stop.

The longer I stand still, the more the ache in my shoulder grows. Resonating through the bone and down my arm.

"I don't need public school philosophy classes. We need to fucking go. They'll hear you."

"I'm sure they will. Father told me about a group of hunters running away from a bear. One of them turns to his friend struggling at the back of the group and says, "The good thing is, I don't need to be the fastest, I just need to be faster than you." A hollow laugh escapes him.

"What the fuck are you talking about?"

I barely finish the sentence when a torchlight blasts my eyes. My hands fly up in front of my face, heart battering my Adam's apple. But it's not the others. It's Ethan's torch. I squint but yellow flashes dance in front of my eyes.

There's a shadow across the torch beam. Lumbering forwards. Ethan's cologne in my nostrils. A knee to my groin before I can react. The pain and the surprise floor me. The ground rushes up. Mud between my teeth again. Tasting the acrid ground.

There's a rustle of plastic as he reaches down, grabs my arm and wrenches it back. All pretence of keeping quiet is gone. There is only pain and there is only anguish on my tongue now.

Luminous green plastic covers my vision. Ethan's waterproof. Whacking at it with my good arm doesn't help. There's a *zip* behind my head and the fucking thing envelops me. There's no air in there. Just the stale taste of rubber against my lips as I thrash and shout.

"No hard feelings, old boy. I just need to make sure I can outrun someone else." A blow sets my stomach alight with nausea. All the air rushes out of me. Trapped in this luminous cocoon. More blows to my head and neck. I don't see them coming and they hurt more than they should. Struggling against the zips and the cagoule, my right arm lights up with pain like a pinball machine.

Ethan's footsteps nearby, behind me. Fighting against the urge, I flinch. No more blows arrive.

"Got one here for you boys," Ethan shouts. "Gift wrapped. Come and get it."

Shouts from afar. Rushing footsteps. First Ethan's disappearing, replaced by others. Shouting strangers. Voices growing louder. Excitable.

I'm on my feet. Struggling with the plastic. My right arm dangling and useless. I push my head up and the knot Ethan's made in the top of the cagoule gives out. Fresh air gushes in and I gulp it down.

Shouting all around me now, every direction alive with voices. Where to run to? Anywhere but up the hill. I run. Arms still pinned by this luminous jacket. I make it five yards, ten yards, twenty yards. No more shouting. I'm bent double, trying to make myself a smaller target to hit. Zigzagging as I go. But there are no gunshots. The voices are silent now. Watching me, surely, in the trees. Perhaps caught off guard by my speed.

Torches flick on, blinding me. Freezing me in place. I'm a rabbit and they're the ten-tonne truck racing towards me. Two torches at first. Up ahead. When I spin round, two more snap on. All of them no further than ten yards away. A pause, then the rattle of metal. A rifle being cocked. A sound from the movies transplanted into real life.

"Don't fucking move, yeah?"

Gav's voice. Familiar from the pub. The sharp vowels of the local accent.

I do as I'm told. Every second I'm breathing is stolen. But there's still time to get out of this. To turn things around.

I raise my hands as best I can with Ethan's coat tied around me.

"Lads, look. It's okay. You've caught me. But that can be the end of it. Head back to the pub. Talk it out."

Movement behind me, I turn and walk onto a right hook, snapping my head back. Colours appear in flashes against the black sky. Stumbling, I regain my balance. Refusing to go down. Remembering my training. Stay upright as best you can. Once you're on the floor, it's curtains.

Another of them steps forwards. Ploughs a boot into my midriff. Oxygen rushes from me and won't come back. My mouth opens and closes before a *gasp* sneaks in and brings me back to life.

"Come on boys. Stop fucking about. It's time." Gav says.

Three of them circle me. Giving me a wide berth before rushing me as one. Gav chief amongst them. A blow catches me on the shoulder and sends a scream out of me before I realise I've made it. One of them hacks at the back of my knees and there's nothing left to do but fold. I'm down in the mud. Cold seeping up from the ground, through my dirty jeans and into the skin of my knees.

Ethan, that cunt. Doing me over. Leaving me here to die.

"Come on, Wallace. Get it done," Gav says.

Wallace lumbers forward like he's pissed. Long, heavy strides. The rifle hangs from the crook of his arm.

"Lads. Don't do this. This is insane. I've got kids. They need their dad."

"Shut up," one of the others says. His fingers dig into the meat of my shoulder until I call out again.

"We don't need your opinion, *pig*," Gav spits as he speaks, like he's the first person to ever use that term to a copper. "We're just here for the meat," he oinks at me. Right up in my face. Spit from his mouth finding mine before I can turn away from the smell of spirits on his breath.

"Lads, come on. This has gone far enough," it's the tone I use at incidents. My voice for fishing drunks out of pubs. Out here, without my uniform, it sounds weak. Grovelling.

One of the others steps forwards and delivers a backhander to the side of my face. It rocks me. A decent shot. The right side of my face tingles and then roars with pain. I don't go down. Never hit the deck.

"Come on, Wallace," this other man says. "Get him ended. One down, three to go."

Wallace steps forward on command, like a dozy old dog doing what it's told. His eyes don't meet mine. His rifle hangs in front of him, pointing at the ground like a flaccid cock. Wallace's hands shake on the rifle stock. The others don't notice.

There's a chance.

"Wallace, you don't have to do this."

The third man goes to smack me again, I don't flinch, but Gav brings his arm up and blocks it. They snarl at each other like feral dogs until Gav leans in, threatening to stick a nut on the guy. The third man flinches and Gav grins. Still smiling, he turns to Wallace. "Do him and do him now."

Wallace swallows. Brings his rifle up towards my chest, hands still shaking. Gav notices this time. His top lip turns up, his teeth grey in the moonlight as they were in the pub.

"Stop being such a fucking mard arse, Wallace. Get. It. Done."

Wallace fumbles with the rifle, which is still pointing at me. My breath sticks in my chest, everything trapped, I'm unable to move.

"Point it at his head and pull the trigger. It's like a deer. Do it," Gav says.

Seconds pass. There's no shot.

Gav grabs the rifle, wrenching it up and into the air. Wallace gasps, takes a step back. "You know what happens if you can't get this job done, don't you? You know the old lads back in town won't let you walk away?"

"I just don't think it's right," Wallace mumbles.

"It's not fucking right? What's not right?"

"On your stag, you killed the stag, not just someone. It was the main person. It meant something."

"We won't say anything to anyone, please…" I say, shifting forwards and half getting up from my knees.

Without looking, Gav swings the rifle like a baseball bat and full-on twats me under the chin. My teeth slam together and one of the back ones chips. Rocking, I spread my knees apart so I don't fall. A sharp piece of tooth catches my gums and inside of my cheek. The taste of iron coats my tongue.

"Fuck off. This is between me and him," Gav says.

Blood trickles down my chin. Drops onto the luminous cagoule. Another reminder of what Ethan's done to me. If there's a way out of this, I swear to fucking God…

"I'll kill the stag. That's what you did. That's how it should be." Wallace whines like a child in a toy shop, wanting something his parents can't afford.

"You're going to kill the stag? Because I'm not telling Helen she can't marry you. You come out of this forest with something for her or we're all screwed. Got it?"

Wallace nods again. "I promise I'll get the stag."

Gav sighs. "Fine."

He swings the rifle round, it's muzzle inches from my face. He turns square on to me.

And pulls the trigger.

FIFTEEN

Ethan

I run. My ankle isn't that bad. Nowhere near as bad as it looked. The blood was a godsend. Just a scratch, nothing more. But it helped Jay to believe. That's all I needed. An element of surprise. Just enough to catch him off guard. I could've taken him in the end, but it would've been messy and led to too many questions. His little outburst earlier made it easier for me. Funny how these things come back around.

The shitty backpack rustles on my back, my cagoule is now gone for good. Not that a shitty, luminous piece of plastic had many more uses than the one I just gave it. Couldn't have worked out any better. Four protein bars to go. Better make them last.

Pain ripples through various parts of me but there's nothing I can't overcome. Not too bad for someone who is just a pen pusher. A dry ache in my throat. There'll be a stream somewhere to fill up and recharge. Now it's just about putting distance between me and the four of them that captured Jay. There's no point in a human sacrifice if it doesn't bring you any gain.

Head down, focus on what's ahead. An actual broken ankle would be some pretty shitty karma for what happened back there. Still, Jay had it coming. Not just the fight but the whole time since we've left university. His whole fucking God complex about being a cop, being in control. Looking down on me because he works for "society" rather than a company, or whatever shit he was on about. A job is a job.

His endless fucking moaning about the project. The way he looked at me like I owed him a living. I bought the idea, Dad's company did all the work, he just thought up some half-arsed dream, but *we* made it happen. Not him. To expect more money for it is just foolish. *Was* foolish…

Dodging round trees, jumping over fallen branches and upturned roots, eyes constantly scanning the ground. Making good time, good distance, whatever it is. Putting those local nutcases in the rear-view mirror.

He had kids.

Over a fallen tree. Trainers squelching into the ground as I land.

A boy and a girl.

I went to the boy's christening. Can't remember his name for the life of me. Benjamin? Both of them growing up with no dad. His wife going to bed alone tonight, the first night of many.

That's my fault.

I stop. A branch hangs sodden and limp, leaves across my face. Rainwater on my lips, cold and fresh. It trickles down my neck and onto my chest. Cold against my burning skin beneath.

My hands find my knees and I take a deep breath. There's no-one coming, not yet. They'll still be on Jay, taking turns on him. Roughing him up a bit. What was that film, *Deliverance,* or something? Maybe they're doing something worse.

I turn back the way I've come. If I sprint, maybe I can get there, do something. Change this.

Fuck.

I don't know.

No.

It's too late. They've got guns.

Bang.

The shot slams through the forest. There's no doubting what it is. It's further away than I thought it might be but it's still loud. There's no escaping it.

That's Jay gone and it's on me.

I breathe. Calm my heartbeat. Now's not the time for emotion. All that matters is staying alive and staying one step ahead of the others. If one of us can make it out of here alive, then that one of us has to be me. No matter what it takes.

My hands find my face, rubbing at the skin. The scent of mud and moss is overwhelming, calming almost.

What's done is done. Forget going back for Jay. Fuck him. The only way is forward. That's what Dad would say. If you're not moving forwards, you're standing still.

I need to keep going. Find Connor and Luke. See what happens when we all meet up again.

SIXTEEN

Connor

The forest is alive with noise and light. We blunder through the trees, taking turns at the front. It's an unspoken bond, grown from years of practice. We can read each other. It's dangerous to look round running at this speed. A stray root or mistimed sidestep of a tree and any injury is curtains.

In front of me, Luke skids to a stop. I do the same, able to dodge him as I come to a halt. He's panting, face bright red. His pulse visible in his temple.

"They're not following us," he says. "Look." He points past me up the slope.

Following his aim, he's right. They're not on us. Torchlight wobbles as our pursuers traipse off into the woods in completely the wrong direction. Whatever they think they've seen, it's not us.

"Thank fuck," my words are breathy but I'm okay. Not too tired just yet. All those sessions of seven a side football on a Wednesday have paid off. Thankfully, survival requires fitness, not the ability to pass a ball five yards.

Luke's blowing though, bent double. Hands on knees. Sweat beading on his forehead in a way you only see when someone's finished a marathon. The state of him. My lip curls up and I look away, trying to distract myself with our surroundings.

What happened to Luke's gym membership? The promise that he made to Amy to hit better shape before the wedding. It's three months away and he looks like couldn't tell a dumbbell from a treadmill.

I can't help myself.

"That gym membership isn't paying off then?"

"Fuck's that supposed to mean?"

"You're wrecked, look at you. You're supposed to be getting in shape."

"You're not marrying me, get off my case."

"No but now I'm dragging you round these woods like dead weight."

"Fuck you, I've kept up."

"So far. You've got to make it through till Sunday. Got another two days of all this. How are you going to be then?"

"*We've* got another two days of this. We're all in this together."

He's not wrong. All in this because of us. Me for bringing us to this godforsaken shithole in the first place. Him for not being able to be trusted after a few shandies. I rub my temples, muddy fingers sliding over greasy skin, it's impossible to get any purchase and erase this headache that is digging down through my skull and into my neck.

I straighten up, hands pushing my hips forwards until something cracks in the base of my back. At least there's some relief. When I look up, he's staring at me. Eyes red rimmed but fixed on my face.

"What?" I say. Still trying to keep my voice down.

"We need to stick together, alright? None of this shit you're trying to pull, yeah?"

"What shit?"

"Your little digs at me. I'm fat. I'm unfit. I'm not to be trusted after a few beers."

"You aren't. That's why we're here. Amy told me. Specifically asked me to come somewhere like this."

"You think I don't fucking know that? You think she said that to you and not to me? Believe me, there is nothing that you two speak about that I'm not aware of."

"Oh, I know. I know the leash you keep each other on. Don't you worry."

He laughs. Loud. Too loud. I flinch, crouching down. Ready for torch beams to appear and blind me. Waiting for footsteps racing our way. They don't come. Not yet.

"You don't know the first fucking thing about relationships and you don't know anything about Amy either. One date, you had. One shitty, awkward date where you gobbled fried chicken."

"No need for that."

"There's every need when you're lording it over me, making me feel like shit."

"You know I'm your friend. Best mate. Whatever you want to call it, that's me. I'm your best man for fuck's sake. There was no-one else in the conversation. I didn't ask Amy for further details and I wouldn't."

"Well, for your own sake and mine, keep your beak out of what goes on behind closed doors. Yeah? From now on, what I tell you is gospel. No wittering to Amy or texting of an evening, okay? You come through me."

"I'm friends with her too. We're all mates. Together. Aren't we?"

He sighs. Hands on his hips. Face up at the stars. "I've tried to say this kindly. You and I, we're mates. You and Amy are friends. But Amy and me, we're in a relationship. We're going to get married once this fucking weekend is done and dusted. You," he waves a hand at me like he's directing a servant to clean up his mess. "You are *not* in the relationship.

There is no room for three people. There's room for two. You stay out there, on the outside, okay. Better yet, get over whatever is going on in your mind and meet someone else. Doesn't matter who, but you need to get it sorted, sooner than later because all of this stuff between us, it's fucking weird pal. Now I know about the date, it's just making me feel a bit pissed off. It's all a bit sad."

It was easier when he was punching me. It hurt less. It's like he's ripped something out of me, some precious organ and is holding it out for the world to see in glistening detail.

"Thank you for your honesty. Saying it now has really helped matters."

"Con, come on, don't…"

"Don't what? Don't fucking what?"

"Don't build this up into something that ruins the friendship. I'm just setting a few boundaries."

"So, it's easier to ignore it? Pretend that I'm not, what? Annoying you? Wrecking your relationship? Embarrassing myself? Eh?"

"None of those. It's not like that, it's just… Well, we aren't in our twenties anymore. This isn't uni. We can't live in each other's pockets. Sooner or later, we just need to grow up. And that includes you."

"I have moved on. I've got a job. Place of my own. I'm just not seeing anyone. It's not a crime."

"I know, lad. But you more than anyone yap on about the old days, uni days. It's ten years ago, more. Stop living in the past. You're like a Manchester United fan."

It's not the United comment that stings but heat rises up the sides of my neck in spite of the drizzle and cold. As if he's saying that my life is worthless. That I've done nothing for the last two decades.

"It's not what you think. I've just not found the right person. It doesn't come easily to everyone. Some people have to actually try."

"The fuck's that s'posed to mean? Eh?"

A deep breath does nothing to blast the tightness from my ribcage. "Just Amy kinda fell into your lap, didn't she? Gorgeous girl, someone you already kinda knew, fresh from a bad break up and then obviously a rubbish date with me. It wasn't like you had to try that hard."

"You tried it. You screwed it up. Can't be that easy, can it? You're starting to sound a little deluded. Maybe even a little green eyed, yeah?"

"Fuck off. You've no idea what you're on about."

"And neither do you, so let's call it quits before one of these bastards stumbles on us."

I go to say something else. Something to have the final word, score the last point but as I go to speak –

Bang.

The shot rattles through the trees. A sharp crack.

This isn't like the first one. That sounded like something from a film. A shot fired in joy or celebration. It didn't sound *dangerous*. But there's a finality to this sound. Something mean and insistent. There's no doubt – the shot was fired to kill.

Both Luke and I freeze. The shot fades into a few seconds of silence. Then there's the flapping of birds. Wildlife reacting to this noisy invasion of their habitat. Animals scuttling away from the perceived danger. Except for once, they've got nothing to worry about.

Luke wheels round to me, eyes wide. Any semblance of an argument forgotten. My feet are too heavy, rooted in place, like the forest floor is creeping over my shoes and up my legs. The shot came from somewhere off to the right. Everything in me is telling me to go left, to run like fuck because they're going to be coming.

We both stay frozen in place for a few seconds, maybe longer. Time is fluid now. Seconds running over each other like the waves of the sea.

Let's go, let's go, let's go, let's go, let's go…

A frantic pattern skittering around the inside of my head. The words etched into my skull by my fight or flight reflex.

"Con, we need to leave…"

Luke's broken the spell. He's turned to face me, his face whiter than the moon above. His mouth a small, dark hole in the middle of his face. Hanging open. His voice barely audible.

"Come on then," I start to walk away from him. Off to the left, away from the gunshot. My footsteps rustle through the weeds and ferns at ankle height. After the gunshot, every step lingers, the noise hanging in the air around me. Advertising me to everyone in these woods.

Moving as quietly as possible takes its toll. It's not fast and it's not efficient energy wise. It takes too much effort. Too much concentration. The same dilemma is written on the folds of Luke's brow.

Do we run or do we sneak?

We're bent low, watching as carefully as we can. My eyes ache from straining in the half-light. Digging over the details of the forest floor for the inevitable trip hazard. That one twisted ankle that brings my life to an end.

There's shouting in the distance. It doesn't make me stop. Somewhere behind me, I feel rather than see Luke pause for a stride, but I don't. I plough on. The shouting is joyous. Whooping and hollering. Cheering and screaming.

They got someone. No doubt about it now. Ethan or Jay. One of them is either hurt or killed. I edge through the shrubbery and along into a bald patch, dodging through the trees, my mind ticks over with the question – *Jay or Ethan?*

What do we do now? Do we go back? There was just the one shot, is one of them seriously injured? Is there still time to save them? Retrieve the body even?

All of these questions are pushed away by the internal monologue of survival. One foot in front of the other. Head down. Move away from the shot. Keep going. Keep breathing.

Me. Me. Me. Me. Me.

There's no stopping. No turning back. If one or both of them are injured, there'll be more shots. They won't be allowed to survive. If they're already dead, then the savages will already be on our trail too.

Keep moving.

Luke doesn't speak, he keeps pace somewhere in my peripheral vision. We scuttle along, bent double, packs sliding from one shoulder to another. Rustling but keeping going as best we can. My skin tingles, tightening over my bones as it waits for another shot. It doesn't come.

"Where are we heading?" Luke hisses.

Since the shot, there's more urgency to us. As though the very last idea that this could all be a farce is gone. Any doubt there could've been that these psychos are playing for keeps is blown to pieces.

Anything else he needs to say to me can wait, it's time to buckle down and survive.

We plough on in silence, the shouting from behind us fading into nothing. There are no voices, no pursuers. Just rain and the nausea bubbling in my gut like a fountain. I cough and choke and keep it down.

We walk, taking it steady and safe. Not taking any risks.

There's a rustling off to my left. Instinct tells me to pause but I don't. To hesitate is to die. A standing target is an easier target.

"You hear that?" I hiss to Luke.

"Yeah," he grunts back through clenched teeth. Sweat glimmers on his face. There's no chance we'll get to rest for hours yet.

"Keep going and stay down."

"Yeah, yeah."

More rustling. Trampling and crunching. Our pursuers haven't been subtle so far, but this isn't right. Whoever this is thunders onwards. Blundering through the bracken and the ferns. Perhaps a hundred yards away, maybe more.

"Do we stop?" Luke asks.

"Fuck knows. Keep going."

We slow down, trying to make our movements silent but it's impossible. Every step we take disturbs bark or a plant or some gravel. Still the noise from the left keeps coming, insistent and relentless. Whoever it is, they're moving with the kind of confidence that can only come from carrying a weapon.

The noise stays parallel to us, keeping pace the entire time. Luke meets my eye but doesn't say anything. After a few more yards, he puts a hand on my arm and pulls me towards him. Without saying anything, he gestures to the ground, pointing down and then crouching himself. I follow suit, about to tell him this is a stupid idea and staying still is a death sentence, but he meets my eye again and shakes his head.

As quietly as we can, we lie down. Our rucksacks scrape against our clothes, ferns and pointed branches take their swipes at us as we prostrate ourselves on the forest floor. All the time I try not to think about spiders and beetles, whatever the fuck lives here climbing onto us. Their disgusting legs searching for a way into our clothing, or worse, beneath our skin.

"Just wait," Luke mutters. His jaw clenched shut. His eyes searching the forest, keening for any movement between the trees. "Let's see what happens."

We lie still. Breaths bunch in my chest, barely making it out and back in as my heartbeat clatters in the base of my skull. Damp seeps into my crotch and everything shrivels.

More thrashing in the bushes. Someone moving quickly. Pain flares through my back teeth and I unclench my jaw, relief in the lower half of my face. Next to me, Luke pants away like a dog home from a long walk. My resting heartbeat is about eight hundred beats a minute and Luke isn't far behind by the look of him.

We've made our choice, nothing to do but wait now. We might get lucky, we might be missed out and given a clearer path to escape, or we might be found and die like farm animals down in the mud. A shudder runs through me, up from the ground and into my chest. My hands shake and I clench my fists so Luke can't see how they're shaking.

Footsteps closer, the swishing of ferns. Luke mutters something I can't make out. Surely not a prayer. Mumbled last words that not even I can hear from less than a yard away. Meaningless.

What would I say? What should I say? There's no point in praying and I don't want to go out begging for my life. Anything that needs to be said, should be said now. Maybe it's time to settle some old scores, say some of the things we've always held back...

"Luke," I hiss. "I've always thought –"

"Ethan," he says. "It's bloody Ethan."

His face cracks into a smile and following his gaze, he's right. It is Ethan. Stumbling out from between two trees. His eyes scanning for people, for friendly faces.

Luke goes to get up and I put a hand on his arm. "Wait a second, just in case he's being followed."

Luke scowls at me but doesn't shake my hand off his arm. A few seconds pass and then he's had enough, he wrenches himself free and kneels up. "Ethan," he hisses. "Ethan, over here. We're fine. Everything is going to be fine."

I realise what's missing before Luke can start talking again. My stomach drops, a sinking, swooping feeling.

My words are muted and flat.

"Ethan, where's Jay?"

SEVENTEEN

Luke

The question is out of Con's mouth and hangs in the air. I know the answer. We all know the answer.

Me and Con get to our feet. The booze checked out of my system a while back, but I'm unsteady as I walk towards Ethan. Every contour of the ground throws me off balance. Con hangs his head, watching every step he takes.

I can't take my eyes off Ethan.

There's something off. Something wrong. Maybe it's just all this – the woods and the chasing – but he looks broken. Dishevelled. I can't remember seeing him this way before, even in the depths of a mortal hangover he still radiated in a way none of us did. As though nothing could knock that "rich boy" sheen off him.

But something has now.

"What's happened?" Con asks. His voice is gentle, like he's speaking to a child.

Silence. All of us listen out for running footsteps or shouting voices. There's nothing.

Ethan hangs his head. His right hand cupped over his eyes. His shoulders move up and down, a gentle motion. Ethan shakes his head, slowly at first and then more vigorously.

Con beats me to him by a step, puts a hand on his shoulder and pulls Ethan into an awkward hug. Our eyes meet over Ethan's shoulder and another punch lands in my gut.

This is serious, this is wrong.

While Con and Ethan compose themselves, I keep watch. Hunting for movement between the trees. The woods are silent. We've got a window of time here but not long, we need to get moving.

"Lads, we need to walk and talk. Come on."

They break apart, Ethan's face pale. His eyes are dry but red, looking for something far away. A thousand-yard stare.

"This way," Con says, his hand on Ethan's back. "Away from where we... last heard them."

We trudge, walking slowly and carefully through the bushes. Ethan's not watching where he's going, half staggering like he's still pissed. But there's more to it.

Our pace picks up and Con helps Ethan to walk in a straight line. I follow behind, constantly spinning to check no-one's followed us. Whatever's happened since the shot, the lunatics after us are still taking stock. They're not coming for us again, yet.

"Keep going, lads," I urge. "Get as much distance from them as we can."

"That's not all of them though," Con hisses back. "There's more of them out there. We need to still be quick and quiet."

We carry on walking, taking turns to drag Ethan and help him along. There's nothing physically wrong with him that I can see. He's just muddy and damp like the pair of us, but his head's off in fuck knows where.

After a few more minutes, while I'm holding him up, Ethan sinks to his knees and puts his hands over his face. "I need to stop for a minute," he says. His words muted behind his hands.

"Are you alright, lad?" Con asks. Mastering the understatement as fucking per.

"Jay's dead."

"What?"

"He's dead," Ethan repeats.

There's no doubt it's been coming the whole time since Ethan appeared but without confirmation it left hope, the possibility that Jay had just been separated from us, that sooner or later he'd find his way back. But even so, the news is like being kicked in the head. My senses swim and I lean against a tree.

Connor sinks to the ground next to Ethan. His face wet with tears already. What else did he expect?

"How?" My voice is detached from me. Someone else speaking with my lips.

Connor looks at me, his eyes narrow. "How'd you fucking think? Half the county probably heard the shot."

Ethan puts a hand on his arm. Dirty fingers clenching over the checked material of Connor's sleeve. I bite back my reply at this, unable to remember a time that Ethan's ever knowingly touched one of us in this way. Not off his own back at least.

"They cornered us," Ethan says. "We were trying to decide what to do next and they got us in a pincer movement. Came from both sides. I'd seen one of them coming and started running, Jay didn't. I think he must've slipped or something and they just got him. Closed in behind me. Cut him off and then I couldn't do *anything*…"

His hand finds his face again and his shoulders heave, much worse than before.

Connor looks at me over the top of Ethan's head. His face twisted in an ugly cry. His breathing ragged. He's taking this worse than Ethan.

"Did he put up a fight, Eth? Did he go down swinging?"

Ethan shakes his head. "I don't know. I – I didn't stay to watch. I'm so sorry. I should've helped."

"What could you do?" Connor blurts. "They've got guns. We haven't."

"I just wish there was more I could've done. More I could've told Claire and the kids…" Ethan covers his face with both hands and rocks back and forwards on his knees.

"It's all right, mate. Okay. There's nothing else you could do. Try to stay calm." Over the top of Ethan's head, Connor meets my eye. There are times in friendships where you don't need to talk, this is one of them. His gaze says – I hope – what I'm thinking.

How the hell could he just run away and leave Jay to die?

***

We traipse through the forest like the living dead. Branches snag my skin, and I don't mind. Roots make my ankles roll but I don't stop. Mother Nature appears to have sided with these fuckers but nothing she throws at us slows our pace. We don't stop, we just move. Heads on swivels. Ears and eyes wide open.

There's been no concrete signs from the locals since the aftermath of the shot. A shout set us running on two occasions, but we've heard or seen nothing of them for a while now.

It could be an hour later, it could be two, time's meaning is as slippery as the moss beneath our feet. My stomach rumbles, echoing through its own empty cavity. The crisps in the pub didn't touch the sides then and they've long since burned through my system.

"I'm gonna have to stop guys. I need some food."

Ethan and Connor don't say anything, they just collapse into a kneeling position in the mud. There's little point trying to stay dry. Drizzle constantly pisses onto us through the branches above. Water sluices down branches and down our clothing.

Inside the rucksack, I turn on the torch and examine my rations for the evening. Coconut protein flapjacks. Fuck me. I can't stand coconut. Connor rummages in his, a grin turning up one corner of his mouth.

"Chocolate protein," he says as he unwraps his loot.

"Swap us one."

"What for?"

"Coconut."

"Fuck that. You can keep your Bounty to yourself."

"Have a peanut butter," Ethan says. We chuck a bar to each other and ripping off the wrapper, I dig in. It's a mistake. The peanut butter bar is greasy, soft and cloying against the back of my throat as I swallow. I need water. My empty canteen lies on its side. I turn my face up to the sky and open my mouth. Acrid rainwater trickles onto my tongue, nowhere near enough to get the job done.

"I'm fucking gasping," I say. "We need to fill these up soon if we're going to last."

"I'm not drinking mud or whatever," Connor says. "Rots your guts some of that stuff. I read it in a guidebook."

"Die of thirst. Die of gut rot. Get shot in the head. What a weekend," Ethan says. His voice lacking the burnish of his usual confidence.

"I'm so cold," Connor says. "I think we're clear of them for now. Maybe we should put our jackets on, just for a bit. Try to keep warm. Exposure and the cold are big factors now. Might be a risk worth taking."

"Yeah, I'm game. It's brass monkeys out here now and God knows what time the sun will come up. If it ever does." I scrabble in my bag. Connor's still got mine. He chucks it over. Permission from my best man to do something. Does it get any better than that? Grunting, I pull it on. Its warmth is minimal but it's better than nothing.

Ethan looks in his bag and then zips it up, getting to his feet. "Come on then lads. Let's get moving." An echo of his usual swagger in his voice now but nowhere near the normal level.

"Not putting your jacket on?" Connor says.

"Nah. I'm okay for now. Don't want to make myself a sitting duck like you pair." Ethan wipes coconut from the corner of his mouth.

"You'll get ill," Connor says. "Just put it on for half an hour, warm up a bit."

"I can't, okay. I don't have it. I lost it in the chase with Jay."

"How?" I say.

"Just my bag was open when we were running. I'd checked the map. Trying to figure out where the fuck we are. All right? It just fell out."

"Yeah mate. No worries. Just asking." By the time I look away, Ethan's panting. His skin shines in the moonlight, from rainwater or sweat is impossible to say.

I feel Connor's eyes on me, but I don't look at him. Instead, I fall into step with Ethan, and we start walking on, even more desperate for water than I am for understanding how the hell one of my mates just died.

EIGHTEEN

Ethan

I need to keep my temper in check. Outbursts like that don't help matters. They think I don't notice their little glances but they're nowhere near as subtle as they imagine.

There's nothing to do but plough on, to head away from the psychos and see where that takes us. Neither of the budding Sherlock Holmeses I'm with remembered that there wasn't a map in my pack. The thought gives me comfort. They're clueless. At worst they think I'm a coward, they're not capable of imagining what actually happened to Jay. That gives me an advantage at least.

It takes a while, but I hear it before they do.

"Stop," I say. My hand going up like an army sergeant. "Listen."

We stand there, dangling like a bunch of ball bags in the wind. Running water. Somewhere over to the right. The burble of a stream.

"Yeah," Luke nods. "Water. Running bloody water. Come on."

His face lights up like I've told him there's a supermodel waiting to suck him off. He surges ahead and I hang back, letting Connor slip in between us both. Let these two luminous idiots take the lead, that way if there are any hunters nearby, they'll be an easier target than me.

We jog as best we can towards the sound. My throat urges me on, begging me to find it some relief. On through the darkened woods, round trees and shrubs. The ground becomes rockier, slippier. Every step becomes a battle.

"Shit, stop!" Luke shouts.

The first shout since Jay's screams. It's too loud. I do as I'm told, skidding to a halt, and knocking into Connor and Luke. They don't turn around. They continue staring down at the ground. I push round them and see it too.

We're stood on a rocky ledge. Below us, shimmering in the moonlight, is a stream. Water forces its way out from the rocks beneath our feet, sluicing through the mud and trees, winding through the woods.

Spring water in its purest form. Evian can go fuck itself.

The other two stand still, gawping like they've just seen a road traffic accident.

"Come on," I say, already moving past them, sliding down rocks and using branches to slow me down. "Let's get at it."

***

It's a free for all once we've seen the water. Tension shifts from my shoulders and I slide and scoot over the moss-covered rocks. They jut out at odd angles and it's nothing I'd usually do lightly but thirst aches inside me. A primitive need pushes me down on the rocks. Luke and Connor are panting as they scramble down. Their breathing echoes off the faces of the boulders. The trickle of the stream running deep inside my mind, like the blood in my veins.

My shoes slam into thick mud on the banks of the stream. Its grappling, dirty hands clamp round my ankles as cold shoots up my calves and across the tops of my feet. The others pile down before I can move. Someone's knee finds the back of my thigh and I crumple into the mud.

"Sorry," Connor mumbles as he helps me up. I'm coated in slime and moss. My fingers ball into a fist but relax at the sight of him. His face is also splattered with this shit. He laughs and then I do too. It's fucking ridiculous when you think about it. Three grown men, so desperate for a sip of water they've nearly broken their necks in the dark to get it. Three men who if you were being unkind, are nearly forty years old. Definitely old enough to know better.

"Stop hugging each other and get a drink," Luke says. He's crouched like Gollum on the bank of the stream, his hands cupped as he slurps water up from them. He smiles, satisfied. Is this what Amy sees after they've fucked? Absolutely rancid.

"Is it clean?" Connor asks.

"It's cold and wet so I can confirm it's water," Luke says as some dribbles down his chin.

"Let's have a quick look," I say as I stumble out of the bog that's been holding my feet.

Natural caution is kicking back in now that the adrenaline of sliding down the rocks is fading. That little voice in the back of my mind that always wonders – *"how does this affect me?"*

I slide off my bag and pull out the torch. It's heavier than I expect and I almost fumble it into the stream before regaining my composure and flicking it on.

"What the fuck are you doing?" Connor hisses. His hand jumps out and clamps over the torch face. "They'll see us from a mile off."

"Checking there's not a dead sheep or a barrel of fucking rat poison in this stream. It'll take two seconds. Which is probably how long your shits will take if this water's contaminated."

Luke looks over, sodden in the stuff, eyes wide. If this water is diseased, chances are his guts are already starting to rot. The last thing we need right now is sloppy shit running down our legs as a bunch of murderous loons chase us with their rifles. I doubt they'd need dogs to sniff us out after that.

Connor relents and I snatch the torch away and shine it up and down the length of the stream we can see. It's clear. A few branches and a lot of mud at the far end but closer to us, the water bursts out from between the rocks. This is probably the source of some huge local river. Fuck knows which one, but we're lucky. It looks like it's coming up from the ground, no chance of drinking half a dead rat or a pile of sheep shit. I turn the torch off. It's barely been on for ten seconds. I stash it in my bag again.

I nod to Connor, and he dips his hands into the stream and slurps from the cup he makes. Luke's shoulders relax and he abandons all pretence of manners, leaning forward on all fours and lapping at the water like a dog. I let my laughter out.

"Here he is – Lassie. The state of it," I say.

"That'll be one for the wedding album, eh? Shame we don't have a camera," Connor says.

"This is just me in my natural form," Luke says. "I'm pure animal. Amy knows that. She loves it really."

"Fucking pig," I say.

I cup my hands in the water and bring it to my lips. It sparkles in the moonlight. The cold sting down my throat brings me back to life. As though it's frozen everything inside me. Crystallised my thoughts and righted the turmoil. After decades of fancy restaurants, eating the local cuisine in any country you can name, I don't think I've ever tasted anything as life affirming as this water. I take another slurp, then refill my hands for another and another.

"This is genuinely better than cocaine," I blather as water runs down my chin. "It's almost better than sex."

We laugh and for that moment, it's possible to forget why we're here. Forget the reasons why we're filthy and drinking out of a stream like peasants. It's possible to forget the danger.

"Let's get these bottles filled up and go," I say. "And get those fucking jackets off. You're as warm as you're going to get." Coming to my senses as I realise how loud we've been laughing. Turning the torch on was necessary, life or death. But now we're just being careless. At the end of the day, this is all about survival.

They grumble but stash their jackets back in their bags. Job done.

Thirst sated, we form an orderly queue. British sensibilities still hold on even in the woods. I take a final sip of the cool water and stash my canteen in my bag. The weight of it is reassuring. We've got some food and more importantly, a day's worth of water. That adds up to a chance.

"Which way now?" Connor asks. I hear him fumble with his map. When I turn around, he's laid it out on a rock like some demented war general.

We squint at it. Without the torchlight it's hard to make out any detail. You get the broad strokes of objects, trees, bushes, people, but it's difficult to make out this map. Connor moves his head from side to side, as though a different angle will give him more detail. It doesn't.

"Shit," he says. He scrunches up the map, not bothering to fold it this time and stuffs it back into his rucksack.

There's another sound.

"Shut up," I say.

They both look at me, not speaking. I put a finger to my lips, and we press ourselves against the rocks as best we can, getting ourselves out of the open.

The stream still burbles away, water muttering over rocks and branches. There's no doubt about it. I heard someone walking, taking their time but still making noise.

Chilled rocks press through the back of my shirt, the cold seeping through my skin like dirt into an open wound. It holds me tight, arms like a vice. Every muscle in my body is rigid. My jaw clenched, teeth rammed together to stop them chattering.

All three of us stay like this, frozen, heads cocked. Ears craning for a sound from somewhere behind us. There's nothing at first other than the gentle mutter of the water. Gallons of it dribbling out of the rocks and meandering through the dirt as it gathers momentum. The sound becomes insidious. Running water. An urge to piss rises through me. I bite my lip and try to focus on listening out.

Then it comes.

Snap.

Almost cartoonish in its sound. A breaking twig, cracking under the weight of a footstep. Next to me, Connor's eyes widen as he looks round. A barely audible "shit" makes its way out from between his lips. I shake my head. Not now Con, keep it together. Luke is the other side of Connor, mostly hidden from view. He's standing as still as the pair of us.

"Don't think they made it this far."

The words shatter the stillness. I flinch at the sound. Worst fears confirmed. I didn't make it up.

"Well, you never know what you're gonna get, do you?"

"Remember those Scottish cunts on Kevan's stag? Jesus."

"Thought one of 'em had you for a minute, that big lad."

"So, did I. Can't see it with this lot. Bunch of fucking pussies if you ask me."

The piss in my bladder slowly begins to boil. Pussies? What are we supposed to do? Charge in with just our fists? I twist around at their words, trying to get a look at them. Connor grabs my arm, his fingers gripping tightly, digging into the muscle. Surprisingly strong. He puts his finger to his lips and shakes his head.

A crackle of static. Walkie-talkies. Gav's sharp voice.

"We got anything down the far end, Steveo? Over."

"Don't think they made it this far. Over."

"Make another check and swing back this way, yeah? Helen's dad is on his way back up with the jeep. He's taking away that dead pig. Over."

"Aye. On our way back. Over."

"Don't worry. This lot aren't at it. They'll give us something soon. We owe posh boy for getting away. Any cunt who leaves a mate like that has it coming. Over."

"Aye. See you in a few. Out."

Silence. I close my eyes, back pressed against the rocks again. Without looking, I can feel Connor and Luke's eyes on me. Their gaze searching, burning. I don't open my eyes. Don't look at them. There's nothing to feel guilty for. It's about survival now. It's about looking after number one.

They'd do the same and if they say they wouldn't, they're only lying to themselves. I'm the only honest man here.

"I need a piss," one of the voices says. I open my eyes. Footsteps come closer, shuffling through the leaves and mud above. There's a *zip* and a cascade of piss pours down the rocks a couple of feet from my left shoulder. A typical sigh from the man stood a few feet above us. A *hocking* sound and then he launches a ball of spit into the darkness where it disappears into the mud.

I barely breathe, as though I've adapted to my environment of stillness and silence. Another *zip* and he's gone, footsteps crunching away from us.

"Let's get back, do another sweep on the way," the pisser says. "We'll catch them soon, pin them between the two groups."

"Could do with getting this one done tonight," the other one says, their voices fading as they walk away. "Big match on tomorrow lunchtime, don't want to miss United for the sake of chasing these fucking idiots about."

"Get Wallace his prize and get on the fucking ale lad. Best way."

They chuckle. I stay still, muscles still compact. Everything clenched from jaw to arsehole. The footsteps and noises from the pair of them disappear but I don't move. I stare straight ahead at the black tree trunks and the shimmering water in the moonlight. Nothing moves. Nothing makes a sound. The stillness focuses me, centres my mind.

"Fucking close one, that," Luke says. His voice low. It carries none of the enthusiasm it held back when we discovered the stream.

"His piss missed me by about two feet. If he'd taken a proper look, we'd be dead meat by now," I say.

"Saved by a pair of lazy pricks," Connor says. "God bless slackers."

"Yeah, maybe. But we need to be sharper from now on. If they've cleared off, we've got a window. Press on. Maybe get out of these woods. Put some distance between us. Keep them guessing," I say.

Connor nods.

"What did they mean, back there?" Luke says. "About you leaving Jay? Thought you got separated?"

"We did. I've no idea what they're on about. Just banter, most likely." I say.

"Yeah..." Connor says, "sounds about right."

I push off from the wall, both of them watch me without saying anything more. My hands rise into a shrug. They both look at me but still, there's nothing said. Fine. Fuck it. Let's move on.

"Where to now?" I ask.

"Depends where you want to go," Connor says. "Stay in these woods and try to hide it out. Or make a break for it. If we get across the fields, there's another wood further down. That gets my vote. They'll give this another sweep I reckon. We won't be able to hide forever."

"We'll be too exposed out on the fields," Luke says. "The whole idea of this wood was to get some higher ground and ride it out. I say we stay here. Take our chances with hiding."

"The higher ground didn't work," I say. "Now they're swarming the place. We need to get going. Try to find somewhere to properly rest. They will need to soon as well. Use the darkness, get across the fields, and try to take stock when the sun comes up."

Luke grumbles something under his breath but Connor cuts him off. "I'm with you, Eth. Let's do it."

"Which way is out?" Luke asks.

"Follow the stream, I reckon." Connor nods at my words. "It'll run downhill, out of the woods?"

"It's as good a plan as any," Connor says. "We can check the map again when we've done some more walking."

Luke sighs, "let's make a start then."

I hoist my pack onto my back and the others do the same. Luke leads the way, taking the route painfully slowly. The mud around the banks of the stream is thicker, heavier than elsewhere. The moisture seeping into my shoes and dirt caking the bottom of my jeans. It saps energy from my calves, a dead feeling spreading up my legs as we slog on, following the curves of the stream. This archaic route out of these fucking woods.

Every few minutes one of us knocks into the other or stands on someone's foot. We're hurrying even though there's time. An innate panic wells in my chest, my breathing coming too hard. Tree branches try to do the job of our pursuers. They claw at my face, one of them drawing blood from beneath my eye. A copper taste on my lips for the first time since Jay decided to lay the smack down on me.

I push to the front of the group but it's a mistake. The going's tougher up here. My palms take a beating as I push branches and bushes aside. Some of them loiter in the shadows, sharp wood hungry for soft flesh. Luke and Connor pant behind me. Exertion and desperation hand in hand. A stitch burns its way up my side, making me regret every session I spent working on my arms instead of cardio.

I reach out, place both hands on a thick branch and bend it forwards, using a few precious grams of strength to hold it back for the others to pass. They duck under it, and I release the branch, dead leaves cascade to the floor with a rustle. I turn to follow the others and slam straight into the back of Connor. His skull makes my nose sing in the blackness.

"What the fuck is that?" Luke says. His arm outstretched, pointing.

Connor stands next to him, his hand cupped over his eyes even though there's no sun. I follow their gaze. Out between the trees and over the curve of the fields, a single light burns in the distance. A house.

A good few miles away. Its yellow light is a beacon to us, asking me a question across the space.

Salvation or damnation?

NINETEEN

Connor

If something seems too good to be true, then it probably is.

Since breaking the treeline and leaving the woods, I've been running bent double. All the time expecting a spotlight to come on and point us out or for a bullet to fizz across the grass and explode someone's head.

Luke and Ethan run free. Heads up, arms pumping. Galloping like young horses allowed to run free for the first time. All caution gone. It's ridiculous. It's fucking stupid. The forest isn't in a vacuum, they can still hear us if we're too loud or too stupid to stay quiet.

It's not just that, it's the light itself. At this distance, it's hard to tell. Chances are, it's a farmhouse. But it could be anything. Another pub. A garage. Whatever it is, it's close enough to the village that whoever we meet will know about this "tradition". Running behind the others, I feel like the only one who's considering that possibility.

Typical.

Cautious Con. Too scared to take a chance on anything, even if his life literally depends on it. My stomach churns as I run, a hollow rumble that's nothing to do with hunger. Protein bar swirling around in there, doing me a mischief. This place, this community, it's too close-knit for this to be a good thing. It'll be someone's Mum or Uncle or ex-girlfriend or whoever waiting for us. One phone call away from execution.

Past halfway there, I pull up. It takes the other two a few hundred yards of running to take notice and stop. Ethan stands there, hands on hips, silhouetted against the growing light ahead of us. Luke bends double, knackered as per. They watch me approach. Shoulders bent forward.

"What is it. Con?" Luke asks when I'm a few yards away.

"We shouldn't do this," I say.

"For fuck's sake," Ethan says. He keeps his hands on his hips and walks around in a tight circle, kicking at the ground. "Every time there's a bloody problem isn't there?"

"I'm not creating, lads. Just think it through. We can only be what, six or seven miles from the pub, tops? As if this farmhouse or whatever isn't going to be owned by someone who knows Wallace or his mates?"

"You can't know that," Ethan says. "Think about London, nobody knows anyone, and they all live on top of each other. They're all miles apart out here. There's no way. No bloody way."

"You're joking aren't you? They *rely on each other* out here. Do things for each other. How do you think all this is still going on after generations? They're all in it together. I'm fucking telling you."

Ethan sneers at me, shakes his head.

"What do you want to do then, Con?" Luke says. He's turned away from Ethan. His attention is solely on me now. "Turn back? Head into the woods and the arms of those fuckwits that killed our mate?"

"I'm not saying go back, all right?"

What am I saying?

I scratch the back of my head, sweat slides down my skin. Greasy and thick. Dirt on my fingertips. Nails digging into the skin as I rub harder and harder.

"I think we should ride it out here until morning. Find the longest grass we can to hide in. Get some rest. Take it in turns to keep watch. In the morning, we can see what we're dealing with and go from there. What do you reckon?"

"No," Ethan says. His voice flat. "We're sitting ducks in the daylight. We go now, speak to whoever we find. Reason with them like civilised people and not fucking animals. And if not, we'll overpower them. Chances are it's some old couple. All the young ones are out here trying to find us."

My head starts shaking before I can stop it. "Fucking nonsense, mate."

"What?" Ethan says, the word a snarl.

"Fucking hell, lads. Just chill out, all right?" Luke says. "It's one vote each. I get to choose." He looks from me to Ethan. "We should do what Connor says, okay?"

Ethan growls. "This how it is, eh? Best buddies playing politics against me? Ooh, ooh." He makes little kissing noises with his lips like we're back in high school.

"Oh, shut up, Eth. We're playing the percentages, okay. There could be anyone in there. Do you even know what building it is?" Luke says.

"Farm, I'm guessing."

"Guessing," Luke says. "Let's get closer, bed down for the night. Christ knows I'm shattered. If we can get a bit of rest and survey the situation in the morning, why not? Then we can start on your plan if we need to. But to go charging in now, it feels doomed, mate."

"Doomed. Nice word for it all," Ethan says. "Jay is dead. I don't want to be next, and neither should you."

"That's why I'm not charging into someone's house and hoping they don't tie me up or shoot me in the face. Just be patient. If we work together, we can get out of this. Come on," I say.

There's a moment of silence, then Ethan nods. "Yeah, okay. Things will seem better with some sleep."

He says that like there's much chance of us getting any.

***

We bed down in long grass about half a mile from the farmhouse. Its structures revealed themselves the closer we got. The single light we saw across the fields burns next to the front door, lighting the entryway to the farmhouse. Two barns loom on either side. Cavernous and empty. There's low noise from the cattle shed, beasts settling and moving in the night. There's nothing to reveal whether the farmer is hostile or not. Whether we could take the farmer, or not.

The long grass is damp from the rain. Its shoulder high stalks fold beneath my weight as I sit down, giving way to mud that seeps into my clothes. These things are a write off. Bought brand new for this weekend and then straight in the bin. As though that matters right now.

"I'll take the first watch," Luke says. "I'll do a couple of hours then one of you can take over. Can't be all that long until it starts getting light. Farmers start early. I'll wake you if I see anyone."

"Fine by me," Ethan says, collapsing to the ground, using his rucksack as a pillow.

Hidden in the long grass, I pull out my cagoule as a blanket and wrap it around my legs. Under and over. A groundsheet and a duvet all in one shitty luminous package.

"Good idea," Ethan says, rustling round and digging into his bag. "Ah yeah. It's gone. Never mind."

I expect Luke to offer his to Ethan, but he doesn't, he just stays sentinel. He's crouching, his head barely poking out over the long grass. His eyes fixed on the farmhouse. Nobody could see him at this distance, could they?

I lie on my back and look up at the dark sky. The moonlight gives me enough to go on as my eyes scan the long grass for spiders or something else that might crawl over me while I sleep. Beggars can't be choosers apparently, and right now, we're the biggest beggars there are.

TWENTY

WALLACE

He lumbers into the house, the drink long since gone from his system, snatched away with the adrenaline of the hunt. Things fell apart after they killed the big man. The night descending into a wild goose chase. By the time Wallace called it off for the night, the lads were pissed off. Chasing shadows and running in circles.

Helen's dad drove him and Gav back in silence. He'd smiled at the news they'd bagged one of the four, but his brow and his jaw formed parallel hard lines as he learned the other three were currently unaccounted for.

Shaking his head, Wallace remembers the whine in his voice, the insistence as he pleaded to his future father-in-law that going home and getting some rest would serve him better than staying in the woods charging round all night.

The sight of his own front door caused tension to bunch in his shoulders, a knot in his stomach. He'd let himself in as quietly as he could but his body never did listen properly to the commands he gave it. He'd made too much noise, trodden too heavily on the wonky floorboards.

"Wally," comes the voice from the doorway.

He stops stirring the cup of tea he's been trying to make quietly. The clatter of the spoon on the countertop, like everything, is too loud. Wallace turns to look at her, his Helen, stood leaning against the doorway. She's wearing the red pyjamas, the one's he's always loved. The way they feel when they lie next to each other. The way they reveal just enough skin at the shoulders to get him going.

The look on her face kills any other thoughts stone dead. Her arms are crossed tight against her chest. Her features knitted into the same lines her father's were just minutes before.

"Is it done with then? You all finished?"

He turns back to his tea, fiddling with the spoon on the counter. "Not quite, but it's going okay. Don't worry."

"Don't worry? You turn up back home hours, days before you should. You sneak in here in the night and make yourself a brew like there's no issue? What the hell is going on, Wally?"

He stares at the closed blinds over the kitchen window. Their beige texture. The blackness that fills in the gaps between slats. "I just needed a little rest. We're going to have a recharge and hit it hard in the morning."

Still the blinds interest him, even as he feels Helen's gaze burrowing into the back of his skull. "I don't remember this happening on Gav's stag party, or John's, or Steveo's. Daddy certainly never mentioned it when he talked about his, or Uncle Roger…"

"I just needed a little time to get myself together. All right? That's it. Just some rest. I'm up every bloody morning with the sheep and the cows and working all bastard day. Sometimes a man just needs to rest. Okay? Not that you'd understand."

His lips move after he finishes speaking, as though trying to bite off the last part of what he's said, to swallow it down before it reaches her ears.

When she speaks, her voice is lower. The growl it takes on during an argument. A pitch that gives him no hint at winning a dispute.

"Oh, I know what being a man is all about. I see it every day written across your face as you drag yourself from our bed. Is it being a man when I find you messing about on your phone in the cattle sheds? Or is it being a man when you can't fix the tractor?"

"If I'm so useless, why do you even want to marry me?"

He doesn't hear her approach and flinches when the back of one of her soft hands grazes the skin on his neck. Her voice is breathy in his ear. Her lips grazing the lobe as she stretches on tiptoes.

"I love you despite and because of these flaws, Wally. I love you for what you are, not what you're supposed to be."

He turns to face her, towering over her. His arms slide around her waist, pulling her close. He smiles down at her and she smiles back. For a second. Then her face changes.

"But you know how it works and you know every one of those rules. You've been there when others have got the job done. You bring me what's mine, you bring that offering to Daddy's house or believe me, there is no wedding, there's no us." She removes his hands from her arse, "and there's definitely none of that. Got it?"

He nods and watches her as she stomps out of the kitchen, her footsteps receding up the stairs before the bedroom door slams, shutting him out.

TWENTY-ONE

Gav

Gav stares up at the darkened ceiling. Everything about it is wrong, he shouldn't be here. Even with Abby's form shaped around his and the intoxicating scent of her apricot shampoo filling his senses, he can't relax, can't shut off.

Lying here with his wife is wrong when there's a job to do. His jaw set, he stares at the ceiling, mind churning.

Abby stirs from her slumber and looks up at him, blinking and then rubbing her eyes, blinking again.

"What are you doing here, babe?"

He'd expected her to wake up the moment he entered the house, but even as he ate and then showered, she didn't show. When he'd slid into bed beside her, she'd not woken, not properly, just slid over to reciprocate their warmth.

Her voice is drowsy with sleep, thick and low. The contact that would usually stir him from the waist down is floundering. He lies stock still. Tensed and awake.

She repeats her question, shuffling around and away from him. Her bedside lamp snaps on revealing the rest of the room. His heart sinks, the conversation is about to start. Abby looks at him, skin pale and blonde hair straggled in a way nobody but him would ever be allowed to see. There's an intimacy to her appearance, her guard down, that reminds him of how much he loves her. The affection brings a tightness to his chest, the same feeling he experiences every time he sees her.

"Wallace got his offering then?" Abby says, leaning away from him and flicking her phone screen to life. "Helen will be pleased. Done nice and quickly."

"What are you doing?"

"Seeing if Helen has messaged me. We'll have plenty to celebrate on the hen party."

"She hasn't. If she has, she won't be saying owt good. Useless clown ain't done it yet."

Abby lies back, head and neck sinking into the pillows. Her gaze meeting Gav's on the ceiling. "Jesus. What happened? Why are you home if he's not done it?"

"It's what he wanted. We lost the scent and he lost his bottle. Wants to start again in the morning."

"Lost the scent? That isn't like you lot."

"Ain't been a good one. Right from the start this time. Wallace been throwing us all off. Been harder to get him going than it should be, you get me? Weird."

"Not a total surprise though? After how he was on Steveo's it was always going to be a problem."

"Aye. But I didn't think he'd be this bad like. There was an... There was an incident." Gav sits up in the bed, he wants to spit on the ground at the memory, but not in his own home. He's not an animal. Not in here at least.

"Did he?"

Gav nods. "Bottled it big time. We had one of 'em. One of the sneaky little cunts gift-wrapped him for us. Left his own mate to die. No questions asked."

"Wow."

"Yeah. Not had that for a while, like. But we've got this fella, the biggest one, on his knees. Wallace has Phillip's gun in his fucking hands. Starts shaking like a shittin dog, yeah, starts whimpering. Hector and Nige are there. Watching him. Starts getting a bit embarrassing so I have a word. Tell him it ain't on, it ain't good enough. He gets worse. Clams up. Can't get himself together at all."

Abby looks at him, her blue eyes shine even in the low light. Her brow furrows and then smooths again. Gav meets her gaze for a second and then looks away. "So, you did it, didn't you?"

He nods. He stares into the far corner of the room. There are no cobwebs there, not like other people's homes. Not like Wallace and Helen's house. Abby despises mess. Despises feeling unclean. He wonders if a part of her psyche is now embedded in his. That hatred for dirt and for feeling unclean. Is that how he feels now, after pulling the trigger? He's not sure. He bites the inside of his cheek.

"Yeah. I'm the best man, I did it. A copper. Wife. Two kids." He mimes a gun with the two forefingers of his right hand. Pretends to shoot and feel the recoil.

Abby stares at him, her eyes searching his face. He keeps his eyes on the duvet and she reaches out to touch his arm.

"You don't have to do all this, not for me. You can be yourself in this house."

"What if this is who I am though? What if I enjoyed it?"

"Did you?"

"I don't know. I don't let myself think about it."

"You shouldn't be like that, Gav. You should be kinder to yourself."

"I'm not being unkind. I don't think about it when I put an animal down. It just needs doing. It's part of my job."

"But this was a person. A person with a career and a family. Doesn't that bother you?"

"Not if I don't let it."

She sighs, rubs her temples. She turns the bedside lamp off, plunging the room into darkness. No light makes its way around the blackout blinds, but Gav stays sat upright in the bed, staring into the same corner as before.

"And if Wallace can't get the job done this weekend, how will you feel about "doing your job" then? Will you not let yourself think about it?"

He takes his time before he answers. His voice comes out harder than he means it to. "If he can't get the job done, then I'll do what's necessary. Just like I did tonight. Wallace is a friend but he's no exception. Nobody is."

"We could've left. We didn't have to do this. We didn't have to stay here."

"This is our home, Abs. Even if things are a bit heavy here, this is all we have. This is all I know how to do."

"Well, when you're finished with it all, make sure you still know yourself. That's the only thing I ever ask."

Her hand finds his under the duvet, their fingers intertwine as Gav continues to stare into the black.

TWENTY-TWO

Luke

Morning breaks ugly and slow, pale light seeping across everything like filthy water. Slowly, as though teasing us, it reveals the details of the buildings. Everything the night hinted at is there. To call this place dilapidated would be too kind. It's an absolute wreck.

Moss stains the walls of the house, weeds teeter in the garden, almost as high as the windows. Sheets of corrugated metal hang from the cattle sheds. Rust colours every inch of the outbuildings.

I don't remember sleeping but feel like I must have. There's energy in my legs. My thoughts running clearer. Connor and Ethan lie in the long grass, dozing amongst the sodden green stalks. The daylight gives me hope. Back in our uni days, waking up in a field at ridiculous o'clock in the morning would've been the stuff of legend, now it's just a secret that we'll have to keep for a long, long time.

Connor blinks himself awake, rubbing at his eyes and looking at the overgrown grass as though he's never seen it before.

"Yeah, mate," I say. "None of that shit was a dream."

"Fuck me."

I reach down, offering a hand and pull him up to his haunches. A waft of his body odour swings across my senses, and I bite my lip against taking the piss. Chances are I smell at least as bad. He meets my eye and there's a second where some of the things we said last night taunt me.

"We good?" He says.

"Yeah, yeah. As if we wouldn't be?" I force out a smile which he returns.

"I'm fucking starving," he says, rummaging in his bag for a protein bar. He rips one open and starts cramming it into his mouth, washing it down with spring water from his canteen.

The sound wakes Ethan. Despite sleeping in a field, he still looks more presentable than I do most mornings. His clothes are caked in mud, but his hair is almost perfect. He blinks, gets to his knees. "What did I miss?" He still smells of aftershave.

"Nothing. Just breakfast."

He grunts and we both follow Con's lead of chewing down processed protein. The spring water washes away the last of the taste and also the fog from my head. Turning away, I piss into the grass.

Connor's voice wobbles as he speaks. "About last night lads, about this weekend. I know I fucked it up, yeah? I know Jay is dead because of me. And I'll do whatever I can to make it up to Claire and the kids. Don't hold any of this against me. Let's just focus on trying to get home. Is that okay?"

Ethan smiles, holding back a laugh. "Well, I wasn't going to blame you but now you brought it up?" He lets his laugh out but nobody joins him.

All I can do is to pat Connor on the shoulder. A wooden, fatherly gesture. "Let's just focus on getting home. We need to decide what to do about this," I jerk a thumb over my shoulder at the house.

"It's a complete shit-bin," Ethan says. "Imagine living like that."

"We need to be careful, farmers have guns. They protect their livestock from all sorts of threats. Let's not give whoever it is a reason," Connor says.

"If his gun is as rusty as his barn, I don't think that's going to be an issue."

Ignoring their chatter, I crawl away from them through the grass. I'm careful where I place my hands. The ground is sodden and uneven. My rucksack rolls from side to side on my back, desperate to escape me.

"What are you doing?" Connor hisses.

"We need to see the rest of it. Come on."

Without saying anything else, the whisper of moving grass tells me that they're following. The curve and undulations of the land make it slow going, after a hundred yards I rise to a crouch and make better progress. We move in a wide circle around the house and outbuildings. The land is higher here, and we settle in to watch, as close as we dare.

Peering over the top of the long grass, the yard behind the house reveals itself. More rust and sheet metal. A filthy tractor idles, its engine a low grunt. A deep blue cattle transporter is hitched to the back of it. The gaping mouth of the thing hanging down into the dirt.

A man wanders out of the farmhouse, he leaves the front door open and shouts something backwards over his shoulder, I don't catch. He's in his fifties with grey hair. He's not ripped but he's got that sinewy muscle that comes from working outdoors and lugging heavy stuff around all day. He's in overalls. Deep green, stained black at the knees and brown in other places. His boots splatter through the mud in the yard, past the tractor and he disappears out of sight into one of the cattle sheds.

A minute later, a woman appears in the doorway. Similar age. Similar build. She's like a tree root, gnarled and stubborn. A cloud of smoke billows from her and she leans back against the doorframe as a pair of border collies bound out of the space and into the yard. There's a whistle from the cattle shed making the dogs stop dead and lie down in the muck.

"I bet those dogs don't even shit without permission," Ethan mutters in my ear.

"This is a problem," I say.

We're well hidden up here in the long grass. This isn't like a terrible bad guy in a James Bond film where the light catches the lenses of binoculars, so Bond knows where to shoot. There's no way either of them could see us from there, but now there are dogs involved, everything becomes more complicated.

"We can't rush them with dogs there," Connor says, like he's ever rushed anyone in his life. "Those dogs will do anything for their master. They'll rip our bloody faces off."

"All it will take is for the dogs to keep us busy whilst Old Farmer Giles here runs inside for the shotgun to finish us off," Ethan says. There's none of his usual sparkle as he speaks, his eyes remain hard. Dulled somehow.

"Or worse," I say. "We need another plan."

Without warning, sheep amble from one of the sheds towards the open gate on the trailer. They're not the cute cartoon sheep from kid's books, these are mangy, grey, dirty beasts. Like everything else on this farm, they're stained and decrepit. They march towards the trailer, heads down, like commuters piling onto a morning train. One of them, a smaller one, makes a bolt for it. Without a word from the farmer or his wife, the dogs spring into action, circling the sheep and guiding it back into line with the others. Once it's taken its place again, the dogs lie back down, satisfied.

"Yeah, there's no way we're getting at these two," Connor says. There's a relief there, he's been scared of dogs since we were kids.

"Where do you think they're taking them?" Connor continues.

"A market? An auction? To the abattoir?" I say.

"He's probably taking them round the local pub for a big woolly orgy based on some of the pricks we saw last night," Ethan says.

I laugh into my sleeve. A schoolboy's joke but after the previous night, I'll take any comfort I can get.

"Wait," I say. "We don't need to rush the farmer. No, no."

The sheep are inside the trailer and the farmer hoists the door shut. There must be fifty of them in there. The trailer's far from full. The door is blue sheet metal that covers the lower half of the gap, blocking the sheep from view.

"We can climb in with them. Look." The other two follow my finger and pick up on the size of the gap.

"How the hell are we going to get in there without being seen?" Connor says, his voice high and I wonder if he's got a childhood fear of sheep he's not dealt with yet.

"Hope to God that the dogs go away and then we're sorted," Ethan says.

"And if they don't?" Connor says.

"We're screwed, aren't we? We can't be seen by this fella, we don't know whose side he's on," I say.

"I think we can safely bet that it won't be ours. We're just going to have to avoid him and hope for the best," Ethan says, his eyes scanning the yard. "Maybe we need to create a diversion. Get him and the dogs distracted then jump into the back while they're not paying attention."

"Not the worst idea you've had to be fair," I say.

"No. My worst idea was going dressed as Jeffrey Dahmer to the Economics Faculty Fancy Dress Ball," Ethan says. He doesn't smile as he says it and neither do we

"Let's get down there and see what we can find. Maybe slash a tyre or something?" Connor says.

"Slashing his tyres won't get us anywhere will it, but keep your eyes peeled. Let's head for that far cattle shed, yeah?" I signal and start scuttling through the long grass. The slope and curve of the hill makes a steady speed difficult. The ground's uneven and my trainers are completely wrecked.

The closer we get to the shed, the worse the smell becomes. Cow shit. The scent so pungent the air feels hot, as though it's coating my tongue. I clear my throat a few times until Connor taps me on the shoulder and whispers for me to cut it out. I take a breath through my mouth and get myself together.

At the far side of the cattle shed, we straighten up and leave the long grass. Flattened against the rusted metal wall, I do a quick scan of the yard. There's no visible CCTV, at least that's something. Just the problem of the dogs and the likely insane farmer and his wife.

I'm closest to the yard, I poke my head round to get a better look. We're further away from the house now, which is good but further from the trailer. The sheep are out of sight, bleating away. Occasionally one of them clangs into the metal. Even if we can get into the trailer, it's going to be a horrific ride out of here. One last step to freedom, hopefully.

The farmer is in the sheep shed. It's hard to see what he's doing properly from this angle. There's a scraping sound which cuts out, then he marches into view. Closer up, he's wild. He looks borderline rabid. Wide eyes and unbrushed hair.

"Sheila, where's the fuckin dip at, eh?" He shouts across the yard.

His wife, on what must be her third ciggie, gives him a shrug and carries on smoking, eyes fixed firmly on the dog. "How the fuck should I know?"

He grunts and waves her away. "I'll get some more at market. Thought we had some. Fucks sake."

"And don't you be going the pub on the way home, only so long you can drive that fuckin thing down them lanes after a few beers without crashing it and doing yourself some damage."

"Oh, you'd like that, wouldn't you?"

"About as much as I'd like three arseholes."

"You know how to fuckin sweet talk me woman," he grins at her. They kiss on the doorstep of the house before he disappears inside, leaving his wife smoking in the yard.

I lean back behind the cattle shed, away from this bizarre romance. It's a grey day but sweat beads along my hairline at the top of my neck. I wipe it away with the back of my hand.

"There's no doubt, this pair are fucking nuts. They wouldn't hesitate to shop us or shoot us," I say. "We can't be seen. No way."

We shuffle in position so Ethan and Connor can take a look at the situation.

"Doesn't feel like we've got long," Ethan says. His mouth set after his view. "These farmers start early. Can't even tell you what time it is. If we're going, we're going now."

"Agreed," Connor says. "If we run across the yard, they'll see us straight off. It needs to be a short run out in the open. If a dog barks at us, we're fucked. Shortest run is from next to the house."

Jesus. Near the house. As if anything good can happen there. Which film was it where they have those lamps and stuff made from human skin? Texas Chainsaw Massacre? Halloween?

"It'll be fine," I say. My voice is steel. Unbreakable. This is it. Probably our best chance to get out of here. "There's no other way. We've just got to do it. Come on."

Signal unspoken, I crouch and start to manoeuvre my way through the long grass again.

***

The closer we get to the house, the louder the blood thunders in my ears. When we were kids, we got fed up with knock a door run and we graduated to knock a door hide. It's the same principle, knock on some poor sap's door but instead of legging it down the street, you hide somewhere close by to watch their fury or bewilderment. Hide too cautiously and your mates rip you. Hide badly and there's no head start if they want to chase you.

There'll be no head start if we're discovered here. No margin for error. Not with two dogs involved. They're hardly drooling pit bulls but there'll be no outrunning them if we need to escape.

I lead the way. Thirteen again and approaching a neighbour's door to play a game. That's what I tell myself, let myself believe. I crawl through the long grass which creeps up, barely five yards from the back of the house, like the tide slowly coming in. From the line of the grass, there's nothing to do but run, bent double, to the gap between the house and some old shed. There are boxes and old pallets stacked there, not enough cover really, but something to work with at least.

We can't linger here, on the edge of the grass. Anyone at the back of the house, either upstairs or down, would see us straight off. I signal to the others where we're heading, then make a break for it. My heart pounds, slapping away like I'm running a mile when it's barely ten yards. I make it to the pallets and kneel behind them, looking forwards into the yard and not back at the lads.

The couple are out there, doing something between the tractor and the trailer. I wave to the others to follow me but push my hands down to calm them. We can't make any noise, and this is something that can't be rushed. The right moment will reveal itself and we must be ready.

Ethan comes first, not bending double, just that usual confident stroll of his. Connor follows on. Halfway across, he stops and runs to the window of the house, out of my sight. He appears a few seconds later. His face is drained and tight, as though someone's got a handful of his skin and is yanking it away from his skull.

"Jesus. Jesus. Fucking Jesus."

"What is it, Con? Why did you look in there?" I ask.

"Just wanted to see if they've got a gun or anything, you know. Cabinets. Racks. See what we're up against."

"Have they?"

"Dunno. I couldn't see anything past what was above the fireplace. These people round here, they're fucking sick. He's in on it! They had a fucking skull on there. Mounted like a stag's head on like a wooden shield. There were all branches and herbs or something all round it. Like decorating it and that."

"What the fuck?" I say.

"I told you, we should never have come up North for this stag party. The absolute state of these people." Ethan's trying for his usual sarcastic tone, but it doesn't hit the mark. There's a quaver to his pitch that's off.

"We need to get out of here. That could be us," Connor says. "Any of us."

I swallow. "That could be Jay."

Ethan looks down at his hands, not meeting anyone's gaze. Now's not the time for all this. We need to be ready to move. "Keep your heads screwed on, yeah," I say as I lean round the house again.

Whatever they've been doing to the tractor, it's done. The man sits in the cab, the door open. The woman stands in the mud looking up at him.

"Try it now then," she calls up.

He presses a couple of buttons and there's a clunk from the tractor, a hiss and then silence.

"That's done it," she says, giving him a thumbs up.

"Beauty," he says, climbing down from the cab. His boots splatter into the filth of the yard. "I'll get in for a piss, then I'll be off."

He walks towards the house, and I disappear back behind the wall. I hear him thud in through the front door and stomp up the stairs. There's the squelch of the woman's footsteps as she approaches the front door, followed by the clink of her lighter and a waft of cigarette smoke. I stand frozen, separated from this maniac by a couple of feet of brickwork.

From the bowels of the house, there's a yell. "Make me a butty will yer, Gerty? Cheese or whatever."

"Yeah, yeah," she shouts back before muttering to herself, "fuck's sake". The cigarette lands in a pile of others in the dirt near my feet. More footsteps disappearing into the house.

"We've got to go now," I say.

"Where are the dogs?" Ethan says, his voice higher than usual.

I shake my head. "Couldn't see them. But they've both fucked off inside. Let's go."

Without waiting to see if they're ready, I step out from behind the house and splash my way across the mud to the back of the trailer. Sliding footsteps behind me let me know the others are there too.

We're brutally exposed here. Nothing to hide behind between the house and the trailer. If one of these freaks looks out a window, it's game over. The half-door on the back of the trailer towers over us. I reach up, my fingertips skim the lip when I stretch but there's no purchase. Connor fumbles with the mechanism to open the door, a rusted latch, and an iron bar.

Ethan grips Con's arm. "Don't. All those sheep will come flying out. It'll be too noisy."

"How will we get in?" Connor whines.

"Old school. I'll give you a boost. Come on." I kneel in the mud, hands cupped. Connor hesitates. We don't have time for this shit. "Come on!" I grunt.

Connor's sole, dripping with cow shit skids across my palms and I lift, standing with his weight on my hands. My wrists scream but the momentum of his step lets me lift him up enough that he can grip the top of the door and pull himself over. He dangles there for a second, only his hands visible and then drops. His feet land with a metallic thud.

Ethan stares at me. If I boost him now, there's nobody to lift me up. He nods at me, pointing with his head for me to kneel again. "I'll stay at the top and pull you up, old boy."

There's no time for my suspicions about Jay's demise to take root, we have to do this now. "Okay," I kneel again and hoist Ethan up. He pulls himself up and sits, one leg each side of the door. Sheep start to shuffle and fuss in the trailer. They're making too much noise.

Wiping his hands on my already filthy keks, Ethan grasps my outstretched hands, his fingers tight round the wrists. "Pull," I groan. He does. He's strong, lifting me off the floor with the joints of my shoulders screaming as I rise. My feet scrabble against the trailer, finding purchase on a metal shelf above the number plate. We both wail as he pulls me up, my trainers slipping over the sheet metal before I'm able to hook an arm over the door. In the edge of my peripheral vision, there's a flash of movement in one of the house windows. Please, no.

"Shit," Ethan mutters. His hand grabs the belt loops on my jeans and thrusts me up and over the door. I grab the top, barely breaking my fall. My knees moaning as I land full pelt on the metallic floor of the trailer.

There's the scuttling of footsteps outside the trailer and then barking cuts through the air. A high, urgent sound that's too loud for this enclosed space. Ethan drops down with another thud. Connor is already huddled in the corner by the door. Curled up in a ball, wedged in. Hands over his face. There are gaps in the metal at waist height. Enough to let air in and give the sheep a view at their eye level.

Those fucking dogs. They go off. Their barking more and more frequent. There are no gaps in the door so it's impossible to see them. Instead, I peer through one of the slats on the sides, kneeling down. The dogs continue to bark. The farmer hares out of the front door, arms raised. Face etched in rage.

"Shurrup. Fucking shurrup. Alright? Knock it fuckin off," he shouts.

The dogs fall silent. He's ten yards from the trailer. Behind me, the sheep are still baaing and scraping. Without looking round, I wave the other two over to me. We need to hide. The farmer's coming. I motion for them to get down below the level of the gaps. If he looks in from this side, he'll never see us. They do as they're told as I keep an eye on the farmer.

After a couple of seconds of giving his dogs shitty looks, he races over to the trailer. I duck. Curled in a ball. Sheep shit and straw clinging to me, coating my jeans. The stench almost visible in the air around me, the taste of something acidic on my lips.

Dirty fingers in the gap above my head as the farmer peers in. The sheep huddle in the far corner. They fidget. Their wide, black eyes fixed on us. There's a fleeting urge to put my finger to my lips and the thought of telling such a dumb animal what to do almost makes me burst out laughing. I bite the inside of my cheek and duck my head down to curl into a tighter ball.

Blam. Blam. Blam.

The farmers fist on the steel side of the trailer. The impact inches from my ear. The sheep fall silent, just as the dogs did.

"Good," comes the mumbled response. Then footsteps squelching away across the yard followed by a whistle and the scampering of the dogs.

I let myself breathe. After a few seconds, I unfurl myself from the ball. My back finds the cool metal of the trailer wall and I slump there, spent, heart racing like I've been sprinting. Sweat slides down Ethan's face and Connor stares into the middle distance.

"Thought he fucking had us then," I mutter.

"I hate dogs," Connor says. "Fucking hate them."

Ethan doesn't say anything, just continues to pant and slouch back against the metal.

The farmer's voice in the doorway of the house again. "I'll be back when I'm back, woman. Okay? Leave it be. Got one stop to make on the way out there, then to the market."

"Don't come home pissed or you're sleeping out with the cows."

"Yeah, yeah."

"And good luck with the drop off," Gerty says.

"Yeah, yeah. See yer later."

There's a second of silence and then footsteps. Presumably a gruff, bestial kiss took place on the doorstep. A worse thought than my parents kissing. The tractor cab door swings open with a creak, then the engine rumbles into life drowning out even the thoughts in my head.

"Hold on," Ethan shouts, fingers gripping the metal through the sheep's air gap. I do the same. Connor too. The tractor pulls off and we lurch forward, clinging on by our fingertips to stay balanced. The sheep stumble and recover, never coming closer to us than they have to. They continue to baa and fidget as they regain their balance. The trailer bangs and shudders over potholes and dips in the mud path to the road.

We lurch to a stop as the farmer pauses, then accelerates out onto the lane by the house. Stone walls blast past as we make our way out of the hell hole farm and away to freedom.

TWENTY-THREE

Ethan

This is what it's come to, being carted out of this place in a trailer filled with livestock and covered in shit. Christ, I'll need a week off work to get hosed down and get the smell off me. Dad will lap all this up when I tell him.

His voice rings in my head.

"What did I tell you about going up there? Nothing but sheep fuckers and piles of shit. You're lucky you didn't come back married to your own cousin."

Not that he'd know or that he'd have any clue what it's taken for me to even make it this far. Even if he could imagine it, he'd never understand. Dad doesn't really "do" empathy. Maybe that's one good thing he's done for me. Helped me to shut off, to do whatever needs to be done to get the deal done or the project over the line. When you shut down and view things analytically, that's all anything is. A job, a task, a project. Things to tick off and complete.

The task was to escape from a tricky situation.

Did I manage it? Yes.

Was the cost more than I could stand to bear? No.

Was the outcome positive and sustainable? Yes.

If need be, it can be repeated another couple of times until closure is complete.

Every pothole and bump in the road sends a thud and jump through the trailer. It doesn't matter how we sit, crouch, or lie down, there's no way to stay still in this trailer. Huddled over in the far corner, the sheep stand up fine. Their brown eyes turned towards us. They oscillate between periods of tense silence and incessant bleating.

We wind down this shitty one-track country lane. It's barely paved. Stone walls line the route. Brambles and trees lean over to scratch the metal sides of the trailer. This could be one of the roads we drove down, it might not. Everything out here looks the same. Sprawling fields, rolling hills, lakes and streams glistening. Every inch of this place crawling with absolute fucking maniacs. They don't tell you this shit in Lonely Planet.

The other two sit and cling onto the walls of the trailer. Luke's face set in a stare, fixed somewhere beyond the horizon. Connor is so pale he's almost green. His head twisted so his mouth and nose are in the air gap. The breeze pushes his hair away from his face. A pair of weaklings. Runts of the litter these two. Much easier to handle than Jay if need be. Neither of them has seen a gym in a decade, if not longer. I flex my fingers and bunch them up again, the muscles on my forearms pulse and tighten.

Another few corners and then the tractor stops. Idling. From his vigil by the air holes, Connor calls over. "There's a main road here, think he's turning right." As if that means anything to anyone. "My map's in my bag, why don't one of you have a look. See where we're heading."

Luke fumbles it out of the rucksack, Connor remaining by the air holes, not even looking. The tractor lurches forward and we slip and bang into the metal door behind us. The sheep continue to baa and stare. We pick up speed, nothing in the trailer staying still. The map vibrating in front of my eyes in Luke's hands.

"I think we're here," Luke says, his finger wobbling on a line. "Heading towards Gowerstone. The nearest town? Maybe."

"How far is it from the B&B?" Connor asks.

"Christ knows, I mean about as far as my hand maybe on the map? In terms of scale."

"Far enough," I say. "I think if we get out there, then we're okay. Looks like we're out of this little valley of lunatics. Put it that way."

"Nice one," Connor says. "Let's stay on it then. Stay alert. When we get there, we'll rush him when he opens the door and find our way on, the train, coaches. Anything."

"And if that doesn't work?" I say.

"We've got nothing else," Luke says, stashing the map again.

We ride in silence for a few minutes. The bumps are less frequent on the main road, lacking their previous teeth-shattering strength. I settle back, wedged into the corner, managing to find a position that's almost tolerable. A protruding metal bolt near my shoulder reminding me to keep it real and not fully relax.

The tractor slows, gradually at first but then more forcefully. Without warning it swings to the left and crunches onto gravel. Pointed branches scrape the trailer, one of them sneaking into an air hole before being snatched away. I'm the first on my feet, followed by the other two.

"He's stopped to let traffic past," Connor says, stretching his back. "Don't worry."

"An unusually polite farmer. Normally these pricks just plough on with eight miles of traffic behind them," Luke says.

More tyres on the gravel. Pulling to a stop. A door opening with a squeak of a hinge and shutting with the dull slap of metal. Footsteps through the stones.

The farmer walks into view and some other guy. A tingle of memory. The shape of the person he's talking to. The patter of his voice. They shake hands and take up a position to talk that's outside the sliver of vision the air holes give us. We duck down below the line of it. Backs against the metal, ears trained like radar on the conversation.

"Thought it was you, Colin," the familiar voice says. "I'm off down Gowerstone market. Same as you?"

"Aye. You know how it is. Sheep need shipping out and don't care who takes 'em. You sold many this year, Phillip?" Colin, the farmer says.

"Lambs for me. All done now like. Gotta get my mind off it all," Phillip says. "The hunt. Hard to not get involved."

"We done our time," Colin says. "Nowt to do but sit back and see how they handle it. Heard they got a couple already?"

"Just one, the others don't seem imminent if you can follow me," Phillip's voice lowers, difficult to hear over the traffic. "If they need us to step in, can you manage a shift this weekend?"

Colin mumbles something. The roar of a passing motorbike drowns it out, the noise fading to reveal the rest of his words. "I told 'em. Dunno why they ain't told you. Don't you worry. They ain't gonna be needing us. It's all in hand. You don't have to take your own action. Your daughter will get her offerin'."

"I've always liked you, Colin. Next weekend, when it's done, you and Gerty come up to our place. I got some of that good whisky, the peaty one you like and a few other things, okay?"

"I'm gonna take you for all you've got after this one," Colin laughs. A harsh sound. Like a dog's bark. "And more."

"Bastard," Phillip laughs.

There's more muttering, beyond our hearing, as though their heads are together and they're speaking low. I half rise to my feet, cram an eye into the air hole. Doing my best to be subtle but something isn't right.

I can't see them until the farmer lurches into view. I drop down onto my knees, below the slots in the metal. Alarm paints the faces of the other two, but I shake my head at them, finger on my lips. The farmer's footsteps stop and so does my heart, then they resume. My life momentarily pauses while the farmer fumbles with his phone or whatever the hell he did out there. Air comes cold and fresh into my lungs as the farmer makes a meal of climbing up into the cab and getting the engine started.

Over the noise, we speak.

"Did he see you?" Luke says.

"No. Close one though."

"What the hell was all that about out there?" Connor asks.

"Fuck knows. Probably married each other's mums or something. You know what it's like round here. Inbred to fuck." In answer to my words a sheep bleats and we all laugh. Tension still squeezes me tight around the ribs, a chuckle doing nothing to alleviate it.

The tractor lurches forward and I grab onto a bolt on the side of the trailer to steady myself. Connor and Luke slide down into the straw and mud. Hands slithering for purchase until they straighten themselves up.

"We're going to make it," Luke says. There's the twinge of a smile on his face. A nick at the corner of his mouth. "Once we get to Gowerstone, we rush this prick up front and make off, yeah?"

"Yeah," Connor agrees. His eyes shine like a little boy staring through a toyshop window.

I click my fingers in front of their faces. Over and over. They're both staring at me. Eyebrows drawn into harsh angles. "Keep your minds on it. We're not there yet. We're bloody miles away from Gowerstone. Stay sharp and stay in the game. Okay?"

"Yes, coach," Luke mumbles.

I dig a fingernail into the side of my thumb, enjoying the pain that stops me ramming his head into the sheet metal behind him. My eyes find the gap above his head, watching trees and streetlights cut across the open square. A familiar, calming pattern. Everything on repeat like a Scooby-Doo background.

"Why are we slowing?" Connor asks after a while. His hands scrabble in his bag for his map. He looks at it and swallows heavily. Rubs at his temples, tries again. Luke and I crowd round, looking at the map from our different angles. Connor's finger quavers over a line indicating the road we're on. He traces it from our starting point to where he thinks we are now. Shakes his head. "I think we're about here. Roughly."

"So, we should be in Gowerstone soon?" Luke asks.

"Another half an hour, forty minutes," Connor says.

"And it's a straight run?" I say.

"Well, yeah. As straight as this road goes but we're supposed to stay on it," Connor replies. He looks at each of us in turn.

Without warning, the tractor swings to the right and we're all shunted against the sheet metal sides. Connor scrambles for the map as we recover ourselves, the trailer bouncing over the uneven ground. He brushes straw off it. Eyes searching for the location.

Connor shakes his head. "What the fuck? This makes no sense."

"What doesn't?" I say, trying to keep my voice steady.

"There's no road here," Connor replies.

He looks to the slots in the sides of the trailer, and I beat him to it. Thrusting my face into the gap, my stomach lurches. We're bouncing across a field. The farmer's pulled in through a gate in the drystone wall. Mud coats the sides of the trailer, water splashing up from where it's pooled in ruts. We're going as fast across the field as we were on the main road. The sheep bleat and stumble around. There's a hammering sound from the tractor. The farmer's fist on the window of the cab telling them to shut the fuck up.

Connor's gone green and turned away from the map. I wobble over to him, grabbing his face with one hand, turning it back to the map. "Connor, we're going over fields. Where's he taking us?"

"I can't," Connor says. "I'm going to be sick."

"I don't care if you spew an organ out, where are we going?"

"Connor, come on lad," Luke says. His voice calm. Ever the pragmatist.

Connor turns back to the map. Traces a line with his finger. His skin shines with sweat. He wretches and turns away. He crawls into the opposite corner of the trailer and spews. The sound of his sickness quickly giving way to the stench. The sheep stamp and whinny. Idiotic creatures.

Connor props himself up, back with us now, his skin almost green, his eyes shimmering wet. "The village. That's where he's taking us. Back across the fields to the village. By the look of this, we've got about five minutes before we're pulling up outside the B&B."

Now he's not the only one who needs to be sick.

"Shit, shit, shit," Luke says to absolutely no use whatsoever. "Shit!"

"We've got to get out of here," Connor mumbles, his hand on his stomach. "We can't go back there. Not after being so close."

My eyes search the sheet metal walls, floor and ceiling of the trailer. There's nothing but badly painted, rusted steel. No mechanism to open the door. No way out other than the way we came in. "We'll have to climb up the gate and jump down," I say.

As though hearing me, the farmer accelerates, and I put my hand out to steady myself. Outside, the scenery becomes a blur of green and brown. All detail fading. It's hard to stand, hard to hear ourselves over the engine and the rush of the wheels. A chorus of sheep bleating away behind us. None of my thoughts take hold as they should.

"That's a ten-foot drop to the floor, lads." I say. "Minimum."

"Jesus. I could barely do that again with the thing standing still," Luke says.

"If we jump down and break our legs, we're totally fucked. A zero percent chance of survival," I say. "They'll put us down like a crippled racehorse."

"We've got to stay then," Connor says. "Fight him. The farmer. When he opens the trailer, we've just got to rush him. Just overpower him and try to get away. It's all we can do right now." He looks to me first and then Luke for approval.

I nod. There's nothing else for it. We stand and fight. That's the only option we have now.

The tractor vibrates and clangs as we pile over ruts and bumps. A sick, heavy feeling in my guts. An executioner's axe hanging over me. Hanging over us all. Back to the village. The tractor slows, leaves the field and swings onto another small road. After a few seconds, it jerks round to the right. A familiar tree and a concrete expanse. Connor's next to me, face poked through the air slots. He groans.

"The pub," he says. "The fucking pub, that's where he brought us back to."

"Square one," I say.

Luke doesn't say anything. He's sitting, hunched in a pile of sheep shit, hugging his knees to his chest. I turn away from him, my eyes combing the car park for other people. There's nobody. Just us and this shitbag of a farmer. The tractor swings round, parking up. The wrench and grind of a handbrake and the engine goes silent.

"Rush him," I say. "We've got to rush him. When he opens the trailer, we fucking go for it, yeah?"

"What if he's armed?" Connor says.

"Doesn't matter. We've got to go for it. This is our last chance. All the boys will be here soon once they've finished fucking their sheep or wanking off their cows, whatever they do round here. If we're getting out of this, we have to do it now."

Connor looks at me when I finish speaking, his jaw set like he's carved from stone. He nods.

Luke remains in his ball in the corner. Head hanging down.

"Luke, get up, we've got to do this now," I say.

Luke shakes his head.

I go to speak again but Connor surges forwards. Reaching down, he grabs Luke by the front of his stained shirt and hoists him to his feet. "Get yourself together, Luke. Get it fucking sorted."

Luke goes limp in his hands, weighted like a corpse. His head lolling, never lifting his gaze off the floor.

"It's now or never. Do it. Get your head in the fucking game. This is it." Connor trots out a few sports cliches but no dice.

The tractor cab door swings open, boots on the metal steps down to the tarmac.

Connor grabs Luke by the throat, pins him against the side of the trailer. "Get yourself together. Don't you want to see Amy again?" He slaps Luke round the face with the back of his hand. The slap echoes round the cavernous trailer. Even the sheep fall silent. "You piece of shit," Connor pants, as though the exertion of twatting his mate is too much to bear.

Luke looks up at him. His left cheek kissed in scarlet. Eyes wet, either from the pain of the slap or from wherever his head's been the last couple of minutes. "That's the last free shot you'll ever get," he says. His voice trembles.

My face fills the air slot, crammed into the gap, as I look out. There's no point hiding, he knows we're here. The farmer walks down the side of the trailer, his bare palm slapping the steel. The dull thudding setting the sheep off. They skitter and step with wide eyes.

"You nearly got there lads, so close. Would've got to Gowerstone. Might've found someone who cared. They share our ways. Not many would've helped you there. Touch and go. Before you snuff it, you wanna know what did for you? Eh?"

We don't answer so he just ploughs on.

"My dogs don't bark for nothing. That was a clue but Gerty, she seen you. One of you, jumping in the back. She called me on the way here. I made a little call of my own. I could've wasted all three of you back at my place. Plenty of fun to be had, could've kept my dogs in raw feed for quite some time. But no, this here's Wallace's weekend. I've had mine. Almost all of us have had ours round here. Time for the new generation to show us what they're made of." He chuckles to himself like he's been told an obvious Dad joke over a pint of bitter.

There's no-one else with him. All the time he's been talking I've been half-listening, looking behind him. Senses keening for the movement of others. Nothing. We can take him. He's going to release us.

"Take the tractor," I mutter to Connor. "They can't stop us in a vehicle."

He nods. "Got it."

"Anyway," says the farmer, "time for the whole show to get back on the road."

There's the squeal of metal, long overdue for an oiling. A bang and what sounds like a kick, boot on steel. The gate drops down, slowly at first, then gathering momentum. It bangs on the solid tarmac of the car park. Bouncing back up a couple of inches before settling. The farmer stands in front of us, arms crossed. Grizzled face staring, one eyebrow raised.

"Is this where you rush me?" he says.

We don't wait. I lead the way, running down the ramp, trying to keep my balance with the mud clogging the grips of my shoes. I plough into the farmer, and he wraps me up in his thick arms, drags me to the ground. I squirm out of his grip, bucking and kicking. I'm on my knees, then all fours. Connor and Luke race round the side of the tractor. Connor first up the steps to the cabin, Luke behind. The cabin doors wangs shut. I wrestle with the farmer, slapping his hands off my arms and legs. I'm on my feet delivering a kick to his shoulder. He grunts but doesn't let up. I land another few kicks.

"Start the fucking thing!" I shout to the dozy pair in the tractor. Nothing indicates they've heard me.

The farmer stops scrabbling at my leg and gets to his feet. His movements are the considered, hesitant moves dictated by middle-age. He smiles at me, puts his hand in his pocket. Pulls out the keys and gives them a jangle.

"How stupid do you think I am?"

He puts two fingers between his lips and whistles. From behind the stonewalls and the pub, they emerge. Wallace and Gav, all their little cronies and a few old boys I dimly recognise from last night. Most of them are carrying weapons. Rifles held out, pointed at me. A couple of them carry bats. One lad taps a crowbar against his palm, like an extra from a Jason Statham film.

None of them are smiling. They move forward quickly. Eager to close the gap on me. The sight of them makes my shoulders sag, my fingers relax from fists. It's true what they say, it's the hope that kills you. Hope guts you and leaves you there, gasping and alone.

Fuck this. Fuck these people. All of them. The only thing for a hopeless situation is to go down swinging. Try and take someone with me.

Gav, that ratty best man gives a thin smile. There's no humour in that face, no joy. He looks like he's chewing a wasp. Next to him, Wallace's eyes find only the floor. His gigantic, flabby frame is stooped. The others move in quickly, eager. Waiting their turn to provoke and to torment. Electricity ripples between them.

"Down you come," Gav says, the wave of his rifle guiding me down into the car park. One of the other lads watches Luke and Connor down from the tractor cab. Herds us together.

"Tricky lot, eh?" The farmer says. "Mugged you off, I'd heard." A superior chuckle. The farmer with his hands in his pockets and leaning back. An old timer's laugh.

Gav's side-eye is so sharp it could almost break the flesh. "Doubt it's been the first time it's happened over the years."

"Keep telling yourself that, sunshine," the farmer says. He jerks a thumb at Wallace. "Dozy arse's father-in-law has already made this right with me. I expect you pair to do the same. Get your thinking caps on, eh? Bring me something I'm really gonna like."

At the mention of his father-in-law, Wallace shrivels even more. His shoulders find his ears as his head sinks. "Yeah, yeah, sure," he mumbles.

"Good boys," the farmer walks up to Wallace and cups a hand on his cheek. Wallace fights a flinch. "Don't fuck it up this time if you can help it, yeah? You know what'll happen if you do." He grins and walks back towards his tractor.

As the farmer passes us, he shrugs. "What can you do? You came so close. If you'd have been a bit quicker into that trailer, maybe. But probably not. Good luck boys."

He doesn't laugh, just steps past us and slams the trailer shut. His sheep bleat and stamp around inside the thing, their voices echoing off the metal. He whacks the gate with the side of his fist. "Shut up, will ya?" Then he's standing on the steps to the cab and makes a show of pulling the tractor key out of his pocket. He jangles the metal at us and climbs in. The tractor roars into life and pulls in a wide circle out of the car park and onto the main road.

He accelerates away, the trailer clanging behind. The sound of the tractor's horn splits the air. Three blasts. All tuneless and soulless, a corporeal march rescinding into the distance. As the sound rescinds, all that's left for me to focus on are the guns pointing straight in our faces.

TWENTY-FOUR

Luke

They wait like statues until the farmer is out of sight. All of us watching him go. The tractor's engine fades into silence, leaving us stranded in the car park staring down the barrel of rifles and into the black eyes of people that want us dead. People that might even need us dead.

"Back at it again, eh?" Ethan says, his spread wide. "Did you miss us boys? Couldn't let us out of your sight? Oh wait…"

Gav steps forward and lands an uppercut into Ethan's stomach. The air leaves Ethan in a gasp and he bends double but doesn't sink to the floor. Gav looks to me and I flinch, instinct kicking in. He smirks and walks back a few paces, keeping his gun trained on me.

"This ain't the way any of us wanted it, boys. You know that," Gav says. "We wanted to hunt, like our fathers and their fathers and all that. The thrill of the chase, they call it. We've done it all before, seen it all before round these parts. Back in the Seventies, someone like you boys even killed someone like us. Did you know that? Course not. Not like you can Google it. It ain't making no newspapers."

"Fuck off," Ethan grunts, still holding his stomach.

Gav ignores him. "Nearly got away. Imagine that! Hoo boy. That would've been a bad one. Never happened. Not once. See, I thought you didn't have the balls for all this stuff, if I'm being honest. When I clapped eyes on you in that pub, I knew you were the biggest bunch of pussies I'd seen in years. Even worse than the pricks we did on Hector's stag." He jerks a thumb at the lad holding the crowbar. "But you surprised me. Good on you. I thought we'd find you dead this morning. Cold got you or being away from your mobile phones or whatever. You stuck it all out." He gives us a smile and a big thumbs up.

Next to him, Wallace chuckles. Gav silences him with a look. Wallace may be the one taking the spoils but there's no doubt who's running the show. "I made an error of judgement last night. I didn't listen to my gut. I listened to his guts," he slaps Wallace's belly. "I shouldn't have done that. And I won't be doing it again."

"What about –" Wallace says.

"Shut it," Gav cuts him off. "You ain't going back into the woods right now. Not at all if I don't choose it. Yeah?"

He walks close to us. Close enough that I could slap him, headbutt him. Cause him pain in some way. I don't do anything. My hands ball into fists. My teeth gnaw on each other. I stay still. Cowed. Bent by what's happened.

"What about you, posh boy? Anything to say?"

Ethan shakes his head. Gav stands in front of me. Toe to toe. "The stag. Oof. What a man." He pats my belly. "It's rare the stag survives. He didn't on mine, or Hector's. Maybe this time, maybe, maybe."

Then he moves on to Connor, patting him on the shoulder. Connor flinches again. A burst of heat across my face. A physical reaction to the shame Connor should be feeling. "The best man. It's a lot of pressure, isn't it? Until you've done it, you can't know. Not really. Imagine the pressure of getting the stag to kill a man. Is it more or less pressure than trying to get your stag home alive? Who knows? Who can say?"

He steps back and looks us all up and down. The rest are just his hareem. His stooges. Even Wallace. They all defer to Gav. All hang on his every word. A breeze picks up. Two crisp packets chase each other across the car park. My skin crackles with gooseflesh.

Gav shakes his head. Slaps a hand on his thigh. "I feel like we need to lighten this up, you know. Get everyone pumped again. Make this feel like a real stag party." He clicks his fingers and points at me. "A game. That's it. A game."

His fake spontaneity is killing me. Like it's all off the cuff. He's being a smug little cunt. Toying with us. They know what they're going to do so just get on with it. Stop all this pissing about. Let's get down to it.

"Last night, it seemed that you boys loved a little gamble. That's what got you into this little mess. Well, kind of. You'd have found yourselves in this one way or another." That sharp smile. "We'll give you another go. Another chance at freedom. See if you can finally make it out this time. Hey?"

I bite my lip. Holding back all the abuse and the bile that needs to come out of me. Twenty-four hours of pent-up rage. Maybe more. The rifles are still trained on us. None of us move or say anything. The only way this game ends is with two of us face down in a ditch somewhere. The rules are almost irrelevant, it's the outcome that matters. I need to get home to Amy, to make things right. It can't be me left to rot. It's not fair. My teeth sink harder into my lip, threatening to draw blood.

"We're going to gamble with some lives. Well, your lives." A toothy grimace. Faked shock in his eyes. "You ever see that show Game of Thrones?"

We all nod, who didn't watch it? Although it's a surprise they have broadband and Sky TV round this way.

"They do that thing, don't they? That funny little lad, he was on trial and got to choose a champion, someone to fight for him. If the champion wins, he's free but if the champion loses, he gets executed."

He stops talking and looks each of us up and down, his black eyes alight with electricity now.

"Here's what we're gonna do. We're gonna do that. Youse boys choose your champion," he winks at me. "I know who I'd choose." He mutters. "We'll choose ours. Doesn't have to be the hardest, just someone who's tough and quick and all that. Then the two of 'em will fight. If your lad wins, I swear on everything I am, Old Gods and all, that you'll walk out of here alive. Our lad wins, well, there's no mercy is there? Nowt changes for you lot, apart from the one who's dead innit?"

"What d'yer reckon? You game?" He smiles. "Course you are. Not like there's anything else is there?" His hand finds his chin and then drops to his side. "I know who I'd choose, but what do I know? You've got two minutes and then I want a decision."

He turns away as the locals form a huddle. Two of them stand on the edge of the group, rifles and eyes still trained on us, their heads leaned in towards the discussion. There's nothing else for it. We need to choose.

We turn away from the locals into our own huddle. We don't put our arms around each other like a football team before a penalty shootout, but we're close enough that the reek of the other two is alive in my senses. Not that I've got any room to talk.

The best man takes over. Connor getting animated. Talking with his hands. "We need to choose. We've all got strengths and weaknesses, haven't we? Does anyone not want to do it?"

Silence. It's not that I want to fight but we've all got to pretend we do.

"Fine." Connor continues. Every inch a middle manager trying to decide who to fire. "We've all got our strengths. I'm quick, I think. Ethan, you're in the gym a lot. Luke, you're... determined. You've got more to lose than most."

Determined?

That's the best thing he's got to say. Cheeky twat.

"I decked you back in high school," I say. Regretting it at the sound of Ethan's snigger. "Fuck it, I can do it." I wave them both away but that's pretty much put me out of the running. There's no problem with that. My limbs ache, hanging heavy as bags of spuds from my body. My back sings a chorus of bruises. I won't last long in a fight. Not like this.

I look from Connor to Ethan, both of their jaws set tight. Puffed up like a pair of stray cats in an alleyway. It would be easier if they just took their dicks out and started measuring them. It'd probably save us some time.

"Going to have to rush you, lads," Gav calls out from over in his huddle.

"I'm the best man. I know you think this is all my fault so it should be me that does this, wins us back our freedom and gets us home. I can do it," Connor says. It's his turn to look childish. In all the time I've known him, he's never looked younger. More naïve.

"Come on, boys," Gav calls over. "We've chosen and we need to get started."

"What about you, Eth?" I say. "Do you think it should be Connor?"

"No," he says, not looking at me. He doesn't take his eyes off Connor. "We're dead either way. May as well back myself."

Without a word, he steps forward and goes to smack Connor in the stomach. Connor flinches back and then his face crumples, realising what's happened.

Ethan turns to me and I flinch before he even pulls his arm back. "It's me," is all he says. He plants a hand on my shoulder and his fingers knead the skin beneath my sodden shirt, his gaze not quite meeting mine. Then he reaches out to Connor, pats him on the cheek. "Nothing personal, but we have to back the best horse. We just need to win."

Connor says nothing.

"Make it happen then," I say. Ethan just nods and turns away. Ready to face whoever these maniacs have chosen.

Con turns to face me but I keep my eyes on Ethan. He's the one who needs to fight now, not us. Connor's pride is likely hurt but he couldn't take Ethan if it came to it and we need clear heads, not delusion if we're going to get away from this weekend alive.

"It's me," Ethan says. His voice strong. The same confident cadence that he used to have when he'd approach women in the student bar. There's no swagger to him as he marches away from us. He doesn't look back. Chin up, shoulders pinned back, Ethan makes himself look as big as possible.

None of the locals give him a second look. They huddle together, apart from the two of them holding rifles pointed at us. They don't respond to Ethan. Silence elongates.

"Are we doing this?" Ethan says.

More silence, the group huddled together and muttering away. Then, they break. Gav steps forward, same sneer on his sharp features. A stoat of a man. Vermin.

"Picked the posh lad, eh? Don't say much for youse two, does it?" He says. "If he's the best you've got, you two may as well just kill yourselves."

"Are we doing this?" Ethan says.

Gav gives him a long look. Eyebrows pointing like daggers. "Aye. We are."

Ethan positions himself into a fighting stance. Feet shoulder with apart. Left side turned towards Gav, hands up in a defensive stance. Right hand cocked and ready.

Gav looks him up and down. "This is going to be fun," he says. Then turns away from Ethan. "Hector? Come on lad, look fuckin lively, yeah?"

Hector lumbers forwards. His crowbar dangles from one of his meaty hands. Everything about him is huge, like a giant born premature. Not quite gigantic but too big to be a real man.

I keep my eyes on Ethan. He doesn't shrink when Hector steps in front of him. Doesn't deviate from his stance. Muscles tensed. Concentration set.

"Be a good lad and put the fucking bar down," Ethan says. "You're an enormous freak, at least pretend to make this fair."

Hector doesn't respond, just looks to Gav, who nods. The crowbar clanks onto the tarmac.

"Good boy," Ethan says.

"Not yet," Gav says. It's hard to tell whether he's saying it to Hector or Ethan as well.

The locals fan out, creating a circle around the two fighters. Their faces are pale. Hard eyes and tight mouths. Fists bunched at their sides. The sky hangs grey over us all and it's as though I can see everything through a filter. All the colour is washed out of people, clothes, scenery.

There's a jab in my back, something hard and cold between my ribs. One of the locals smiles when I turn around, his rifle jammed into my back. Next to me, another of them has Connor in the same position.

"No funny business," this lad says. "Either of youse."

There's no point in responding.

Gav eyes up Ethan and then Hector. "You know what to do lads. Get at it."

His words are snatched away by the breeze and as the two fighters start to circle each other, my stomach drops away. The most important fight of our lives is underway and we're only one win away from going home.

TWENTY-FIVE

Connor

My pride aches after Ethan's fake punch. That familiar feeling of shame running through me. That knowledge of being second best, yet again. His indifference to anything we've said or done this weekend.

There's a fine line between wanting to survive and not wanting to live in a world where we've survived because of Ethan. The thought of his smug face every time we meet for a pint. His swaggering at the wedding.

Christ...

No.

None of that matters now.

What matters is Ethan ending this prick and letting us all go home. No matter what threats they leave us with, no matter how they interfere in our lives, no matter what it takes, we just need to get home. Get the hell out of here and never come back.

"Fuckin do him Hector," the lad holding the rifle behind me shouts. His words rattle down my ear, leaving my hearing stunted for a few seconds.

I keep my eyes on the fight. Ethan steps forwards, body set in a fighting stance. Left hand extended out in front of him. Finding his range. If this was a boxing match on pay per view, the commentators would be chatting about how Ethan gives away so much in height, weight, reach. What they'd be talking up is his speed. It's clear, watching them both move.

Hector's strong, no doubt about it. But he's built like Wallace. Broad shoulders and thick muscles on his arms and legs. But he's no athlete. He's flabby around the middle. Doughy. He's like a dinosaur. Enormous body, tiny brain. Slow to react.

Definitely.

Ethan circles Hector, testing him. Watching how Hector moves. Never letting him settle. Hector turns on the spot, his footwork sloppy, his balance off. He snarls and swings for Ethan once, twice. Both punches aren't even close. All he damages is fresh air.

Ethan feints left, then goes right as Hector tries to adjust.

Bam. Bam.

Two punches to Hector's face and then out of reach again. Hector shakes his head as though a gnat just buzzed past his ear. He lumbers forwards and swings a fist at Ethan. Eth dodges it, kicks Hector in the stomach. The big man grunts again. Annoyed more than hurt.

"Come on, Hector," the lad with the gun at Luke's back shouts. "Stop pissing around and end the twat."

Hector doesn't look over, but Gav does, shooting daggers at the lad. He cowers behind Luke, tightening his grip on the rifle.

Hector lumbers forwards again. Ethan fakes one way and goes the other but Hector's got him sussed. Lands a massive uppercut into Ethan's chest. Ethan staggers backwards, the air audibly leaving his lungs. His arms pinwheel and for a moment it looks like he's going over. If he hits the deck, he's never getting up, Hector won't let him. Ethan regains his balance. Tears in his eyes. His cheeks red. He circles Hector, bent double. One hand on his chest as he gulps in air, gasping and choking. One hell of a body blow.

Hector lunges forward again. Blood in the air and in his brain. His teeth are bared, long yellow squares. He grunts before he swings, like the effort is too much for him. Telegraphing what's coming. Ethan dodges away. Still struggling but too quick for this gangly freak.

The other locals hiss at Ethan. Close to booing him. As though his chosen fighting style isn't good enough for them. Fuck them. All that matters is who comes out alive.

Ethan continues his dance. The blows that landed a memory now. It's not quite the old boxing tactic of rope a dope but it's similar. A smaller, quicker lad keeping the stronger, bigger opponent moving. Tiring him out. It's not like prizefighters stay up all night in a field after being chased by gun wielding psychopaths but last night might've sharpened Ethan's mind in some way.

The rifle presses harder into my ribs as Ethan dances round, swerving away from direct confrontation with Hector over and over again.

"Fucking do him, Hector," the lad behind me shouts.

I wonder whether the safety is on the gun. That'd be typical of me. Ethan beats his opponent to a pulp, and I end up accidentally getting blown away by some crazy local who can't keep his emotions in check. I sneak a look at the lad over my shoulder. He's amped on something. Maybe just blood lust. Wide eyes punctuated with red veins.

A couple of the other maniacs pipe up then, egging on their man to kill. To get it finished. If Hector hears them, he doesn't let on. His eyes never leave Ethan as he spins and steps, trying to keep up. Hector's breath comes in noisy bursts. His mouth is hanging open, his footwork slowing.

"Shut up!" Gav calls to his mates, not wanting any more distractions. It's written on Gav's ratty features – his man's tiring.

Ethan steps in close as Hector's balance struggles to keep up with his movements. Light on his feet, Ethan lands two punches into Hector's stomach and one to the side of his head. Then he nips back out of range. Hector doesn't look like he's noticed. His expression doesn't change. But his next punch is slower, less ferocious. A lazy, petulant swing that's nowhere near his target.

Ethan wipes sweat out of his eyes with the back of his hand. He smiles. Skips away from Hector again. I find myself smiling too. I watch Luke until he turns his head towards me. There's a glimmer of it on his face too. There's no doubt. The longer this goes on, the more chance Ethan has of winning.

There's silence over the car park as the dance continues. Hector swinging and missing like a blind man trying to whack a pinata. Ethan uses his speed to stay clear of any haymakers. He lands the occasional blow which is more than Hector's doing. But Ethan's not managed to hurt the big man yet. His punches aren't carrying any weight. It's like watching a child fight his dad.

On it goes. Just the scuffing steps and panting breaths of the combatants. Then it happens. The chance. After a few more errant punches, Hector growls up at the grey sky. Roaring like a caged animal. Ethan watches him. Poised. Hector charges forwards, growling as he does so. Arms stretched out in front of him, grasping for his prey. Ethan steps one way, then another, then back. Hector's foot slides on the gravel and he crashes to his knees. Skidding and trying to get up.

Ethan's on him. Racing over and landing a running knee to Hector's face. Hector's head snaps back. His eyes wide and confused, pupils losing their relationship as they roll in different directions. His weight tips over to one side and he props himself up with one enormous hand. Ethan lands blow after blow to Hector's face. Fists battering his head and neck. Losing control as he does. Losing accuracy in his urge to punish.

The locals are all shouting now. A couple bordering on screams. Panic in their voices. Their mouths jagged black slashes in their faces. Eyes watering as their friend takes a beating. The possibility they'd never banked on coming true in front of their stupid faces.

"Go on," I shout. "Fucking do him. Finish him." My hands are in fists and I surge forwards towards the action on instinct. Pain in the side of my head as the lad with the rifle cuffs me. I sway on the spot and try to focus on the fight in front of me as pain slides down the side of my face and neck.

Ethan nips round behind Hector as the big man struggles to get up from his knees. He slides his arms round Hector's neck. The crook of his right arm under Hector's chin. Both arms pulling tightly on the big man's windpipe. A classic UFC chokehold. If he can get Hector on his back, it's lights out. Game over and we're going home.

Hector fights back, swinging elbows into Ethan's sides but he can't make Ethan let go. Hector's tree trunk arms flail. Hands searching for anywhere he can get purchase. Eyes. Face. Ethan sees them all coming, dodging every time. Hector resorts to more blows to Ethan's ribs but they're slower now, less frequent. His light is waning. Leaving his eyes. A glaze appearing over his baby blues.

Ethan tightens his grip, stepping and manoeuvring, trying to swing Hector to the ground. "Do it Eth," Luke shouts. "Finish the twat off right now. Get him fucking gone." A yelp from Luke as his captor slams the butt of the rifle between Luke's shoulder blades. Luke sinks to his knees before he gets pulled back to his feet.

Ethan's momentum takes Hector down. Not onto his back but onto his side. Ethan curls round him like a lover. Their legs folded in the same way. Hector tries kicking Ethan's legs, but it doesn't work. Ethan wrenches his arms tighter. Adjusting his hold now they're down on the floor. A grimace on his face that suggests victory is coming. His eyes somewhere off in the middle distance as he squeezes the life out of this inbred freak.

I notice the bar before even Hector does.

His thick, black crowbar lies a couple of feet away. I go to shout a warning and the lad behind me slaps me quiet. My head ringing from his blow.

Hector opens his eyes, focus coming back to them. He takes a deep breath, forcing himself forwards. Hands reaching and dragging, fingers scraping the concrete beneath them.

"No!" Luke shouts as Hector's ham like fingers tighten on the metal.

Before the words are out of Luke's mouth, Hector's swung the crowbar round in an arc, whacking it into Ethan's back. The air leaves Ethan in a whoosh and then a yell as the pain kicks in. His grip relaxes but doesn't release. Hector pulls in a deep breath.

Ethan tightens his grip again, moving his arms to reaffirm the chokehold. His face is puce, reddened with pain. Both men lie on the ground, facing me and Luke but Ethan's gaze is above our heads somewhere as he holds on. With his knees, Ethan lands blows to the back of Hector's legs, grunting as they hit home. But Hector doesn't release the crowbar.

"Argh!" Ethan shouts into the grey sky, pulling his arms as tight as they'll go around Hector's windpipe. It's the bigger man's turn to redden. One arm is pinned underneath his massive body, the other, wielding the crowbar, swings wildly around searching for purchase. Hector's eyes water. His tongue lolls like a dog on a hot day. Sweat mottling his skin. Shimmering even in this dull light.

He's going. His gaze settling and stilling. His arm relaxes, drops to the tarmac. Ethan gives one more yank on his hold and then lets go slightly, leaning back and gulping in air.

Out of nowhere, the crowbar comes swinging up.

Ethan's not huddled behind Hector as well as he was. His face is exposed. The crowbar catches him above the left eye. A dull thud as the metal meets his brow. Blood explodes out of Ethan's skin, immediately soaking his eye. Claret blots out one side of his face and he shouts, all pain and surprise.

"Fuck!" I find myself yelling. Next to me, Luke's shouting something I can't understand. Sound rushes around me like the echoes in a cave. "Fuck! Fuck! Fuck!"

Hector's scrambling to his feet, crowbar in his hands. Ethan's trying to do the same but he's woozy, not moving as quickly as he was. The gash above his eye is deep, perhaps three inches long. The deep red of his blood glows, vivid colour on this endless grey pallet.

"Get up, get up, get up," I grunt under my breath.

Without realising, I surge forward but the lad holding onto me anticipates it. There's a swift kick to the back of my knees and I collapse to the ground. One strong hand pulls me into a kneeling position. The muzzle of the rifle is cold against my temple.

"Don't give me a reason to spoil this party," the lad says.

I don't take my eyes off the fight.

Hector swings the crowbar in huge, desperate arcs. Ethan staggers around, staying out of reach but not moving with the grace or speed he had previously.

"Fight me, you pussy!" Hector yells. His cronies cheer like they've forgotten this tosser was about three seconds away from dying. Like he's been winning all along.

More swings of the crowbar. His form is like an amateur golfer, hacking his way round the course. Ethan settles himself, wiping more blood away with the sleeve of his filthy shirt. There's a grimace on his face. Lines etched into his skin with blood, his mouth a red slash. He's feral. His head's gone. He's already killed this bastard once – he can do it again.

Ethan dodges one swing and then as Hector's off balance, darts into range. He lands a punch in Hector's gut but his shoe slips on the concrete as he goes to dodge away. Hector's other hand grabs hold of Ethan's elbow, pulling him back in.

My heart thunders in my chest. I try to move but the muzzle of the gun presses in harder.

Hector spins Ethan round and headbutts him in the face. Both men grunt but only Hector remains standing, blood from Ethan's cut splattered across his face. Ethan tries to scramble backwards out of range again but Hector boots him in the side. A groan escapes Ethan. He tries to move but it's slower.

Hector smiles now. Like he's been enjoying this all along. He brings down the crowbar on Ethan's knee and the only sound is a scream sharp enough to cut glass.

"Do it, Hector!" Wallace yells. "Fucking do it!"

Hector doesn't take his eyes off Ethan. He steps over him, watching Ethan writhe between his legs. Like a baseball player, he gathers his momentum and swings hard and true. The flat of the crowbar smashing into Ethan's face, cracking across his forehead. The crumpled sound of Ethan's head smacking onto the tarmac. Killing his screams stone dead.

He lies still for a moment, and I think that's it. That he's dead. Then he spits out a mouthful of blood and tries to scramble away from

Hector. Ethan's trying to speak but his words aren't forming. They're all half words. Unfinished thoughts and sentences.

Hector swings again. Ethan doesn't put an arm up to block the blow. He raises his chin. Defiant. The metal smacks into his head again and he collapses onto his back. His head bounces back up off the car park surface and then lies still. Arms down by his sides. Not moving.

"Ethan!" Luke shouts. "Eth!"

Nothing.

Hector looks over at Gav first and then turns to us. Smiles a smile painted in Ethan's blood. Then he smashes the crowbar down again and again into Ethan's head. Every blow landing with a wet squelch. I close my eyes, but the sound tells me everything I need to know as the blows go on and on and on.

After what feels like a hundred blows, there's the clank of the crowbar hitting the ground. I open my eyes as Hector steps away from what's left of Ethan. He wipes his forehead with a sleeve of his flannel shirt and raises his eyebrows at the sight of blood. Gav gives him a slap on the arm as he walks past before Wallace runs over and starts hugging Hector like he's a soldier back on leave.

Behind me, the two gun-toting freaks laugh and cheer with the rest of them. Chanting "get in" like they're watching a football match. Gav is the only one who doesn't join in. He stands alone, in front of the others, staring down at Ethan's body and the puddle it's slowly becoming. His face relaxes. There's no scowl there. As though sensing me looking, he meets my eye. He doesn't rub it in, doesn't gloat. Just nods once and turns back to his friends.

"Stop all your fuckin cheering. Hector could've fuckin died. Would you be cheering then? When the consequences are coming in for you? Nah. So shut it. Still two of them left. We're only half done."

He turns to us, and the familiar scowl makes its way back to his features. "Big question is, how're we gonna decide which one of you gets to go home?"

TWENTY-SIX

Luke

Ethan's face is jam on the car park, his skull a hollow mess. It catches my eye and I look away. It doesn't make me nauseous like it should, I'm just as empty and hollow as the cavity I've seen.

Connor is on his knees next to me. His face grey, eyes focused on something miles away. His whole body is bent and slumped, like the wind's gone out of him. Can't say I blame him.

Ignoring the clown standing behind me with a rifle, I sit down on the concrete. A shudder rises through my spine. It's nothing to do with what we've just witnessed, how close we've come to escape, I'm just fucking freezing.

Next to me, Connor also sits. He pulls his rucksack off under careful supervision and extracts his canteen of water. His hands shake as he removes the lid and brings it to his lips. He drinks deeply, gulping like a child. I do the same, the chill of the water almost burning on its way down, me wishing it was something stronger the whole time. Longing for whisky or tequila. Even a Jager. Just something to take the edge off.

Gav comes over. They all linger behind him, they've cracked open a tin of beer each. They're toasting Hector and slapping him on the back. Gav takes his time, walking slowly. The rifle propped against his right shoulder, like a soldier on parade. When he reaches us, he squats down on his haunches. He's barely five yards away, close enough that the scent of him reaches me. A familiar tang of deodorant, Lynx or something they sell in all the supermarkets. Innocuous and mainstream. It's difficult to picture this maniac doing his grocery shop once a week like the rest of us. Plodding down the aisles at Aldi with a blue plastic basket in his hands.

"I ain't come over to gloat, boys. This lot are enjoying it cos they know what a close-run thing that was. Your boy was about ten seconds away from putting Hector's lights out for good. He's never had a fight like that before and I doubt he will again. District boxing champ, that lad. He's battered every one of us at some point, either in the ring or round the back of this gaff," he points to the pub.

"The fuck do you want, Gav?" Connor spits but all the piss and bile in him has leaked away. He's not threatening, he's like a spoiled kid who can't get what he wants.

"All I'm saying is, don't you pair go weeping too hard for old posh boy." Gav jerks a thumb at what's left of Ethan. "Bet you he's been blaming himself the whole time for taking the bets but that don't matter. You were always gonna be part of this from the second you booked that B&B," he shakes his head at me. "If you wanna blame anyone, blame the guy who booked it." A thin smile as he sees my eyes find their way to Connor.

"I blame you," I say. "I blame you and Wallace and every other cunt here. You're all as bad as each other."

"Nah. Cunts is harsh. We're just doing what we need to do to get by. Very particular way of living round here lad. Very special. Traditions don't make people bad. Sometimes, that's all they have."

"You can stop any time you want," Connor says. "You do it because you like it."

"Like it?" Gav shakes his head, a wider smile revealing itself now. One we've yet to see before. "Think I like blasting your copper mate in the face point blank? Seeing all that fuckin terror on his face before I pulled the trigger? Eh? Or how about watching one of me oldest mates nearly getting strangled to fuckin death? That your idea of a laugh? Nah. You know it ain't."

"Don't do this then. If you hate it so much."

Gav looks up at the two lads with rifles standing behind us. His features are set again. Neutral and flat. "I don't enjoy this shit, lads. But you've gotta admit, you ain't ever felt as alive as you do this weekend. Come on."

He waits for an answer, but I don't oblige him.

"Round here, see, it's different to what you're like down there in your cities – Manchester. Liverpool. Birmingham. London. Down there, you do the things you want to do. Your career. Your qualifications. All that. Round here, we do what we're told. We take on our family's land or the family business. If our fathers tell us to do something, we fuckin well do it. None of this running off and doing your own stuff. You following me?"

His watery blue eyes search for my gaze until I meet them.

"We do what we're told and that means keeping our traditions alive. Keeping this place going. We do what we're asked because we can't let the old dreams die. Can't let those old ways fall apart. And when we do want something for ourselves, we want ourselves a wife, then we do what we're asked and we blow away a few lads like you when the time comes. But enjoy it? Nah. We're just better at doing what needs to be done than a bunch of fannies like you."

"You don't know anything about us," I spit.

"I know a lot about you, Luke. And you Connor. I know a lot about Jay, and I know an awful lot about your recently deceased friend Ethan. I know he never did one damn thing he was ever told to do. Even in his father's business. I know he never grew a proper spine because if he had, if he'd grown a pair, he wouldn't have given Hector a chance to come back. He'd have gone through the pain barrier to kill a man. Cos let me tell you this, not one man here would've paused to adjust his grip before making that kill." He holds up a filthy finger. "Not one fuckin man here would've thought twice about putting you away."

"You don't know shit about us. I'll put you all away first chance I get," the words taste strange on my tongue.

Another smile from Gav. "Course you will, stag. Course you will. Maybe you can learn a little lesson from your Tory mate there though. Before we pack him away, let me tell you this. When we found the copper in the woods, you know what'd happened to him? No? We found him with posh boy's cagoule pulled over his head and tied in a fuckin knot so he couldn't see where he was going."

"You're lying," Connor shouts.

"He ain't" says the lad holding the rifle to my head. "I was with him. Good strong knot too."

"Just you think about that if you're thinking you're going to do me or any of these lads," Gav says. "Until this second, we knew more about you than you knew about each other. Accept that and maybe you've got a chance." He winks at me and gets to his feet again. Turning to Ethan's body, he points down at it.

"Joshua, Kevin, Al. You're on clean-up duty. I want this gone right fuckin now. Not when your cans are done. Now."

Grumbles from the three lads. "Thought this was a stag party, if I wanted to clean up, I could go home and see the missus."

Electricity crackles behind Gav's eyes. "Ain't no rules about who's hunted on one of these things, yeah. Nowt saying we can't sub one of you moaning little ninnies in. You wanna take their places?"

Silence in response.

"Just as I fuckin thought, so keep it zipped."

The three lads take a last pull on their cans and place them down out of the way. One of them casts a look back over his shoulder at his tin, as though leaving a loved one behind. The three of them wander over to Ethan's body. Two stop by his head, the other by his legs. Up by his head, the pair turn away, hands over their mouths.

"Sweet fucking Christ, Hector, state of this." One of them shouts. "You're an absolute animal, lad. Get it sorted. Fucking tapped."

"Shut it and clean up my mess," Hector grins. Lager spills from between his teeth and onto his chin. He wipes at it with a grazed, red hand. The other lads laugh and clap him on the back.

Wallace chuckles along. At the sound of his laughter, Gav prickles. His eyes narrow. He mumbles something to himself that I can't pick up. He gets to his feet. Turns around and barks orders at the three lads assigned to dispose of Ethan.

They do as they're told. Two lads taking an arm each, one of them taking both legs, Gav directing and abusing them the whole time. They hoist Ethan into the air and move him with slow, stuttering steps. Grunting the whole time, they carry Ethan towards the break in the low stone wall that acts as an exit. Something deep red and grey drips from Ethan's dangling head. They turn and Ethan's head lolls back, his face level with mine. The carnage of what's left makes me taste bile. I look away and take a sip from my canteen to swill it all away.

They dump Ethan's body by the wall, the three of them panting by the time they get there. They've barely moved him twenty yards.

There's no dignity in death for the lad. Parts of him that nobody should ever be seen are laid bare. Left alone long enough, he'll become carrion. Everything he ever was reduced to bone and meat.

His body lies broken. Head caved in. It's hard to know how to feel about the lad now he's gone. Hard not to think about memories of better times, easier days. University when we spent time pissed up and chasing girls, lounging about in pubs and skipping lectures. Disposable barbecues on summer fields. Playing video games all night instead of studying. Every single time Ethan lent us a tenner or paid for the taxi. Yeah, he lorded it, but he'd earned that right – he'd bought that right.

The later years. As we drifted apart. Me up North with Amy. Him down South earning wedge for his dad's company. The disdainful replies to our invitations to come and stay for the weekend. Those mad weekends we spent down in London with him. Being offered coke and all sorts on the side. Free tickets to the rugby and the football. Best seats in the house. Swings and roundabouts of friendship with him.

And then what he did to Jay. What he might've done to Jay. We never saw it ourselves. There're no witnesses apart from those biased against him. Why would they tell us the truth? But then, why would they make this up? It's not hard to imagine it happening. He's always been selfish, self-absorbed, even downright fucking rude to us all.

But he stood up for us. He fought for us. Right here. He took on Hector toe to toe and nearly won. Nearly booked our ticket out of this shit hole. Nearly killed someone so that we could all go back to our lives. He stepped up, pushed us aside and tried to get the dirty work done. He didn't need to do that. Didn't need to gamble like he did.

Fuck.

Tears sting my eyes and I look over at Ethan's body. The way it lies alone on the far side of the car park. It's not him anymore. And then it all hits me. What's just happened. Jay's gone, something we've had no time to take in. The fact that these psychos are playing for keeps. That two of my friends are dead and there's a fifty-fifty chance I'll be next. And even if I survive, it'll be at the expense of my best mate.

I turn to Connor. He's sitting with his knees pulled up, his head dangling down between them. He's refusing to look at Ethan or at me. Lost in his own world.

A Land Rover pulls up in a squeal of brakes. Two older men get out, one of them dressed in tweed like he lives in a stately home. The other is caked in mud. They look like something from a BBC sitcom. The fella in tweed smiles benevolently at the others, like he owns them.

They step round the stone wall and look down at Ethan.

"Jesus Christ, who's done that?" Shouts the tweed wearer.

"Hector," Wallace says. "Got him good in the end."

"Close run thing," Gav shouts over. "Always nice to see you, Phillip."

"Aye," shouts the tweed wearer. "Not sure I can say the same, young Gavin."

Gav chuckles to himself and walks over to the rest of them. Behind me, the lad with the rifle to the back of my neck lets it relax an inch or two. Probably desperate to get over there and kiss some arse like the rest of them.

"That's why I had 'em tell you about the plastic tarps. You don't want this on your seats, Phil," Gav says.

"Nah," Tweedy says. "Absolutely vile, that."

"And you're okay to set up the fire later? With the car?"

"Yes, of course. It's all ready to go. Whenever you deliver the next body, we'll set it up. All pencilled in for autopsies and police reports. You know the drill, Gav."

"I like to be sure. I don't want no mistakes."

"You're thorough, Gav. Best thing I'll say about you."

Gav snorts and points to the three corpse carriers. "Go on then, Phillip ain't getting blood and brains on his fuckin tweed, is he? Get it in the back. And don't go making no mess."

The three pallbearers do as they're told, heaving Ethan up again. It takes them a couple of goes to swing him high enough to clear the threshold of the Land Rover. Ethan's body lands with a thud, the vehicle shakes on its suspension and then settles. Breathing hard, one of the lads slams the door shut. My last view of Ethan, gone.

"Stay for a tin, Phillip?" Wallace asks.

"No, no. It's a young man's game all of this. We've done our time, haven't we Robbie?"

The man covered in mud looks up like he's shocked to be spoken to. "Oh aye. Done our time, Phil."

"I bring him along for his sparkling conversation," Phillip says to laughs from the others. Then his face changes, the hint of a smile on his lips passes. His eyes harden. "This all looks a little bit like fun and games lads. And that's okay. But don't forget the task at hand." He points over at me and Connor. "I still see two alive. Don't get sloppy. Don't make mistakes. You know what's at stake here. You don't get it done…" He slides his hand across his neck.

"Yeah, bloody yeah," Gav says. "We know the rules. We ain't rookies. We got it. One tin here and then we're getting them sorted. Just keep an eye on that phone of yours. Won't be long till we need you again."

"I hope not. Get it done early so I'm not up all night. Be a good lad."

Phillip slaps Gav on the shoulder and clambers into the Land Rover. The fella caked in mud follows suit and the engine roars as the vehicle skids off down the narrow lane. I watch it go, fleeting glimpses of it appearing between trees and bushes, windows reflecting the meagre light of the day.

When I lose sight of it and turn my attention back to the car park, the locals have put their cans down and every single one of them is looking at me with the same hungry eyes.

TWENTY-SEVEN

Connor

The rifle jabs me in the back as they pull me to my feet. Strong arms hook under mine. I think about going limp, making them drag me along but it'll only lead to more digs, to more pain. Best to make my peace with it, get moving of my own accord.

Numbness spreads through me as I walk. My limbs detach from my mind, limited entities in themselves. They make their own decisions about where to go. Even my vision is different. Everything whittled down to a point just in front of me. Enough to keep me moving and nothing more.

I'm not sure what's hit harder, Ethan's death or what they said about Jay. All these hours spent running through the woods. Trying to save our own skins and neglecting a second thought about our dead friend. Shows the power of instinct. And Jay was the best of us too, that's the thing. A copper, putting his body on the line every day to protect others. Some people scoff at the word hero, but he was that to me. Driven and fair, he deserved better than dying alone in some ditch. Mown down by a bunch of scum like this lot.

Ethan. The thought of him makes me shake my head. He'd never done anything that didn't benefit himself in his life. Whether he was getting a round in at university or inviting everyone down to London, there was always an angle. You'd provide him with something, even if you were just meat in the room to make him look more popular. Everything came back to him and what he wanted.

What they said about him is true. He hung Jay out to dry. No doubt about it. The missing cagoule. The evasive answers. Contradicting himself. He did it. Set up someone he lived with for three years and fucked off, leaving them to face down a bunch of guys with rifles. It's sick. And selfishly, the worst of it is, there's no question that he'd have done it to me and to Luke. If it was the difference between him getting out of here and not, we'd have been a footnote in his story.

Even standing up and taking on the fight, he didn't do it for us. He did it for himself. To be the big man, the one who got us out of here. Yeah, he had the best chance of winning, sure, but he put himself forward out of arrogance, nothing more.

I take a deep breath. Maybe Ethan had the right view of it. He's gone now. He took his shot and burned out. We're still here, alive, suffering. Maybe doing what he thought was best to end was the right way to go, but probably, almost certainly not.

Another jab in my back and I look up from the floor. They've taken us round the back of the pub. My feet clang over the metal cellar doors. They're followed by another clang as the lads dragging Luke bring up the rear. Gav leads the way. I blink at him, like I've woken from a dream and found myself here, somehow still at their mercy and still at risk.

A third jab from the rifle but it doesn't make me walk any faster. Like everything else in life, you can become desensitised to the sight of guns, to the feel of one in your back or pressed against your head. The first time, the whole world feels like it's going to fall out of your arse, but not even twenty-four hours later and the fear's fallen away. Maybe right now, it'd just be a mercy to have it all ended, to put me on ice and let me get some rest.

Round the back of the pub is a wreck. Bricks tumble from the stone wall, creating piles of broken masonry and dust. A rusted bike is chained to the pub wall, both wheels missing and the frame bent beyond repair. An old car sits alone, the dirt on its windows at least an inch thick. Its tyres sag, lifeless black rubber.

And there's a shipping container.

Corrugated black metal. Rust patches on the corners. A faded company logo that I don't recognise. Fuck knows what they're keeping here. If they unleashed some sort of genetically altered freak to rip our heads off, it wouldn't surprise me.

Gav stops at the doors of the shipping container. Luke is shoved forwards, so we're standing next to each other in front of him. The familiar clicking of the rifles being cocked. Cold metal shoved against the back of my neck. I don't flinch.

"Here's where the story ends, lads." Gav slaps a hand on the front door of the shipping container. There's a hollow boom that resonates from within. "Not luxury accommodation but better than sleeping in your own shit like you did last night. Maybe."

Titters from the assorted goons.

"Your lad fought well before. Nearly got the job done." He waggles a finger at us. "Ain't been as simple as we thought, this one. I thought we'd be done by breakfast once we knew who was coming. And to get the copper first and all, the only dangerous one. Sloppy, sloppy work."

More titters from behind us.

"The fuck you laughing at, eh? It's down to all of you. Me and all. Fuckin slipping. Piss poor. That ain't happening again. There're only two stag parties left after this one and we will not be making fucking mistakes on them. But it's okay. We're gonna fucking get it sorted now. Wallace is gonna get his little decoration for his house. He's gonna impress his new bride and her Daddy dearest. He's gonna step up and be a man." He looks from me to Luke and back again. "But first, one of you pair is. You're gonna be clever and brave and all those lovely things that people like you imagine you are when you're sat in your offices thinking you're better than people like us."

I go to speak but he cuts me off.

"Don't lie to us, Connor. Fuckin hell lad. We've come this far. Speak some fuckin truth if you open your mouth."

I don't say anything.

"Thought as much," Gav says. He claps his hands together, rubs them like he's warming himself in front of a fire. "Keep your fuckin lies for each other. Not that you're gonna be short of things to talk about."

"You can't make us do anything," Luke says. Like we've not spent all weekend being ordered around and manipulated by these twats. The growing a spine act looks a little thin right now, pal.

Gav smirks. He tries to hold it in but gives up. "Yeah. Right."

Guns pressed harder into our backs now. Luke stumbles forwards under the pressure on his neck. Fuck that. I stand my ground, leaning back into the rifle's muzzle. What're they gonna do about it? Shoot me? The end is inevitable at this point. Surely.

Gav fumbles with a ring of keys and then unlocks the industrial sized padlock on the container. My stomach tightens as a sliver of blackness appears. He swings the doors open, the metal whining like a beaten dog. The sound makes me wince but nobody else reacts. Christ knows what they've got in there. Some assault rifles or medieval torture devices. A pack of wild, starving dogs ready to rip our guts out.

The light reveals a grotty, empty shipping container. Water stains cover half the chipboard floor. I squint into the dimness, eyes searching for traps or blood stains or hidden cameras. There's nothing.

"The fuck's this?" The words are out of my mouth before I realise. They're answered with a cuff to the back of the head from behind me.

"Speak when you're spoken to," comes the grunt from my captor.

"Fuck you."

Another cuff to the back of the head, this one sends me stumbling. Hands clutching the back of my head. They don't come away wet, but the bastard got me with the rifle butt. I turn and face him. Walking onto a sneer and the deep, dark of the rifle's mouth.

"Do it," the grunt says. "Give me a reason."

I shake my head. Nothing this maggot has to say matters. There's only one person in charge here and I've got my back to him. When I turn back around, Gav raises an eyebrow.

"When you're quite done, pal," he says.

"Yeah. I'm done."

"Right you are. Not just your time you're wasting. I'll have him mash your teeth out next time."

I say nothing.

"This is it lads, the fortress of solitude. We don't roll this one out very often, but sometimes, it works a charm. Besides, it gives fat arse Wallace here the chance to rest. Maybe chasing you through the woods like the old days isn't the best way to do it for him. It's about tradition and hunting. The tradition is that the stag makes the kill. Takes home the prize for his wife. But you look at how meat's produced these days, Greg will tell you, there ain't a whole lot of chasing being done. Am I right?"

"Aye, Gav," intones one of the grunts.

"You had your chance to go free range. Now you're gonna be battery farmed."

The locals chuckle at his farming terminology. Referring to people like animals and meat, further proof that this lot are completely tapped. Whatever happens in there isn't going to be fun. They'll probably lock the doors and fill it with water or heat the thing from the outside like an oven.

"I look at both of you proud specimens and I can't decide which one of you is more worthy." He looks from me to Luke and then to the rest of his lads. "Tricky one, ain't it?" The lads mumble their responses. Some saying I'm more of a catch, others saying it's Luke.

Gav smiles. That small, sharp grin. "See. We can't decide. It's a score draw. But if we can't decide, then that means you'll have to. Both of you."

"Fuck off," I shout.

"Fuck you," Luke shouts.

"Our tradition says one of you is allowed to go home. There's a reason for it, trust me. But that means one of you becomes meat for us. We've been a bit silly. I blew your copper mate's head off and Hector caved in the face of your posh chum, so if you can try not to damage your skulls in there, we'd appreciate it."

"What the fuck do you want us to do?" Luke shouts.

"Whatever it takes for you to decide who lives and who doesn't," Gav says. "Talk it out. Fight it out. But don't you fuckin dare let one of you die in there. Whatever happens. If one of you is chosen or one of you gets knocked out, you bang on the door and the winner gets to go home." He spits on the ground. "I swear on me Mum's grave. One of you is going home."

"Come on, man. This isn't fair," Luke says.

"You wanna fight, Hector?"

"No. But..."

"But nothing. Now fuckin get in there."

A jab to the back of my head. The cool steel of the rifle jarring into the back of my skull. I take a step forward and stop. Another jab. Then another. My head is ringing, pain circling through me before dropping down my neck.

"All right, all right," I say and walk into the container.

Luke gets chucked in after me, he stumbles forwards and puts a hand on the wall to steady himself. They crowd the entrance of the container. Blocking out most of the meagre light. Gav at the front, his boots on the threshold of the door. The rest line up around him, Wallace and Hector looming. The two minders are still pointing their rifles at us.

"This is your last chance, lads. Time to be brave. Time to step up. Time to die – for one of you. It's nowt personal, but one of you, well… you ain't gonna enjoy seeing these faces again." He smiles. "Just bang on the walls three times when you're done. Someone'll be here the whole time."

Gav steps back and swings the doors closed.

"No!" Luke shouts. "No!"

"You giving yourself up, Mr Stag?" Gav asks, his face barely fitting in the gap between the doors.

"No," Luke says.

"Shut the fuck up then," Gav says.

The doors swing closed, thudding metal-on-metal echoes off the walls. The darkness is almost absolute apart from a hole the size of a golf ball in the far-right corner. A tiny patch of grey against a blanket of black.

I put a hand against the wall, the metal cool, peeling paint rough beneath my fingers. It orientates me, knowing where this wall is. With that knowledge I build a picture of the rest of the container. Using my hands, I feel the wall and slide my back down it until I'm sitting on the floor.

Luke's by the door, stomping and thrashing around. Pacing backwards and forwards. His footsteps sound unsteady, like he can't find his rhythm. Like he's somehow still pissed. The container reeks of metal and dirt. Dust is thick on the air. I wipe it away from my lips with the back of my hand before pulling my knees closer to my chest. It's colder in here than outside, it doesn't make sense, but gooseflesh runs from my hairline to the top of my jeans. Maybe it's the adrenaline leaving my system, taking my warmth as well as my hope.

Luke shouts and swears and bangs his palms against the doors. There's no squeak of metal or indication they move at all. There's the jangle of chains from the other side of the doors. Another security measure. As if there's any hope of getting out of here anyway.

"Let us out you fucking cowards. You shithouse bastards."

Slap. Slap. Slap.

Palms on the metal doors, his blows slowing down. The fight is draining from him just like with me. Then they stop altogether. The only sound in the darkness is Luke's panting. Hard and wet. I can't make him out properly but there's a slump to his form. His shoulders angled down to the ground. His head bent forward. If I was a betting man, I'd wager there's tears in his eyes. This is how he always is. Overemotional. Not grasping the gravity of situations until it's too late.

There's the scuffing of his footsteps on the chipboard, the drag of his back down the metal wall opposite me. He's only two, three feet away from me now. We're halfway back in the container, the measly light showing outlines but no details. I can see enough that I notice when his hands find his face. He tries to hide his sniffling, the audible cues of his lack of backbone. But he doesn't manage it. In this confined space, there's no chance he's keeping his blubbing a secret.

I don't say anything. I can judge in silence although questions flood my mind as he lets it all hang out.

How did he think things were going to get better?

Did he ever think we were all just going home?

What part of him thinks that crying is going to help?

I don't say anything because there's nothing worth saying. I just sit here in the darkness and let a grown man cry.

TWENTY-EIGHT

Luke

I don't think Connor can see me crying. I've been as quiet as I can but the occasional sob sneaks out. After everything we've been through this weekend and as friends over the years, this is the first time I've cried in front of him. Thank fuck for the pitch black. It hides my shame. It's done a good job all weekend of preserving my dignity.

I don't know how long we've been in here or how long we're expected to stay in here either.

Until one of us is left?

Until one of us dies of starvation or thirst?

Are we supposed to be fighting right now?

The only thing I know for certain is when one of us goes home from this place, it'll be me, not Connor. The other two are already out of the equation. Propped up in some parody of a car crash that's just waiting for the third and final victim to come and join the fun.

Good lads those pair but they don't matter now. What matters now is getting home and back to Amy. Getting on with my career and my life. All those things I'd taken for granted for the last thirty years. Normality. Safety. Stability. After a few pints, I'd bitch about those things. Call my life boring. Worry that staying with one woman forever would somehow tame me as a person. That I'd never be free, not like I used to be, back in the day at uni when I could do whatever I wanted. Get up when I wanted, go out when I wanted. All that stuff.

But I'd got it all wrong. Made a right dog's dinner of it all. Because it's not those connections that tie you down and break you apart – they build you up. It's Amy who's there for me. She's the wind in my sails. She's the fire that burns in my chest. It's her that lights me up and makes me want to get promoted or earn that bonus, to give her all the things she dreams about. If it wasn't for her, if it wasn't for the marriage, I'd have no will to survive. There'd be no need for me to live.

I'd be directionless without her.

Like Connor.

I take a deep breath and try to still the hitching in my chest. My throat constricts, begging me to clear it, but I don't want to draw attention to myself. Connor hasn't spoken either. My words need to be the first that puncture the silence between us.

"I think you should do the decent thing and agree to let me go home."

The echoes off the container walls add a metallic bass note to my words. Silence expands like a balloon, taking over the gap it so recently vacated.

"How'd you figure that?" Connor replies.

I don't know how long it's been since I spoke, could be seconds, minutes, could be an hour.

"When you look at the two of us, I think objectively you'd have to say it's the fairer choice. I've got a fiancé. I've got a career that's going pretty well. I'm on the property ladder. In terms of society, I'm bringing more to the table. With due respect."

"With due respect? Sorry Connor, do you mind if you fuck off and die, please? With due respect, of course. As if that makes it all right. Everything is totally cool now you've said that. What next? No offence?"

"You don't need to be like that about it, bloody hell."

"You've literally told me that I need to die so you can live. How can I not be offended about that?"

"I don't know. Maybe it came out wrong. I'm sorry, lad. But –"

"No buts about it. Amy's right. You can be an insensitive arsehole sometimes, Luke. You need to watch that. It'll cost you one of these days."

"I didn't mean to upset you."

"Christ, now you're making me feel like it's me who's marrying you. Knock it off. You've slugged me in the face this weekend too and you haven't apologised for that so don't go getting all over-emotional now."

"Sorry."

Connor laughs. "You're forgiven, babe." Silence again, then he continues. His words coming out of the black to me. Darkness obscuring his form. "Do you not think I've chewed this over in my own head, the whole time we've been here? Literally since this thing started. When I looked at you all, do you not think I found myself wanting? That I just didn't measure up?"

"Con, come on lad."

"Jay was a copper. Giving something back to society. He had a wife and kids, had a career path at his feet, Who knows where he could've got to? Maybe to the top job? Made a real difference. But he was cut down before he could.

"Ethan was a success. Whichever way you look at it. He made a fortune for himself and for his dad's company. Sure, he started halfway up the ladder, but he made the most of it all. He lived for the now. There's barely a day he didn't do something he enjoyed.

"And there's you. You're right. You have more to live for than me. The woman of your dreams. The wedding, the mortgage. One day you'll probably have kids and dogs and all sorts. That's the full package mate.

"And then there's me."

"Con. Don't do this to yourself. It's not like that."

"It is though, isn't it? That's what you were saying yourself. You did the sums and weighed up our lives. It took you about two minutes. You totalled up the things we've both got going for us. Tell me, Luke, what is it I've got? What were the positives you put in my column?"

Truth be told, I didn't even consider them. I find myself scrambling for an answer. "You're close with your family. Your brother would miss you."

"I'm sure he would. Adam would miss me. Score one in the box for Connor. The most minimal requirement for a human being on this planet – your family loves you. Christ on a bike. Even Hitler had a family. I'm sure they liked him once too. Anything else? Or does my reason for living die with that pathetic attempt?"

"I don't know what else to say."

"What you want to say is this – Connor, you've got no girlfriend or partner. You've never managed to be in a relationship worth a damn in your entire life. You talked the big talk about moving away and travelling the world, but you bottled it. You live alone in a tiny apartment that you hate. Oh, and your job is a boring admin job where you'd need literally six people to die on your team before they'd even consider you for a promotion. Am I right?"

"No, Con. You're projecting on me. That's not fair. These are things you think about yourself, not things I think about you."

"Really? So, you can't deny that being my friend comes with the upside of it making you feel better about yourself?"

I make sure I don't pause. "No, Con. We're friends on our own merits. We always have been. It's just been unfortunate the way things have worked out at times. That things have gone better for me than they have for you recently."

"Recently? You mean ever. Say what you fucking mean, Luke. Don't be such a coward the whole time. You're asking me to die so you can go home after a fucking mental weekend where people have been literally murdered but somehow, you've survived without doing one brave thing. That is so you. It really is."

"And what does that mean?"

"It means this is how your life goes. Stumbling into success without ever trying, without ever grafting for it."

"This is about Amy. Still. Jesus Christ." My fingers pinch the bridge of my nose. Pressure builds inside my head. "It's been years. You can't still think you have a shot with her. We're getting married. You're the best man. This is sick."

"It's not about Amy. It's not like that. But she is an example of how everything just goes your way. Here's Luke, the lovable slacker who actually, when you look at it, has ended up successful through no fault of his own."

"Oh, piss off, I work hard."

I can't fully make him out but I'm sure he's counting things off on his fingers as he goes. "University – fluked your way to a 2:1. You couldn't be arsed revising the whole course but guess what – here are questions on all the topics you did actually learn. Luck."

"Could've happened to anyone."

"Your job. You didn't have the grades for the graduate scheme, but you chanced your arm anyway. Called up on the exact same day that someone else dropped out. You didn't get there on merit, you got there because of timing. Luck."

"Better to be lucky than good."

"Getting on the property ladder. You've never saved any money in your life. You don't have the discipline to save. You're always half-skint before pay day is even over. I know you. But Amy, she's got it. She's like me, she hasn't been brought up to waste things. She scrimps and saves and squirrels away her part of a house deposit. And you? Do you remember what happened?"

"Yes. I inherited some money."

"Bingo. Like you won the world's easiest game show. Great Aunt Penny, who you met once as a five-year-old, dies alone and probably doolally leaving you ten grand. House deposit secured. You can't fucking make it up."

"But we got the house. That's what matters. Never mind the how and the why. We're making a life. A life I need to get back to."

"A life you didn't even seem to want at some points. Those other girls Amy suspected, did they ever happen?"

My fingers curl and I try to stop myself from making fists. Once I make fists, I'm not going to be able to stop myself from using them. "No. Sure, I made mistakes. You have a go at me like you've never done anything wrong in your life. But I never went that far. I never went too far."

"And Amy, she's the one, is she? That's how it's going to be?"

"Yes. It'll be me and her. Always."

"My worry is that she's not best off with you, Luke."

"I knew it. I fucking knew it."

"I don't mean she's better off with me. But maybe she needs a fresh start. Maybe someone new. Maybe that's what you should do. Step aside. Let her get on with her life. Stop dragging her down. You're only going to hurt her in the end. Your luck can't last forever. One day you'll make a mistake, you'll break her heart. And I think if you're honest with yourself, you know it."

"I won't let her down. We're building a life together. We've got something proper, something solid."

"Stop taking it for fucking granted then!" His voice rattles round the container, hitting me from all sides.

"I'm not. Not any more."

Connor sighs. "How do I know I can trust you? That you won't let her down, that you won't fuck it up one day?"

"Because I promise you, Connor. Once I get out of here, things are different. Work – I'll take it more seriously. Put a shift in. Get promoted. The house – we'll do it up properly. Sell it on when the time comes. Amy – I'll do right by her, man. I promise you. You say all this shit about me being lucky and me not caring. Maybe I have been lucky in the past but you're wrong about the other thing. I've always cared. Always tried. And maybe I have in the past sometimes, hell, even this weekend, but I've never meant to let you down. It's not who I am."

"We can't both walk out of here, Luke. You know that. These fuckers, they aren't messing about. You saw Ethan, you heard about Jay. This isn't acting. They'll keep watching you. They know all about you and Amy. I'll tell them about this deal. They'll keep you honest."

"I don't need them to. I got this." A smile breaches the corners of my lips. He can't see it in the darkness. That tingle of getting what you want, that buzz that makes your fingertips waggle.

"You better had. This isn't about you, Luke. It's about her. You're right about her and right about me. All this time, I kept chewing down on it, keeping it in. But I love her. For all those years since university. So many times, I played back that date we had, tried to figure out what went wrong. You know the only thing I've got?"

"What?"

"That it wasn't meant to be. Not then. You know how little that is to go on? How little comfort that gives you?"

I don't want to say anything, the momentum's there. He's going to do it. He's going to give in and let me win it all. "I don't, mate."

"Fuck all. When no-one else measures up, it gives you nothing. That's why I don't date much. That's why there's no wife or whatever. Nobody else is quite on that level of her." He clears his throat. "Of what you have. And I know I'll never get that with anyone else. That's the baggage I've carried all this time."

"I'm sorry, Con. Truly. I never did anything to hurt you. Never on purpose."

There's a clumping of shoes on the chipboard floor. I feel rather than see his movement in the darkness. His breath on my cheek. The outline of him giving way to more detail as he stands barely a foot away from me. Everything tenses in my body. An instinct brought on by this weekend. An instinct to flinch away even from those closest to you.

As I reach my hand out, there's a touch on my shoulder. Fingers gripping my skin through my filthy shirt. Connor pulling me closer. My hands find the shape of him, the small of his back. We pull each other in close. It's not that laddish hug where you grab each other, smash your chests together so hard that the air leaves your lungs and then slap each other on the back. It's more than that. It's real. My chin on his shoulder. His on mine.

I don't know how long we stay like that until we break apart. Even in the darkness, I scratch at the back of my head, look down at shoes I can barely see. Heat rises up one side of my neck. What a pair of soft twats. After everything this weekend and we hold each other in the darkness. Somewhere, Ethan is looking down on us, a barbed insult on his heavenly tongue and I bite my lip at the thought. It's all too real still.

"Don't let me down, man." Connor says. His voice still close by but softer now, cowed. "You make the most of everything. Do all those things you said you would. Look after Amy how she deserves. Don't you ever let a day end when she doesn't feel like a queen. Have you got that?"

"What, so I'm supposed to buy her some Corgis and not let her work a day in her life?"

"Don't be a twat for once, yeah."

"Thought you'd appreciate a smile before... Well, before we get those doors open."

"A joke from you? Got more chance of this bloody Gav busting out a full stand-up routine."

"He's probably got one. Local observational comedy. How his dad fucked a sheep and then his own sister and nine months later, out pops Gav."

"This is the kind of shit you need to wind back in mate. They'll be watching you. No matter what happens and what gets said, don't forget that. They know where you live. They're connected."

"Yeah. I won't forget. I'll always remember."

"And don't forget me either, okay? When the time comes, you don't forget me. Don't you forget what I did here. Please."

"How could I?"

"Talk to the family. Tell them I always cared. Don't forget."

"I won't, Con. I won't."

His shape moves in the darkness and for a second I think I'm going to have to hug him again. But he leans past me, the scent of shit and mud and sweat lingering. He slaps a palm against the walls of the container.

Blam, blam, blam.

Footsteps outside, scuffing on the gravel. A couple of sets. Maybe more. My breath hitches in my throat. I need to get out of here.

"What d'you want?" An unfamiliar voice. Must be one of the grunts.

"We're ready. We want out."

"You know you're not both going to carry on. Right? Once those doors open, one of you is going to die." A pause and a sharp breath. "You're both still alive?"

"Yes," we both say.

"Right, you are then. Stand back. We're fucking armed so don't get any ideas." Then the voice drops. "Get Gav and the others round here before we open the doors." The sound of running footsteps making their way away from the container. After a few seconds of silence, there are more footsteps. Many pairs. The rest of these inbreds are racing round to the container, smelling blood and punishment.

"You ready for it?" Gav's voice. The master of these sick ceremonies.

"Yes." Only me responding.

Scuttling outside as they remove the chains, the clink of metal on concrete. There's a second of silence. The doors are unlocked but aren't open. We stand in the blackness. Side by side with my best friend, my best man laying down his life so that I can carry on with mine. I need to say something to him, something profound and important. But the words are miles away from me. Unformed things, worms of ideas.

With a squeal the doors part and daylight blasts in. Even this dull day is blinding in contrast to the container and its shadows. There's a slice of light and then the doors swing open to reveal Gav and Wallace and Hector and all these other ugly fucks. The sight of them prompts me into words.

All I can think of to say is "thank you".

TWENTY-NINE

Connor

Guns meet us when the doors open. Gav and the whole crew. Every twisted, bloodthirsty bastard in the local area waiting for us. My breath hitches in my throat at the thought of what we're going to do. What they're going to do to me. My fingernails find the soft flesh of my palm and I squeeze them against the skin until I can't take it anymore.

"Looks like we've got a winner and in record time as well. I though you cunts were gonna keep us waiting here all night. You were what, about ninety minutes? Who knows, we might end up getting to watch the match after all. Depends whether Wallace can get his shit together and do what he needs to do."

"I can do it," Wallace says. His voice steady. His eyes meeting mine and then Luke's.

"Let's get on with it then," Gav says. He uses his rifle to gesture us both out of the container.

Everything is as flat and grey as before. I'd read something once about the moments before people's death being the most vivid of their lives but nothing's different. I look at Luke and then at the pub, my vision is the same. There's a tang of old leaves on the air but it's not incendiary. It's not evocative or bringing back childhood memories.

If my life is going to flash before my eyes, someone had better tell it that the reels have stuck.

I'm going to do this. There's no backing down and no changing my mind. We're out now. If anything, we were safer in the dingy, rusted prison they'd shoved us in. There were no guns in there. No psychos. Just old friends.

"Come on, come on. We ain't got all day. We need to get on. Get young Wallace here blooded so we can all get on with our lives. Well, not all of us, hey lads? Sorry about that."

His gaggle of admirers snort and chuckle at his little joke and I bite the inside of my cheek to stop all the bitterness inside me from spilling out.

"You've got what you wanted, but don't take the piss. People have died this weekend, people we care about. There's no fucking need all right?" Luke says.

There's silence for a second and then one of them goes "oooh," like some camp guy from an Eighties sitcom and they all start pissing themselves again. Laughing in our faces. Showing us no respect even though they know one of us is going to die. Even though it's fucking imminent.

"Pipe down," Gav says and they fall silent again but a few of them are jostling, digging each other in the ribs and laughing behind their hands like schoolboys. Maybe they've put a few beers away in the meantime or sucked down a couple of joints. Not that they did it anywhere I could smell it. Tight bastards keeping us in our places until the bitter end.

No last drag. No last tin of beer. No last goodbye to loved ones.

Just the clunk of the rifle being cocked and then a bang before infinity. What a way to go.

I keep my eyes on the ground. Cowed and bent like the prisoner I am. Next to me, Luke walks differently. Defiantly. He's the cock of the walk now, king of the world. One of us is guaranteed to be going home. Tradition dictates.

They march us out of the container and over the metal cellar doors. Our footsteps clanging as we go. We stop at the side of the pub, still in sight of the container but not directly in front of the doors. I guess it wouldn't do to have two bloodstains on the car park. What would their occasional tourists think? But this is no quaint Lake District pub. We're a million miles from Windermere and ice creams and family boat rides. There're no gastropubs here. Just a bunch of maniacs living in plain sight.

We stop and they circle us, Luke not yet extracted and moved away to safety. He'll never be one of them but he's a million miles away from me now. Every pair of eyes is on us. Almost all of them wearing the same hungry look. That burning for violence. Most of these lads don't have a dog in the fight. Not really. There's been big talk of "consequences" if they don't deliver all weekend but who for? Only for Wallace and Gav by the look of it. Most of these lads wouldn't lose anything if they fucked off home now. The main thing is, they don't want to. It's written on their wet lips and wide eyes. They need this. Deep down. On an animalistic level.

The two exceptions are Gav and Wallace. Gav's shifting on the spot. Not staying still. His eyes constantly aware of everyone. Looking for reasons to snap or to react. He's amped. I doubt it's drugs but he's on the edge. Eager.

Wallace is the opposite. His doughy, over-large body moves slower than ever. His gaze doesn't leave the floor. Everything about him is slumped. The rifle hangs limp in his hands. There isn't the soldier's steel about him that the others have. He looks like an overgrown little boy who doesn't want to be playing with the bigger lads.

"Which one of you is it then?" Gav says. "I thought we'd have to drag one of you out of there half conscious and finish him off. I didn't think it would all be so fuckin amicable." He gives us a look like he's walked through shit. As though us not resorting to violence is the most repellent thing he's ever seen.

"It's me," I say. I don't meet Gav's eye. I keep looking at Wallace. He's miles away. Wanting to be anywhere but here with that cold steel in his hands. All his mates are watching while he does what he needs to do and put me out of my misery.

"The stag survives," Gav says, sounding like a snooker commentator. "Who'd have thought? Wallace will be so disappointed, he really had his heart set on it, didn't you mate?" He puts on a babying voice for his friend.

Wallace nods. Still not part of this conversation.

"But it's the best man, proving his worth. Stepping up and sending the stag home to the arms of his fiancé. How delightful. How noble can you be? What a fuckin great man you must be, Connor. Fair play to you." He wedges his rifle under his arm and gives a solitary, slow clap.

"It's nothing. Was never a choice, was it? You know us. Who would you have chosen?" I say.

"We wanted the stag. Really. We all had a little chat. We backed you if it came to fisticuffs in there. Guess you're a bigger, braver man than we thought. Good for you."

"People are full of surprises."

I'm trying to be defiant, but I feel like a teenager again, spouting a load of shit to my parents, trying to be a rebel. Christ, my parents. I'd not even thought about it. What they're going to think when they hear, what they're going to say. How the news is going to hit them.

I straighten up. Pulling my shoulders back, jutting out my chin. Making myself as big and as real as possible. It's doubtful I could take many of these lads in a fight, but this is about pride. About looking the part, no matter what happens next.

"Got anything you'd like to say, best man?" Gav asks. "A fuckin rare one this. Normally you just see some fucker bleeding on the floor saying "please" over and over before you have to blow his head off or whatever. Like your mate, Jay. That copper. He didn't have much to say. You gonna be the same? This is your chance. Think big. Think Hollywood."

He watches me with indifference. With that simmering rage of the pisshead in the pub just before it kicks off. That "calm before the storm" anger. Next to him, Wallace still isn't watching. The rifle hangs limply in his hands.

"If I had to say anything right now, I'd probably just say sorry. That's it."

"Sorry?" Luke says.

"Sorry?" Gav says.

"Yup. Sorry."

Before anyone can react, I set off. I cross the two yards between me and Wallace. He only looks up at the sound of my last step. He's too slow to bring the rifle up and I lower my shoulder. The impact hits him right in the sternum. A jolt hammers through me, but he loses his balance and his grip on the rifle.

I lean through my charge, one arm pushing Wallace back, the other hand closing round the rifle. Snatching it from his chunky fingers. He makes a groan of surprise as he stumbles backwards. But the rifle is in my hands now, not his.

I adjust my hold on the weapon. Turning it in my hands like every action hero I've ever seen. It can't be that hard to manage. Just find your target. Aim. Squeeze the trigger. But I've got to be quick as every fucker with a weapon is now aiming them at me.

Everything slows down.

I look up. Meet Luke's eye. I pull the trigger.

Luke's stomach explodes in a burst of claret.

And everything in the world goes on fast forward around me. Screaming back to normal. Sound rushing in. My vision settling.

Luke drops to the ground. His scream is primal, almost beyond human. He writhes, shouting and crying, arms and legs flailing like a trapped insect. My hands go slack around the gun, its muzzle pointing to the floor. Someone slaps it out of my grasp, and it clatters onto the concrete.

Three punches land to the right side of my face. The first two barely register before the third knocks me sideways. My balance slips away and I stumble, pushing myself up from hitting the deck with one hand.

Everyone's shouting at once. Me included although I don't know what words are forming. Everything's rushing by me. People, time, thoughts.

Wallace is up at me. His pudgy face pressing close to mine as he screams, his skin already a livid red and getting worse with every word. My hands find the front of his flannel shirt, grabbing, pleading with him. Two quick punches to my gut drop me to my knees and end the conversation.

"Wallace, get over here," Gav calls from his position kneeling next to the prone Luke. He waves the big man over. "Bring your rifle. You don't have long."

Wallace tears himself away from me. Eyes blazing. He snatches up the rifle and runs the few yards to the scrum around Luke.

My breathing starts to slow down from the winded panting it's been since the punches landed. I heave in lungfuls of air, fighting against the pain. My eyes water and I wipe them as I stagger to my feet. The exertions of the last two days catching up with me. My arms hang limply by my sides, too heavy to be of any use.

Nobody is looking at me. If I had the strength, I'd make a break for it but there's no chance of that now. I wouldn't make it to the door of the pub, let alone any further. I take a couple of steps towards the crowd but stop as Gav shouts.

"It's gotta be now, Wallace. No fuckin about lad. This is it. You do him here and now or we all fuckin get it. He ain't lasting long. Just hit his chest and it's all over."

Wallace stammers something, mumbling in that deep voice of his. Words coming out slow and disjointed. His hands shake on the rifle.

Gav's on his feet. Wallace towers over his best man but cowers as Gav moves in close. "I ain't suffering for you, Wallace. None of us are. Get this done. Do your duty to your men and to your wife. End this little cunt now."

Gav reaches up and slaps Wallace across the face. The crack is like a rifle shot itself. Wallace's head jerks to the side. "Do it now. Do it fuckin now."

The others join in, a chorus of screams and obscenities, jostling the big man. Hector's shouting loudest of all, his bruised face twisted into a savage grin as he howls at his friend. Wallace shakes his head, his lips are moving but I can't hear what he's saying.

On the ground, Luke has stopped shouting. His movements are slow and small. Through a gap in the crowd, our eyes meet. His skin is drained, as grey as the concrete beneath his head. Blood pours from his mouth, coating his teeth in deep crimson. His eyes widen as he meets my stare and I wonder what he sees written on my face.

"Just fucking stand back," Wallace shouts. The crowd of locals does as it's told. Gav lingers on Wallace's shoulder as the big man steps forwards, rifle poised. He whispers into Wallace's ear, his mouth inches from the flabby ear.

"Leave it, Gaz. Watch." Wallace yells.

My eyes find Luke. His gaze still on mine. Those blue eyes I know so well. That familiar face that's been with me since childhood.

The rifle cracks and Luke's body jerks. His eyes don't leave mine. Another crack and another jerk. The next time I blink, there's no light left in Luke's eyes. They stare through me, glassy and vacant. He's not getting up, not this time. He's lying in a grave that I kicked him into.

I stand there, alone and ignored on the fringe of their group. I can't take my eyes off Luke but somewhere in my peripheral vision, the locals are clapping Wallace on the back and hugging him. The air's full of their noise. Satisfied and gloating. Their mission completed and all of their lives off the hook.

All our lives off the hook it seems.

Gav breaks ranks and strides over to me. Violence in the way he moves, everything about him angular and up for it. He shoves me. His bony hands pushing flat against my ribs.

"Think you're some kind of hero, do you?"

Shove.

"Think you're a little legend for saving yourself?"

Another shove.

"You put everyone here at risk. Even yourself. You've got no fuckin idea how close you came to getting us all killed."

The third shove sends me stumbling backwards.

"Selfish, fuckin coward."

There is no fourth shove.

"I thought it was the maddest thing I've ever seen," Hector says. He shakes his battered head. "All these years Gav and we got ourselves one for the ages. We ain't ever had to lock two of 'em up to decide who dies and who doesn't. We ain't ever had a lad be so fucking cowardly and sneaky before. There's never been a stag like this one. It's fucking wild."

"You know what happens if the rules get broken, Heck. If that little pussy of a groom had bled out before our big pussy of a groom finished him off, we were all fuckin for it."

"Yeah. But he didn't. You got Wally there. You helped him get the job done. So, what's the fucking problem? We got it all done. Just calm down. Relax. Enjoy a few beers and know you'll be sleeping off a massive night with that lovely wife of yours."

"He doesn't understand the consequences," Gav growls. His dark eyes burn, a scowl never leaving his features.

Hector laughs. "Always so tightly wound, lad. There are no consequences now. It's done. Wally's got his offering. Helen's got her gift. We're all good. All you need to worry about is doing a good speech now and fuck me, you could do with some help on the jokes."

Gav doesn't smile. Doesn't look away from his eye contact with me.

"Whatever lad, we've still got work to do here. Don't go switching off until it's all sorted. Come on." Hector tugs at Gav's arm but Gav doesn't move.

"In a second," Gav grunts. "Call the in-laws, get them up here to come and collect the prize. Tell 'em to make it snappy, yeah. We can still make it inside to watch the match if they get a shift on."

"Good lad," Hector says, walking away from us.

Gav's hand shoots up and grabs my throat. His fingers tighten around my windpipe.

"Maybe Hector's right. Maybe this was epic. Maybe it's just lucky that you didn't blow that lad's fuckin head off. I dunno. Guess it doesn't matter now."

"It doesn't," I choke. "It's over."

He smiles then. "Is it? Is that how you see it?" He squeezes my windpipe harder and then lets go, transferring his hand to the scruff of my neck. His fingers pinch a combination of skin and clothing, digging deep into both filthy surfaces. He drags me over towards where the locals still buzz around Luke's body. They're flies, vermin, salivating as they prepare to pick through the bones of the corpse.

They part at Gav's instructions, each of them stepping back. Their eyes comb my face, their looks almost physical on my skin. My gaze stays on the concrete, not lifting, not rising. None of them says anything as we pass. Their silence is worse than insults, even worse than taking a kicking.

"Look at him," Gav says.

I close my eyes.

Gav's voice shifts, moves closer to my face. "Open your fuckin eyes and look at him."

When I open my eyes, Gav's face is inches from mine. His skin blotched red. His eyes crackle. His breath brushes my cheeks. At least he's brushed his teeth. That's something.

"This is what you've done," he points down at Luke. I keep my focus on Gav's elbow, trying to make it look as though I'm doing as I'm told.

Gav's hand swings up and grabs me by the face. His thumb pressing into one cheek, his fingers into the other. He tries to drag me, but I hold my ground, like a dog that won't go into its kennel. I shake my head, crushing my eyes shut, and that means I don't see the punch coming. Square onto my nose. Pain makes me open my eyes, unbidden. Water streams across my vision. I blink it away. Gav's face fills my view. Scowling. His jaw working as he tries to hold it all in.

"Look at your friend. Now."

I shake my head.

"We're going to start cutting pieces off you if you don't get the message."

"You can't. You said one of us has to make it home alive. That's your tradition."

"Our tradition is that someone makes it home alive. There's nothing about what state they have to be in."

"It's more to explain away. Another lie to make up."

"Your friends died in a car crash. People can get seriously fuckin maimed in those as well. Now look at your friend."

I do as I'm told. There's only so long I can hold out for.

Luke lies on the concrete, his face still as pale as before. Blood is on his chin and his cheeks, his head turned to the right so that he's making eye contact with me. His eyes are open. Glassy and unreal. There's no mischief in there now. No spark. My eyes drift to the area below his neck. It's just tattered, bloody meat around the bullet wounds. His clothes are soaked with blood, dyed by the life that oozed out of him.

"That's your friend, that. The lad you were gonna be best man for. You've known him what, twenty years?"

"More."

"More," he shakes his head. "And you threw him away like he was a bag of rubbish. Just chucked him into the gutter like a sack of shit. All those years of friendship. Everything you've been through together. You know, I've got this image of you as two teenage spotty virgins, plotting how you could get girls to like you. Very cute mate. Except, one of you managed that, didn't they? It just wasn't you."

"Shut up. You don't know anything about me."

"We do, mate. I do. We only let the right people stay at the B&B. We only let the right groups of lads into this. I know you Connor. Just a shame you don't know yourself."

"What and you do? Do you know what a fucking psycho you are?"

He lets go of me then. Shrugs. "We've all got our own paths, lad. I know who I am. Who I need to be, like when Wally couldn't put your copper mate away. Plenty of lads could've stepped up cos we've all got backbone here, but I did it. I made it right."

"You're a killer and you liked it."

"You're pointing lots of fingers here Connor lad. Lots of 'em. You ever think about turning one round and pointing it at yourself? Taking a long, hard look at who you are and who you think you are. Cos from where I'm stood, there are two best men. One of 'em stepped up and helped out his groom when he needed it, the other only stepped in and helped himself." He spits on the floor in front of me. "And you say that I'm a fuckin psycho."

He walks off then, leaving me alone with the corpse of my best friend. The only person in my life who truly knew me, as he lies with the heat leaving his body. I kneel next to him and close his eyelids. From the outside it probably looks like a tender moment, but I can't stand his gaze on me anymore. That blank stare looking into me. Judging me.

I don't cry. All of the other symptoms are there ,the tight chest, the stifled breathing. But the tears won't come, I won't let them. These fuckers won't see me cry. Gav can say all he wants about me being the psycho, about me killing Luke, but none of the things that happened this weekend would've happened without them. The locals.

That bunch of fuckers. It's their game, their pressure that led to this. Luke's bad choices and Amy's lack of trust in him - that's why we're here. Yes, I made mistakes too, but I just reacted to the hand I've been dealt.

Oh, fuck.

Amy.

What the hell am I going to tell her? How can I look her in the face after all of this? The wedding plans, the honeymoon, all those cancellations. Luke's life insurance or whatever they hopefully have in place. She's going to be a wreck. This will destroy her. This will destroy the whole family.

I bite my lip, the pain distracting me from anything else for a few precious seconds. The locals leave me be. Their eyes crawl over me but I don't turn round, and they don't approach as I grieve.

Three funerals to come. There's going to be plenty of time to mourn.

The crackle of tyres on the concrete breaks the silence, the Land Rover pulling into the car park. The in-laws are here to claim their prize. I don't take my eyes from Luke. The sound of a door opening and being slammed shut. Boots on the concrete, coming closer.

The voice of Wallace's father-in-law. "Wally, you little beauty. Tell me you did this?"

"Yup. I got him."

Scuffing footsteps behind me. I look up and the father-in-law is leaning over me, staring at Luke's body. He's not looking at me. He's peering round me like I'm nothing but an obstruction.

"And the stag as well, nicely done. That's the one you wanted, wasn't it?"

"Yup. The best one, isn't it?"

"Absolutely. Helen will be thrilled. And so am I." The sound of them embracing in that way men do, pulled in tight, hands slapping backs. "It's just great news. The wedding's on after all. I mean, I had my doubts, but you came through, Wally. You're worthy and I'm so proud."

He prattles on like this, as though he's talking about Wallace passing his driving test rather than murdering another human in cold blood. Well, finishing off what I started at the very least.

"Hector and a couple of others, give me a lift with the stag into the boot. Robbie is getting the workshop ready – we'll take him straight there to be prepped. No worries at all."

Hands shove me out of the way and three lads, including Hector, help the father-in-law to pick Luke up. He doesn't drip like Ethan does. He just hangs in the air, head tossed back as they lift him away from me. I watch the whole time as they hoist him and gently place him in the back of the Land Rover. There's new plastic wrap coating the hold. A clinical touch.

They slam the door shut, cutting off my view of Luke. As the engine starts, it dawns that this is the last time I'll see him. We've said everything we'll ever say to each other, done everything we'll ever do. There are two sides to every story, until there aren't. And now we've reached the point where only my memories remain of our friendship.

The Land Rover pulls out of the car park and I follow its path along the winding lane until it disappears from sight. My shoulders slump as it goes. As Luke goes.

"Get the rest of that blood washed off, yeah," Gav says behind me. "Same lads as last time, you did a smashing job on that first one." His voice sounds far away although I'm barely five yards from them, standing alone, facing the view of the fields.

Then there's a hand on my shoulder, hot breath in my ear as Gav speaks softly so only I can hear. "People have asked us in the past why one person is allowed to leave. Why not do you all in? When we first did this, I asked my dad the same thing. Why let people go home when there's a risk we might get caught? He told me there's no risk, he said 'we've got the connections, but that's not the point, son. The point is, the person who goes home is the one you've broken. You've killed the others, but you've broken this one. He's never gonna be the same again. He'll have seen and done things this weekend that he'll never tell anyone about. And you can bet that he'll spend the rest of the time he has left wishing he'd never made it home.' He wasn't wrong, my dad."

THIRTY

WALLACE

He strides up the path to the cottage. His long legs make short work of the distance. On his shoulders, the rucksack is light, lighter than he assumed it would be. He fumbles with the latch of the gate, part nerves, part eagerness. It clacks open and the gate squeaks as he pushes through.

Movement in the windows snatches his attention and he hurries between the stubs of rose bushes and the rest of summer's detritus in the borders. As he raises his hand to knock on the door, it swings inwards and there she is.

Helen.

His Helen.

Her eyes, always his favourite feature of hers, sparkle an almost translucent green in the light. Bright and wide and focused solely on him. When she sees him like this, he knows he can do anything in this world and in this life. All he needs is her approval, he needs her to need him.

"I've got all the girls round. What's going on? Thought you'd be with the lads, like, you know, on your stag."

"I am," he says, then clears his throat. "They've all been taking the piss something rotten, but I couldn't wait no longer. I just can't keep nothing from you, that's my problem. Can't keep anything from you."

"And what would you need to be keeping from me?" Her hands find her hips.

"Nothing. Nothing. Look, this is why I'm here." He pulls an arm out of the rucksack and slides it round to his front.

Behind Helen, there's movement on the stairs. Her friends watch down, not trying to hide their presence. They titter and nudge each other. This isn't how he dreamed it but it's how it'll have to be.

Wallace unzips the rucksack, it's bright yellow, the one carried by that copper Gav finished off. No doubt it'll be used again in the future for the same purpose.

"Your dad and Robbie have just finished up, so I came running over here for you. Should be watching the game and having a pint and that." He nods up the stairs at Abby and smiles. "He said I can come but I've got to pay the price when I get back."

She smiles. "That sounds like him all right, nothing happens without someone paying for it down the line."

"Aye, well I'll be paying for it with a right royal hangover in the morning." He turns to Helen, his fiancé. "Anything they do to me is worth it to share this moment with you, Helen. I love you."

He reaches into the bag and pulls out the prize. His hands move softly over the smooth bone. The weight of it is perfect in his hands, well balanced. It's another of nature's miracles. The colour of the skull surprises him, as it always does when dealing with his sheep. In films, bones are always bleached white but it's not like that when you see them up close and personal. There's an off-white colour to it. A tinge bordering on yellow.

"We can get it mounted ready for the wedding - however you want to do it. You tell me and I'll make it happen. Your dad said he'll let me help him prepare it. Make it a proper family job like."

He holds the skull out to her, and she stands there for a moment, staring up into his doughy face. A split-second passes and he starts to withdraw the skull, unsure whether he's let her down in some way he can't understand. Then her face breaks into a smile and she launches herself at him. Her arms reach up around his neck and she buries her face in his chest, crushing his spoils of victory between them for as long as either of them can stand it before they break apart.

She shrieks and the sound fills him, completes him. The joy in the note flooding his reserves and making him stand up straight.

"You did it, Wal. You did it."

"I did it for you, Helen. I did it for us. I know what you thought about me, I know what people said, but I did it."

"Which one was it?"

"The stag of course. Only the best for you. It could've been the copper, but this just felt right."

Up on the stairs, Abby clears her throat but says nothing. Wallace doesn't look over at her, doesn't want to see through his own white lies by meeting her gaze.

"Wally, I can't believe it. Daddy phoned, said it wasn't going well. What happened?"

"I'll tell you all about it tomorrow, Hels. Okay? I need to be getting back to the boys. The match is on, and it's my stag party, I guess I need to be there."

"You're right, you do." Helen reaches out and takes the skull out of his hands, then leans up and kisses him gently on the lips. He meets her kiss firmly, a hand finding the small of her back as he pulls her in closely. On the stairs the gathered women coo and cheer. He feels his cheeks heat up but continues the kiss until she pulls away from him.

"My husband," she says, her palm finding his cheek. "Hurry back to me."

"I will." He backs out of the front door, not wanting to take his eyes from her before he needs to. She blows him a kiss with one hand, the skull tucked under her other arm. That smile again before she closes the door and he turns away, walking on air.

From behind the closed door there's a cheer from Helen followed by squeals and screams from the other women. He smiles to himself, and wipes sweat from his forehead with the back of his hand. The breeze chills him where more sweat bunches under his arms and at the base of his spine. It's only then that he pumps his fist in relief of a job well done. She's happy, his duty as a future husband fulfilled, his friends safe from the consequences of his lack of action.

Closing the gate behind him, he walks down the narrow stone path to where he parked Gav's Land Rover. He drops into the front seat, the suspension juddering beneath his bulk. He starts the engine and pulls away, following the road as it winds down the hill towards the pub.

It's only as the house disappears in the mirror that he lets his fingers slacken on the steering wheel and his jaw unclench. It's then that the tears sting the corners of his eyes. He knuckles them away with a meaty fist. He drives slowly, giving himself time to digest what he's become, how he got to this point, perhaps even come up with a strategy to help him get through it.

Drink will be the start of accepting who he is now.

Drink will help.

THIRTY-ONE

Connor

Three months later.

I park up on the street outside her house. It isn't their house anymore, just hers. The small, eighties built semi-detached is neater than I remember. A trimmed lawn, its borders sharp and angular, reflecting the house's architecture. Sparkling windows, curtains neatly drawn and tied behind them.

Two cars sit on the driveway. Her smaller, white Volkswagen Polo parked in front of his deep grey Ford Mondeo. There's a film of dust on the Ford and from the stains on the driveway around it, it's clear it's not moved since we went away.

My car locks with a clunk, the only sound breaking the silence on the street. It's late morning on a Tuesday, most people are at work now. But not her. Not me. The flowers in my hand crinkle in their wrapping as I walk up the driveway. The doorbell chimes, incongruous with the mood inside the house.

After a few seconds, the door opens and there she is. Pale, blonde, and thinner than I remember. She's wearing a pink dressing gown and yellow pyjamas. Her hair is pulled into a messy top knot but it kinda suits her. I smile and she doesn't return it. Instead, her brow knits, her eyes looking past me into the garden.

"I didn't think we were meeting until Tuesday, Con?" She says.

"It is Tuesday. Half ten, just like we said."

"Ah, right. You'd better come in then."

She steps aside and I step into the house, wiping my feet and kicking off my shoes onto the cream carpet. She watches me the whole time like she's never seen me before in her life. A blank look across those blue eyes, like she's struggling to wake up from a heavy night.

"I brought you some flowers. Lilies. Your favourite."

A pointless thing to say. I offer them to her, and she looks at them for a second as though I've tried to pass her a bag of human shit. Then she shakes her head and it's as if her personality is suddenly downloaded back into her body.

"You're right. Very kind. Thank you. I'll – erm – put them in some water." She takes them from me, our hands touching as she does. A shock of electricity shoots across my skin and I smile. I follow her down the hallway.

She fills the kettle. "Do you want coffee? Tea? I'm sorry, I can't remember how you take it." Amy lies the flowers in the sink. "All of the vases are being used. But I'll find somewhere for these."

She's not kidding. Through the join between the kitchen and living room, there's a glimpse of the mantelpiece, cluttered with vases full of lilies. She follows my gaze. "People have been very kind. Work. My family. His family. It's a good job I don't have hay fever because the air in this place is about ninety percent pollen."

"I think you could open your own garden centre at this rate," I reply and smooth down the front of my shirt. Watching her move around the kitchen making the drinks, I keep my hands in my pockets, the urge to reach out for her is too great. The timing needs to be right. The correct words need to be said.

We take our drinks into the living room and the waft of pollen brings a rush of sneezes down on me. I struggle to not spill my drink, placing it on the coffee table before lapsing into a sneezing fit. When my eyes clear, she's watching me, not smiling. Just sipping her tea and sitting still.

"How are you holding up?" I say. My voice nasal from the sneezing.

She looks away, watching our reflections in the enormous flatscreen TV. "Fine. As well as can be expected. Okay. Getting there. Whichever one of those you think will make you feel best about it all."

"How are you doing really? You can be honest."

She looks back at me. Her pale blue eyes shining like a violent sea. "Can I? Can I tell you everything? How I don't sleep anymore? How everything in this house makes me want to vomit or smash it to pieces? How the thought of having to go back to work or to do anything normal makes me want to scream or cry or both? Can I tell you all of that?"

"I was there, Amy. I'm with you now. Do you not think I'm going through it all too? That I don't miss him too? All of them?"

She holds my gaze for a minute. "I've tried to keep up appearances, kept the place neat and clean and all that - helped my dad with the garden. All of it is fucking futile. It keeps me busy for seconds, minutes at best, but what about the hours, Con? They stack up, they stretch out. There's so, so many of them."

"I know."

And I do.

Those nights spent not sleeping. The hours at work just staring at a screen and not doing anything at all. Time spent alone at home. But I'm not missing Luke or Jay or Ethan, I'm missing her. I'm missing Amy.

"It's tough," I continue. "There're so many times I've gone to text him or call. To send him a stupid meme I found online or see if he's free for a pint. Every time I stop myself and it all hits home. It's awful. I can't imagine how you must be feeling, still being here."

"My dad listed Luke's car on Auto Trader and I made him take it down. Now it's just sitting there on the driveway, filthy and useless. I hated driving the thing. It's too big for me but the thought of it going to someone else, it just makes me ill, you know."

"I do." I reach out and take her hand, I give it a squeeze. She looks down at her hand, as though it belongs to someone else, but she doesn't pull it away. We sit there in silence like that for a while, minutes stretching away.

Her hand slips out from under mine. "How did you survive the crash, Connor?" She says. She doesn't look at me. "The three other lads in the car all got killed but not you. You walked away, basically unhurt. How did that work?"

"Nothing but pure luck, I don't think. Like I said to you at the funeral, the angle the car hit and then rolled, the driver's side and the front took all the impact. I was sat behind the passenger seat, I was furthest away. That's all I can think of."

"And when you woke up and they were all dead, what happened? How did you feel?"

"Amy, I didn't really come round to talk about all that. It's something I'm trying hard not to think about."

"I know you're not thinking about it. That's why I'm telling you to. Because do you know what I think about all day and all night when I don't sleep? When I lie up in that bed, our bed, staring at the ceiling or the walls or whatever. All I think about is him. And how you came to, woke up, got away but he didn't."

"I'm sorry. It's just dumb luck. Like I said. It's just how it worked out."

"How it worked out. Except it didn't, did it? It didn't work out for anyone apart from you. Three people are dead. Three families are grieving. Yet here you are, walking free."

"You make it sound like I committed a crime. I didn't do anything wrong. Not one thing."

"And that's supposed to make me feel better, is it?"

"Amy, I don't know where all this is coming from."

"Don't you?" She puts her tea on the coffee table, swivels on the sofa so we're facing each other. "You don't know what all this is about?" She gestures with her fingers from herself to me and back again. "Really?"

"Amy, I – I don't know what to say."

"Say you're sorry. And mean it. Tell me that it's wrong that of the four people in the car that night, three of them died. Tell me it's wrong that the man due to be married, due to start a family, due to grow old with the love of his life died while you lived."

"It's not my fault."

"Shut up," she says, her voice more of a slap than anything I received on the stag party. "All anyone's done since Luke died is talk. Yap, yap, fucking yap. You worst of all. You've just blagged away at me, Connor. Trying to "pop round" and see me. Bringing flowers or bland chit-chat that helps no-one. Has it not crossed your mind that maybe I don't want to see you? Maybe I don't want to see anyone for a while?"

"I just thought that I could help you. That maybe I could do or say something to help."

She grimaces. "That's just it. I thought at first that this was a man thing. My dad's the same, bless him. Men do this thing where they try to fix something. A shelf breaks, they fix it. A tap leaks, they fix it. A heart breaks, someone loses the will to live, then guess what? They try to fix that too."

"I'm sorry for trying to fix you. I didn't mean to upset you."

She purses her lips. "Thing is though, Connor. It's not about fixing me, is it? Not with you. It never has been."

My gut slides as she continues to talk. Her eyes wide, white teeth bared with every word.

"Other people laugh off that we went on a date, Con. They think it's funny. But I don't. I think it was a stupid mistake when I look back on it."

"Amy, we went out once, it's not like we were married."

"From the horse's mouth. There it is. We went out once. And to be fair, it wasn't terrible. I joke about it being a KFC but that wasn't the worst of it – everything was just a bit flat. The conversation was ok, you were ok. But most people don't want their lives to only be ok. It's about finding that right person, finding the soulmate or the one or whatever you want to call it. And I did. I found Luke. And despite all our problems whether they were real or problems you imagined, we were perfect together. Perfect."

"I never said otherwise."

"Not to me. Maybe not to Luke but it was always there. Every time we hung out, you were trying to gang up with me against him, picking away at his tiny flaws, alluding to his bigger mistakes. God it was relentless. And your texts, fucking hell. Talk about inappropriate."

"Inappropriate? I never said anything rude or suggestive."

"Connor, it's the sheer volume of them. Half the night my phone was going and if you weren't messaging me, you were messaging him. It was like being bloody cyber stalked or something. You never left us alone, the endless spinning third wheel in the relationship."

"I didn't realise I was doing something wrong. I just wanted to be close to my friends."

"You wanted in, Connor. That's it. Just admit it. You wanted in."

"I just wanted to be friends with you both. Genuinely."

"We talked about it a lot, phasing you out over time, cutting you adrift. I mean really we hoped that you'd end up meeting someone and we could all be friends together, with the pressure off but you never seemed that keen on that."

"It's hard to find someone online, Amy. It's all a bit arm's length, you know?"

"You tell yourself that's it but nobody was ever good enough were they? I think I know why that is, Connor. And I can tell you, Luke knew. It tore him open. Some days it made him so angry he'd scream out loud when you messaged one of us, other days we'd just sit here and laugh."

"If I'm such a joke then why did he make me his best man?"

She rolls her eyes. "Because you needed it, Con. Because you needed something in your life. Nobody can live as empty as you. We felt bad for you. And Luke thought it might help draw a line under everything. You standing there alone, watching us have our first dance as man and wife. Maybe the nail would be driven home, you know." Tears shimmer in her eyes and she wipes them with the back of her hand. "And now he's gone but you're still here. How is that fair?"

She sobs openly as I try to tell her what she's just said isn't fair either. But she's crying and reaching for tissues and my words get lost. I put a hand on her arm, but she shakes it off, scowling at me as she wipes at her nose and calms her breathing.

"I shouldn't have lost it like that, Connor. Sorry. But you need to listen to what I'm saying now and properly understand it. I know why you're here. I know it's more than looking out for a friend. I know you want something to happen here, and I know you always have."

My eyes are on the floor. I've never said this out loud to anyone before. Never let those words slip out of my mouth.

"Connor," she says, "nothing will ever happen between us. When I found out you were Luke's best friend, my heart sank. After that one date, I knew you thought there was something between us even though I never did. I put up with it all for Luke. I answered your messages and smiled at your jokes and invited you to dinner for him. Not for me. And he's gone now. Luke's gone and so is my reason for keeping you around."

"Amy, please. I'm just trying to help you."

"You're not Connor. You're trying to help yourself. In your best shirt and buying these ridiculously expensive flowers. You've come to help yourself. Watch my face, read my lips. It is never going to happen. Luke is dead and you're here, it might not be your fault but your face, everything about you reminds me of what I've lost. I don't want you to call, I don't want you to text. I don't want you coming to this house ever again. Enough is enough. Let me grieve and let me get on with my life. Alone."

I get up, punch drunk like a boxer who's let a jab slip through his guard. The room spins around me. The cloying, sweet scent of the flowers makes my head start to pound. I need oxygen. I need to get out. I pat my jeans pocket, making sure my keys are there and I stumble to the front door.

Amy's saying something in the living room, but I don't hear it. Not properly. The edge of anger's dropped from her voice, but it doesn't matter. The damage is done. I drag on my shoes and fumble at the locks and let myself back out into the world. Fresh air hits me like a slap on the cheeks, detail rushing back into my vision. I pull the door shut and wander down the path to my car, my arms hanging heavy by my sides, my feet moving automatically.

I drop into the front seat of the car and scrabble with the key to get it into the ignition. The car starts with a muted roar, still somehow too loud in my ears. When I look up, Amy's stood in the doorway in her dressing gown. Her arms are folded across her chest. Her cheeks show a tinge of colour for the first time since I arrived. Even now, in her fury at me, she's magnificent.

I reverse away, my eyes still half on her, then swing forward and out of the cul-de-sac. I'm on the main road before I realise the car's beeping to tell me to put my seatbelt on. I clunk it into place. To think I took a day off work for this. To come here and make this mistake. To be this blind for this long.

Down the main roads and out onto the bypass. I could go home but there's nothing in that flat but four walls. Nothing to keep my mind off what happened. Nothing to keep my mind off what I've done.

A sign catches my eye, a small blue box on the larger green sign. Pointing onwards to places like Manchester and Leeds. The small blue box says "M6". The route north, up to the Lakes and beyond. Back up to the B&B. Back up to Gav and his cronies.

Gav's words still hang in my thoughts, how sometimes it's better to die than to be the person left behind. It's not that it hasn't crossed my mind these last few months but there always felt like a chink of light in the gloom, the chance that one day things would work out for me. With that door closed, there is only darkness now. There is only memory and regret. Toxic and churning inside me.

I put my foot down and follow the signs.

Maybe there's a chance to make the right decision after all.

AFTERWORD

Writing comes with a lot of baggage. You fret and worry and wonder about your words constantly. Does this plot point work? Would this character do this? Am I selling enough books? Is my vocabulary too small?

Writing does however give you a lot of freedom. Have you ever been on a night out and seen a bunch of pissed up morons ruining everyone's evening? Do you have the physical strength to batter them all like some sort of John Wick rip-off? No. Neither do I. But what you can do is go home and write about them being slaughtered as some sort of bizarre catharsis. At least, that's what I do, mostly because I'm too pretty to survive for long in jail.

Considering I've just written a book in which men commit a lot of violence against other men, I sure do have a lot of men to thank for guiding me through the process.

A huge thanks to David Moody, Kev Harrison and Wayne Kelly for their blurbs of support for the book. Much appreciated, chaps. A particular extra thank-you to Wayne for reading this book after Harrogate Festival in 2023. I took numerous copies and gave them out to various people, Wayne was the only person I know read it for certain. He's one of the good ones.

A big thanks to the following lovely writers/creatives for their ongoing support – Andy Barker, Stewart Hamilton, Grant Longstaff, Paul Feeney, Michael David Wilson, David Watkins, Dave Jeffery, Adam Hulse, Thomas Joyce, Dan Willcocks, John Crinan, Luke Kondor and Mark Armor.

An extra boatload of thanks is due to Austrian Spencer, who helped shape this novel in the early drafts. Andy – you are one of the good ones!

Special thanks to the magnificent Paul Stephenson from Hollow Stone Press who designed the superb cover for the book. He's slowly building me an author brand, he may be due a sainthood.

Thanks to my parents and to my sister Rachel, who proofread the book. If you find any errors, they are her fault, not mine.

Lastly and most importantly, thank you to Jen and Elsie. For always being there, for always lighting up my life. You both give me purpose. Without you there are no words, no books, no me. I give you everything I am and just hope I can always be enough.

ABOUT THE AUTHOR

Dan Howarth is a writer from the North of England, based on the Wirral – a place which worms its way into his fiction.

Dan's work has been shortlisted for the Northern Debut Award 2021 from New Writing North, as well as placing runner-up in the Writing on the Wall competition Pulp Idol 2024.

Through Northern Republic, Dan has released the short story collection *Dark Missives (2021)*, a novella of snowbound horror *Territory (2022)* and his debut novel *Last Night of Freedom (2024)*.

His short fiction has appeared in *Weird Horror Magazine, Chthonic Matter,* and *The Other Stories* podcast.

Like all Northerners, Dan enjoys rain, pies, and drinking craft ale from the skulls of his vanquished enemies.

www.danhowarthwriter.com

ALSO FROM NORTHERN REPUBLIC

Lionhearts
by Dan Howarth

A politically charged thriller about class, hatred, and second chances.
The Lionhearts show their teeth when they smile, they can't wait to sink them into your flesh...
When Henry Oswald loses everything in a gas explosion in his hometown, he stumbles from disaster to disaster before being picked up by a local community group full of good intentions. Yet beneath their veneer of benevolence lies hatred and division. Half-in and half-out of the group, Henry must make a choice between redemption and darkness, knowing that violence will come with either.
Lionhearts is a violent trip into the backwaters of Northern England, exploring the rage and isolation of the population and delivering a timely message for this broken country of ours.
RELEASE DATE – TBC

The Children's Horror
by Patrick Barb

Imagination is often a wonderful thing, opening doorways of creativity and possibility. But what about the other doors it can open? The ones revealing twisted passageways of corrupted innocence and unfathomable cosmic nothingness. In an elementary school auditorium, on a TV set playing weird and sinister versions of popular children's TV programming, YOU will experience this dark side of the imagination firsthand.

The Children's Horror is a themed short-story collection from horror author Patrick Barb that looks at today's most-popular kids TV franchises through a darker lens. From cities controlled by dogs and children acting as would-be heroes to infant sharks and the strange fates of written-off sitcom characters, this collection provides must-read thrills perfect for your Saturday mourning.

OUT NOW

Society Place
by Andrew David Barker

Set during the blazing English summer of 1976, recently widowed Heather Lowes moves into the house she was supposed to live with her husband. But now she is alone... or at least, she thinks she is.

It is a normal terrace house, on an everyday, run-down working class street in a dying industrial town. A place that seldom sees the extraordinary.

However, when Heather meets her new neighbours – the old woman next door, the kid from a few doors down – they all seem concerned that she has moved into the house at the end of Society Place. They seem to know something.

Heather's nights in the house are troubled. She senses a presence, particularly on the stairs, and down in the cellar. She dare not go down there. As the sweltering summer rages on, Heather experiences supernatural turmoil that tests her sanity and pushes her understanding of reality to its very limits.

She learns that there isn't just one ghost.

There is a Nest of Ghosts that haunt, not just her house, but all the houses on Society Place. She also comes to learn of the Nest's interest in the baby growing inside her, and of the far-reaching consequences of the events of that summer and how they will still be felt into the first decades of the 21st century.

OUT NOW

Printed in Great Britain
by Amazon